I GLANCED IN THE MIRROR—

and got a stabbing pain straight through the temples that made my eyes water. I immediately looked away, as if I'd been blinded by a bright light. The pain faded.

What the . . . ?

I looked in the mirror again, slowly raising my eyes—

When the second headache faded enough to allow me some awareness, I was staring into the sink, gripping the sides of the counter so tightly that my arms were vibrating. The idea of brain damage came to me, even as I draped a towel to cover the top half of the mirror.

I had felt *fine* until I had looked directly at the mirror. Maybe it was just a temporary aberration. I reached over and touched the corner of the towel.

I began to lift it.

Slowly, it revealed my shoulders and a scar on my left pectoral. Then my neck, the cords standing out as I clenched my teeth. My chin dark with a few days' beard. My mouth, pressed into a hard, bloodless line. A nose broken once, severely, and reset. My . . .

. . . eyes . . .

"GOD!"

RAVEN

S.A. SWINIARSKI

DAW BOOKS, INC.
DONALD A. WOLLHEIM, FOUNDER
375 Hudson Street, New York, NY 10014

ELIZABETH R. WOLLHEIM
SHEILA E. GILBERT
PUBLISHERS

First Printing, November 1996
1 2 3 4 5 6 7 8 9

DAW TRADEMARK REGISTERED
U.S. PAT. OFF. AND FOREIGN COUNTRIES
—MARCA REGISTRADA
HECHO EN U.S.A.

PRINTED IN THE U.S.A.

The literate parts of this are dedicated to
Robert E. McDonough.

The bloodthirsty parts of this are dedicated to
Susie Kretschmer.

Acknowledgments to
Astrid, Susie, Charlie, Levin, Mary, Bonnie, Geoff, and
Paula for doing their best to eviscerate this novel in the
manuscript. I also give thanks to Mr. Poe
for the obvious reasons.

PART ONE

PREMATURE BURIAL

Thank Heaven! the crisis—
The danger is past.
And the lingering illness
Is over at last—
And the fever called "Living"
Is conquered at last.
                    —"For Annie"

1

I dreamed of blood, and I awoke in a frozen darkness, wondering why I was not yet dead. As my blood-red dreams faded, cold wrapped my body in a grip severe enough to tear flesh from bone.

"Shit."

My painful whisper was loud enough to frighten me down to my soul.

My back pressed against a wall of curving concrete. Water rushed over me, up to my waist. I opened my eyes, and could barely see a darker shadow where the rest of my body was. The water numbed my body, and my frozen hands couldn't feel the ice on the walls.

My senseless hands slid over the concrete as I tried to push myself upright. When I finally stood, I heard the rip of my clothing tearing from where it had frozen to the wall. When the wall released me, my head slammed into the low ceiling, and dizziness overcame me. I had to crouch and dry-heave until my gut ached and my eyes stopped watering.

I was so *cold*.

My mind flew in chaotic tumbles, the cold and the vertigo making it easy to lose my concentration. My thoughts took a supreme effort to retain, and it was some minutes—too many minutes in this icy tomb—before I had overcome my disorientation long enough to think about where I had awoken.

Once I could concentrate, it was obvious that I stood

in a storm sewer somewhere. But I had no idea where it was, no memory of how I got here.

The more I tried to force my memory, the more traitor my mind became. As I groped for some impression, some image of my life before this icy hell, my mind was gripped by a headache that shot sparks of color before my eyes.

I was in serious trouble. I had no memory. Everything before my awakening, and a sense of a dream, was a void. I felt a sick impression of what was there, like sensing the definition of a forgotten word, but the substance of my memory was gone.

Not only couldn't I remember how I had come to this place, but I couldn't remember who I was.

I put a hand to my head, and while I couldn't find an injury—all parts of my skull throbbed equally—my hair was clotted with frozen blood.

Not good. Possible head injury, nausea, dizziness, amnesia, nightmares—and I was probably going to die of exposure and hypothermia down here. The thought of dying down here, with no memory of who I was, terrified me.

I started downstream, hoping for an exit before the cold finally claimed me. As I duckwalked through the knee-deep current I tried to force a memory of how I'd gotten into this mess.

Had I fallen through an open manhole? Had I collapsed into a drainage ditch to be washed underground? I could not focus on what had happened. Nothing emerged from my memory beyond the impression of violence done to me.

However I had come here, I could not imagine it happening more than a quarter-hour ago. The cold was deadly. It was a miracle that I had not yet died from it. However long I'd been submerged in this icy water, any longer, I felt, and I never would have woken up.

For a moment I took some comfort in being able to

think clearly now. That comfort brought an unbidden thought, *If I am brain damaged, would I know I was thinking like mushy cabbage?* I pushed away the idea.

I slogged downstream, the rushing water cold, deep, and painful. I felt sick that I might have survived whatever accident brought me here only to die of hypothermia, or lose my legs to frostbite.

For some reason, that brought an involuntary laugh which made me dizzy and surprised me by showing me my own breath. My eyes had adjusted to what little light there was, and I could see my misty laughter before me. I hugged myself for warmth—gaining little from it—and slogged on.

The laugh had been for the word "accident."

The word was soaked with irony despite the fact I could remember nothing of what had happened. My subconscious knew, however, that "accident" was the last word to describe what had occurred. What had happened to me was violent, purposeful, and intentional. This had been done *to* me. No faces, no memory of the act itself, only the certainty that some asshole had tried to kill me.

My anger made me a little warmer. So did the movement, the effort easing some of the chill. It helped when I finally walked into a chamber tall enough for me to stand upright.

By now I could nearly see, and I was fighting to stand upright against the current pushing me. The water was up to my chest before I found a ledge lining the tunnel that was high enough for me to stand out of the water. I climbed up on it and stood, shaking, cold, and wet. Sensation, searing cold, returned to my numbed lower body.

I don't know how long I'd walked down that sewer pipe, or how long my legs had been submerged, but when my legs were exposed to the air, cold as it was, it felt as if someone were torching them. The pain was bad enough to make me gasp and nearly pitch headfirst into the torrent below.

Looking down at the water, I couldn't believe I had fought my way out. Now that my eyes could make out this gray subterranean world, I saw how close to death I'd been. The water roared, carrying logs the size of my thigh and battering them against the walls. As I watched, one slime-blackened log slammed into a swamped shopping cart that was wedged against the walls. The sound of the impact echoed through the sewer, and the cart was dented and knocked loose, to clatter along the wall and out of my sight. If I'd been struck by that log, it would have cost me some ribs or possibly my spine.

I must have been unconscious and swept down the sewer by this torrent. Miraculously I hadn't drowned or had parts of me bashed to pulp against the walls.

I felt my head again. Maybe part of me *had* been pulped.

I suddenly realized that I had stopped breathing.

Panic gripped me, slamming the headache back into my skull. I thought I was having a stroke. But once I thought about it, my chest shuddered and I started breathing again. I sucked air in great gulps that had to originate from psychological rather than physical need. I hadn't been consciously holding my breath, and I hadn't stopped long enough for it to cause any pain or discomfort.

It scared me.

It scared me worse than amnesia or possible brain damage. It scared me because I hadn't realized it was happening. I was terribly conscious of my own breathing as I made my way down the storm sewer.

I inched along that concrete ledge, sliding along walls of brick, concrete, and eventually corrugated steel. I managed to avoid immersing myself again.

It seemed an aeon before I finally made it out of that

frigid little hell. Logic told me that the time I spent underground must have been subjective. Had I actually spent the hours down there that I felt I had, I would have been a frozen corpse long before I reached the sewer's outflow.

The outflow I came to emerged from underneath a highway. The echo of traffic reached me through corrugated steel long before I saw the opening. The exit itself was hidden around a bend until I stepped in front of it.

It opened onto a swollen river that snaked away into a frosted ravine. Snow-covered ice began a few feet from the opening, an unbroken blue plain, shimmering in the moonlight.

I inched out of the sewer opening, stepping on rocks and downed trees, trying to avoid dunking myself again. It was colder out here, under a clear black sky, the air sharp enough to shave with.

I pulled myself onto ice that could support my weight, holding on to a tree growing out from the lip of the ravine, and looked up the wall from which I had just emerged. The storm sewer outlet was set into a sloping hillside that went up for maybe a dozen or twenty feet, topped by a guardrail. As I watched, a lonely car sped out of the darkness, passed me, and disappeared back into the darkness, chased by its own bloody taillights.

I moved to the edge of the ravine, holding on to the branch above me until I was certain that I was on firm ground rather than snow-covered ice. Seeing the highway lifted something in me, as if it was a confirmation of my survival. I was going to make it through the snow and the cold. I was going to live, however unlikely that was. I shook in the cold and told myself that I had, finally, made it. I had gotten out of the pit alive.

Whether or not I was in one piece, that was debatable.

I felt around my head again, now that it wasn't throbbing constantly. My hair was a tangled mass of frozen blood. No dangling flaps of skin, no bumps, no holes, no abrasions. I was comforted until I thought that I might have suffered an injury that had frozen under the mat of hair I was prodding. It was cold enough out here to numb anything, and I'd been in the water way too long.

I had to get inside and warm myself up. My legs felt asleep. I thought my pants had dried, but when I felt them with my numbed hand, I found them frozen stiff.

I scrambled up the slope toward the highway, putting my share of bruises on my numbed shins as I started a dozen mini-avalanches. When I got to the top, I had to scramble over the guardrail and six feet of snowplow ejecta. I rolled into the breakdown lane.

I got up and started walking.

As I walked, I searched myself for clues to where I was, what had happened to me, and who I was. I felt desperate for some item my ragged brain could hang a memory on.

I wore well-worn steel-toed work boots—if they didn't have to chop off my toes it was thanks to them—a pair of terribly abused blue jeans, a denim work shirt that, like my hair, was ruined with frozen blood—mostly on the chest and collar—and a black, fleece-lined trenchcoat that would probably never be usable again. Everything had been soaked and frozen stiff. I made cracking and grinding noises when I moved.

My wallet, if I'd had one, had either been stolen or had been lost in the sewer. Same for a watch, or keys. No rings, or any jewelry for that matter. My pockets were almost completely empty.

For a time I felt as if I had been robbed. But something in my void of a memory made me feel that what had happened had been more than a simple mugging.

My hands were clumsy and numb, and found it difficult to manipulate my frozen clothes, which is why one of the last things I discovered was the empty holster. It was clipped to the rear of my belt, hidden from view. I didn't know what I had found until I'd unclipped it and looked at the thing.

It gave me my first memory of something before the icy sewer. I could see the gun that belonged in the holster, a mental image of a blue steel Colt Police .38. It was more than an image. I felt how much it should weigh, how it should fit in my hand. I knew what it was like to load it, by hand and with a speed-loader. The shock of the impressions made me drop the holster.

What had I been doing with a gun?

I bent slowly, my frozen clothes abrading my skin, and fished the holster out of the slush in the breakdown lane. I shoved it in a pocket, for the first time suspecting that I might not be an innocent victim.

No one is innocent, I thought.

I resumed my stumbling progress toward the lights of what I hoped was civilization. I continued examining my pockets, my search taking on an edge of desperation.

I found only one other thing, besides the holster. I felt something in the breast pocket of my shirt. The pocket was buttoned shut and gummed with blood, but I tore it open. Inside was a small plastic card. At first I thought it was a credit card, but there was nothing embossed on the surface.

It took a moment for me to realize that it was a key. The print identified the place as the Woodstar Motel. The key carried a weak visual impression with it. A view of a garish neon sign that could have been as much my imagination as memory.

There was an address on the card and that cheered me, but only for a moment. I had no idea where I was, much less how to find this motel. I looked up and stared down the four lanes of unused asphalt. How did I know I was going in the right direction?

I had yet to pass so much as a sign identifying this road. I pushed my way along the shoulder, leaning into a wind that cut like a razor, dragging my feet through dirty brown snow.

By now, on top of the cold, I was feeling pretty damn weak. I had lost even the pins and needles that reminded me that I still had legs. My fatigue was a dangerous sign. I felt as if I could lie down upon the snowbank and take a nap; the idea was tempting even though I knew I'd never awake from such a nap.

I forced myself to march along the breakdown lane, my boots growing heavier with each step. I had gone maybe another dozen yards when I saw the trees lighten in front of me. I saw my shadow reach out ahead of me, and I turned to see a pair of headlights bright enough to make my eyes water.

Incredibly, my first instinct was to hide from the approaching car. It was an insane impulse, since I was certain to die if I spent much longer out in this cold.

Instead, I gathered my coat about me to hide the bloody shirt I wore, and waved the car down. The car passed me and rolled to a stop on the shoulder. I watched the narrow brake lights ease back toward me as my eyes recovered their night vision. The nearer the car came, the more I was gripped by an insane ambivalence.

I was frightened of being discovered, and I had no memory of why I should be.

The car was a late model Cadillac, black or dark blue in color. It had Ohio plates, Cuyahoga County, up-to-date tags, and a five-digit number. I also noticed the small Enterprise Rent-A-Car logo. I was cataloging all these items by rote before I realized that I was doing it. By then the plate number was fixed in my head.

The Cadillac came to a stop about ten feet away from me. For a few moments I was unable to force myself to move. My hesitation was brief. The wind picked up, driving needles into my exposed skin. If nothing else, the cold pushed me toward the car.

I walked up and opened the passenger door, letting out a blast of heat and the sound of Creedence Clearwater Revival. The driver turned to face me. He was an old Asian gentleman with snow-white hair that contrasted with a very dark face. He wore a dark blue suit that was conservative enough to be three or thirty years old.

He took one look at me and said, "My word . . ."

His accent wasn't foreign, but it wasn't Midwestern. It was only slightly offset from the universal newscaster accent, but it made me think Canada. "Sir," I said, doing my best to sound harmless, "I've had an accident, I need to get back to my motel."

The way he stared at me made me realize just how terrible I must have looked. "Of course," he said. "Certainly. Come in."

I slipped into the passenger seat and pulled the seat belt around myself. In the warmth of the car, my skin began burning, fiery needles racing across my flesh. My clothes began melting immediately.

"Are you certain that you don't need an ambulance?" my benefactor asked. "I can drive you to a hospital—"

"No," I said. It was a reflex, and I said it much too strongly. He turned to face me, and I saw the beginnings of suspicion grow on his face. After a pause, I said, "Look, I'm all right—"

"You don't look all right." I could see his face harden, and I could feel him beginning to perceive me as a threat. His fear began to fill the car like a fog. I could almost breathe it.

On the radio John Fogherty was singing about bad moons rising . . . .

I started talking even before I knew, consciously,

what I was about to say. I ran my fingers over clotted hair and said, "Look, this is embarrassing. I lost my job you see—laid off, downsized, whatever you want to call it—got cut off with no benefits, no nothing. Car's totaled, sent the damn thing into a ditch—black ice. But my insurance lapsed, and hell—I never had any medical insurance to begin with . . ."

I amazed myself by the facility with which the lies came out. I fell into a natural patter where the hesitation stops gave me time to think of the next sentence. It only took a few glances into this guy's eyes to tell I had him convinced.

"I understand," he said, "but don't they have to take you at an emergency room?"

I laughed humorlessly. "Yeah, and what they'd charge'd wipe out what savings I got left. Then I'd probably be arrested for no insurance on that wreck I totaled. I do *not* want to look for work with a suspended license."

"Head wounds can be nasty."

I nodded. "I can go to the free clinic tomorrow. They'll take that long to get to me in an emergency room anyway."

The look of disgust on the man's face now had nothing to do with me. I had sold him, completely, on a story that I'd constructed out of whole cloth, on the spot.

Who in hell was I?

I felt my head again and wondered why I was so terrified of going to a hospital. *"Head wounds can be nasty,"* said my Good Samaritan. The idea did not make me feel good.

"The health care system in this country is insane," he muttered. "Where's your motel?"

I fished in my pocket and retrieved the card key. I read off the address of the Woodstar Motel in the dim glow from the dash.

"Can you give me directions?" he asked.

"No," I said, "I'm from out of town. I was following up a job prospect." The lies were almost easy, as if the conversation was a puzzle and all I had to do was fish out the pieces to fit. He eventually had me fish out a map from the glove compartment. At least I now knew exactly where I was. We were westbound on Route 322, east of Cleveland, Ohio, just outside of Cuyahoga County.

None of that information held a whisper of a memory for me. All I knew for certain was that everything I had told my benefactor had been a lie.

The song changed to "Fortunate Son."

The drive turned out to be a short one, which was fortunate. Even in the warmth of the car, my breath was shallow, my head throbbed, and I seemed to have no feeling below the waist. More than once I reconsidered my attempt to avoid a hospital, but I never voiced my second thoughts. I was going to follow my instincts all the way, and pray that there was a reason for them.

Eventually the neon-chrome sprawl of the motel emerged from the drifts beside Route 332. The neon sign merged with the memory my card key had inspired.

"Here you are," my benefactor held out his hand and said, "My name's Park. Lee Park."

"Damien Castle," I said automatically, knowing it wasn't my name. "Thank you for the lift. I think you saved my life."

He shook my hand and his expression darkened. "That remains to be seen, my friend."

I nodded as I slipped out. The cold was so searing that I nearly collapsed by the car. It was an order of magnitude worse now that my clothes had partially melted. Immediately the moisture on my skin began to freeze again.

The Cadillac drove away and I stumbled through a recently plowed parking lot, realizing that I had no room number. I gripped the key in a numbing hand, and realized that there was no guarantee that I still had a room here. I had the sick feeling that I might have only delayed the inevitable.

The wind sucked my strength as I tried to think. I stumbled toward the motel, leaning on a dirty Chevette that had been half-buried by a snowplow, and was overwhelmed by a sudden stab of aloneness. The night gripped me in a silence so total that I wanted to scream.

Just as suddenly, the sense of isolation was gone, leaving me shaken and empty. I tried to calm myself, to push back the tide of panic that was making it difficult to think.

I looked around the lot, and noticed something. The Chevette was the only car that was buried so badly. It had been here a couple of days at least.

My car, perhaps?

Even better, I looked down and saw that each room had a parking space marked for it. Room numbers were painted on the curb in front of the spaces. The curb by the Chevette was hopelessly buried, so I kicked away the snow around the empty spaces to either side of it.

The numbers were 222 and 224. That meant the Chevette belonged to room 223. It was worth a try. If I was wrong, I'd just have to try every single door until I found the one where the key worked.

I raised my head and began looking in vain for room number 223. I felt a blurry panic when I didn't see that number on any of the doors facing the lot. It took a minute for me to see a set of stairs leading to a balcony and a second story of rooms.

I ascended the stairs, the only sound the crunching of salt under my boots. I passed two doors and stopped in front of 223. My numbed fingers fumbled with the card, and I felt the panic begin again. What if this was the wrong motel, what if the room had been given to someone else?

The card chunked home and a small diode blinked green from the lock.

Behind me, one of the streetlights illuminating the parking lot buzzed and went out. For the first time I noticed that the sky had lightened from black to a deep aqua.

As the door creaked open, the wave of heat that blew from the room felt like a furnace. My refrozen clothes began to melt again. I spared one more look at the lightening sky.

For some unfathomable reason I felt as if I had made it just in time.

I stumbled into the darkened motel room on legs that felt like stilts carved in ice. I slammed the door shut behind me, not caring if someone else was in the room. Though, even in the near pitch black, with the shades drawn, I was sure the room was empty.

I took a step and stumbled over a suitcase. I was shivering violently, and salt was stinging my eyes— sweat or thawing blood.

Ass on the floor, and in total darkness, I began stripping off my frozen clothes. It was a process that felt as though it ripped skin and hair as much as cloth. Wrestling off my boots ignited deep burning pain in my feet, especially my toes.

For a moment I sat there, naked, shivering. Fiery pain washed over me, leaving bone-deep aches in its wake. Ice trickled down my back as my hair melted.

I crawled to the bathroom, not bothering with the light. I could feel my consciousness ebbing. There was actually a bathtub in the bathroom, not simply an abbreviated shower stall. I turned the hot water on full and half climbed, half fell, into the bathtub, barely worried about scalding myself. I felt the steam filling the bathroom.

My last coherent memory of that first night was of killing the water when the tub began to overflow, thinking I was probably going to die.

2

For the second time I woke up in darkness, submerged in cold water.

For an instant I thought I might be caught in some vicious cycle of hallucination—doomed to traverse some private circle of hell, waking in that sewer and stumbling to the motel over and over and over . . . .

I had to clamp down hard to keep myself from flipping out.

Calming down took a minute or ten. It took that long for me to realize that I was still alive. I hadn't stopped breathing in the night. I hadn't slipped down into the water and drowned. I'd avoided hypothermia. My headache was gone for the most part. And, when I conducted a prodding search of my extremities under the tepid bathwater, I could actually *feel*. Sensation was back in my fingers and my lower body.

All things considered, I felt better than I had any right to feel.

I probably *looked* like hell.

I heaved myself out of the tub, carefully, expecting a wave of vertigo that didn't come. I was waking up. I felt alive, alive in a way you can only feel after coming pretty damn close to the alternative.

I stood in the darkened bathroom, dripping, thinking how badly the boys who tried to off me had screwed up. I was going to find them and—

"Calm down," I whispered to myself. It was hard.

Like the panic that had surged in me before, thinking about my hypothetical attackers gave vent to a deep well of raw emotion. A visceral anger gripped me, abnormally intense even after what had happened. Especially since, with my hole of a memory, I couldn't say for certain that I was the victim of *any* sort of attack.

The problem was that I *was* certain.

I shook my head and tried again to force a memory. The strain was almost physical. I clenched my fists and felt a bead of sweat roll off my brow.

I remembered a brief sensation. A smell like rusty leather, and a heavy wet sound of something falling on . . . .

On what?

That was all the memory that would come, the smell of ferric leather and that incongruous, ominous sound. Nothing more would come to me, and my subconscious left me with a deep rage and a feeling that I had been, in some sense, raped.

"Maybe I don't want to remember." I took a deep breath. "Stop talking to yourself in the dark, people will think you're nuts."

I groped for the light switch. A frosty fluorescent flashed a few rattling strobes before it came on.

The bathroom was a mess. Worst was the bathtub. The water was black with dirt and blood. Water had slopped over and drenched the hex-tile floor, streaking it red and brown. A few towels were sopping in the midst of the mess on the floor.

I walked over to the tub and hit the lever for the drain, its only response an anemic gurgle. I had to pull out a tangle of hair and twigs from the drain to get the thing to start. I shook my hand off into the john and glanced in the mirror—

—and got a stabbing pain straight through the temples that made my eyes water. I immediately looked away, as if I'd been blinded by a bright light. The pain faded.

What the. . . ?

I looked into the mirror again, slowly raising my eyes—

When the second headache faded enough to allow me some awareness, I was staring into the sink in front of the mirror and gripping the sides of the counter so tightly that my arms were vibrating. The idea of brain damage came to me again.

But I had felt *fine* until I had looked directly at the mirror.

I cast a furtive glance at the mirror without raising my head. I saw my naked waist sliced by the lines of the sink. I saw my hands, veins standing out on their backs, knuckles white.

I didn't quite have the courage to raise my head all the way.

I thought furiously for a moment and came to the conclusion that it was an effect of the light reflecting off of the mirror. Bright lights could trigger headaches. Strobes could start seizures in epileptics. Maybe some weird angle of reflection hit me just the wrong way when I looked directly in the mirror.

That decided, I grabbed a dry hand towel from the rack and, without looking, hung it up over the bare fluorescent tube that ran along the top of the mirror. Once I was sure it was secure, *then* I slowly raised my gaze.

No migraine struck this time, if that's what had sliced my skull open a few minutes ago. The towel didn't cover the whole mirror, I could see myself from mid-chest down.

On the parts of my body I could see, there was no injury, nothing that looked like frostbite. That was good—or not so good, because that left only one place for all that blood to have come from.

The drain in the tub gurgled as it finally emptied out.

I prodded my skull—with the towel in place I couldn't see my head—and found my hair a crusty mess. No area felt particularly sensitive, but I wasn't going to find any signs with all that clotted hair in the way. I shrugged, sighed, and stepped back into the shower.

After a long time pulling gunk out of my hair, I emerged from the shower. I felt about as good as I could ever remember. Which, of course, wasn't saying much.

As I dried myself off with the only clean towel left in the bathroom, I looked at the hand towel I'd draped over the mirror. I found it disturbing. It was the one concrete sign, other than my memory, that there *was* something wrong with me. I might not have found so much as a bump under my clotted hair, but it wasn't normal to have migraines just from peeking into a mirror.

Maybe it'd just been a temporary aberration.

Yeah, like the blood. If the blood came from you, that bleeding aberration was pretty damn temporary. Wasn't it?

I reached over and touched the corner of the towel. Two ways to test this, lift gently, or yank it away.

I began to lift it.

Slowly, it revealed my shoulders and a scar on my left pectoral. Then my neck, the cords standing out as I clenched my teeth. My chin, dark with a few days' beard. My mouth, pressed into a hard, bloodless line. A nose broken once, severely, and reset. My. . .

. . .eyes. . .

"GOD!"

The pain dropped me on the floor this time. It was as if someone had fired a high-powered laser through my eyes and burned all the way to the back of my head. My palms pressed into the orbits so hard that I felt I might fracture my skull.

It took a while for me to think straight.

As the pain faded, I stared at my hands. I became very conscious of my vision. It seemed normal. Nothing was blurred, nothing doubled, the colors seemed right.

Nothing I remembered seeing in the mirror clued me in either. The reflection that had looked at me, despite the grotesque contortion of pain it had caused, seemed normal. Even the eyes—green, I remember—couldn't account for the blinding stab I'd felt when I made eye contact with my reflection.

It struck me as some sort of psychotic pathology, and that really scared me.

It scared me because I had no obvious injuries. That left me with the strong possibility that the blood wasn't mine. I had refused to be taken the hospital. I was afraid of something. What if it was the police I was afraid of? I was missing a gun. Was it possible that I had killed someone?

I climbed, shaking, to my feet.

Amnesia could be psychological as well as from a blow to the head.

Was I insane? Could I be a serial killer with a few dozen bodies to his credit? Was I—

I put my hands over my face and told myself to cut it out.

I pushed out of the bathroom to get away from that damn mirror. I might be on shaky ground, mentally speaking, but it wasn't time to be sized for a white jacket that buckled up the back.

Fumbling for the light switch, I told myself that, for all my erratic behavior, nothing I'd felt or done yet was more out of line than the situation I found myself in. I needed to give *myself* the benefit of the doubt, since I didn't think anyone else was about to.

I found the lights and flipped them on, hoping that something in my room would pull loose a memory. But

the only thought that crossed my mind upon seeing my
motel room was that the place had been tossed by
amateurs.

There are two ways to search a room: thorough and
subtle. Subtle is supposed to leave the room so the
owner doesn't know it was touched. Thorough is just
like it sounds; you don't give a shit, you trash the place
and sift through the pieces.

This was neither.

I tried to push the thought away, blame it on paranoia, but the certainty gripped me and wouldn't let me
go. The feeling grew as I rummaged through a pair of
suitcases for clothing.

As I dressed, I began cataloging the details that told
me the room had been searched. Furniture had been
moved. The legs of the end table, the wheels of the bed
frame, both were slightly off the divots they had worn
in the motel's carpet. The cushion on the one easy
chair had been compressed by a succession of rear
ends, but the cushion only sat loosely on the chair
itself, as if it had just been placed there. The runners
that held the carpet down at the front door and the
bathroom were loose. The suitcases had been gone
through and hastily repacked.

At least the clothes fit me.

Dressed, I went over the motel room more thor-
oughly. The closer I looked at anything, the more evidence I found of tampering—shiny scratches on dull
screw heads, an absence of dust on the back of the TV
set, nicks on the sides of drawers where they'd been
forced off their tracks and replaced.

I couldn't check around the mirror above the dresser
until I thought of putting on a pair of dark sunglasses
I'd found on the night table. The sunglasses prevented
eye contact with myself, and that prevented the pain.

Once I could check the mirror, I found the tampering
there as well. Along the edge of the mirror, scratches

circled the plugs capping the screws that held the mirror to the wall.

I got the feeling that whoever had done this—and it was obviously not the cops, or, if cops, seriously bent cops—had been rushed. Maybe not amateurs, maybe seriously rushed pros. That didn't make me feel any better.

Then I had a sick paranoid thought to add to all the others. What if all of this was my doing? I had no memory. It could as easily have been me as anyone else. If it had been, what had I been looking for?

Presuming that there was something to find, I proceeded to toss the place myself. I hoped desperately for some clues to who I was, to who searched this room, to what had happened to me . . . .

I checked the doors and windows first and found something truly strange. White crumbs were ground into the carpet by the front door, as if someone had stepped on a cracker. By the window that faced the garage I found another cracker, white, about the size of a Ritz. It lay on the sill where the window opened, and I had to reach behind the chair to retrieve it. When I saw the image of the Lamb embossed on the surface of the thin wafer, I realized what it was.

I held in my hand a holy wafer. Someone, probably myself, had placed the Eucharist across the entrances into this room.

"Why?" I asked. My voice felt hoarse from lack of use. I backed from the window, confused and fearful. Looking at the wafer in my hand, I heard a voice out of my memory—

". . . it is something evil. It is evil and I fear for my daughter's soul . . ."

There was little in the room that gave me any clue to who I was. There was much, however, that implied what I did for a living.

In the closet I found a camcorder, a high-end model with interchangeable lenses; next to it an empty tape case for videos. With the camcorder was a voice-activated microcassette recorder. Again, an empty tape case for the cassettes. I found a very expensive pair of binoculars.

And in the bottom of the closet was a briefcase, aluminum and covered by a matte-black vinyl veneer. It weighed more than it should have. When I placed it on the bed, the mattress sagged. The latches had combination locks set to 537.

When I tried the latches, it opened. Whoever had opened this last hadn't bothered to relock the case. I suspected that my visitors hadn't cared after they'd finessed the combination.

Inside the case, resting on a foam rubber cushion, was a two-thousand-dollar monster: a Desert Eagle and two boxes of shells to go with it.

Its presence scared me more than the missing thirty-eight. The revolver was a reasonable weapon, but a fifty-caliber Desert Eagle is bigger than any handgun had a right to be. It'd throw a magnum bullet through someone, through the guy behind him, through the wall, and crack the engine block on the car parked outside. No one had any business carrying this thing outside a combat zone.

Scarier still was the way my hands knew the weapon, checking the slide and the magazine. The gun was fully loaded, and so new it shone. In the closet hung a shoulder holster that could fit it and an extra magazine.

I would have preferred some form of photo identification.

But in the remainder of the room I found no papers, no keys, no wallet, no checkbook. The closest I came to my identity was in the drawer of the nightstand. Three hundred dollars in cash was weighted down by an expensive-looking watch. I picked up the watch. It was shiny, and old enough to show some wear. On the back was an engraving, "Happy Birthday. Love, Gail."

Something clogged my throat. It came from the same blank place where the anger and the fear had been coming from.

"Gail?" I whispered, not enjoying the sound of my voice.

I put the watch on my wrist. I wondered why I had left it here. Fear of losing it, maybe?

When I lifted the stack of crumpled twenties out of the drawer, something clattered back into the drawer. I picked up a wedding band.

". . . Kate, I'm worried about you and Gail—"

A sigh comes from the other end of the phone. "You're always worried about Gail. That's what your work does to you."

"This is different—"

"It's always different. I'm not like you, I can't live in fear all the time. That's why I left you . . . ."

The memory burned, but even so, I tried to hold on to it. I couldn't and I felt sick and ashamed that I couldn't. I had a family somewhere, and I was certain that I had done evil by them.

I sat on the bed, staring at the night table, trying to remember anything. But forcing did me little good. I sighed and looked at the phone.

For once I seemed to have some luck. The message light was on, I had some voice-mail waiting for me. I picked up the receiver and punched up my messages, hoping for some sort of revelation.

The first message was a voice that was achingly familiar though I had no memory of ever hearing it.

"Okay, Kane, you owe me. I got the information on Childe you wanted. Call my beeper, 216-3839. *Not* my apartment or the station. You better get this cleared up before Internal Affairs eats me alive for not handing you over."

Internal Affairs? That implied police, and that I was dealing with a cop who was risking something by talking to me. Was I wanted for something?

But I had a name now. Somehow that lifted some of the weight off of my soul.

The second voice was still familiar, but I had a more ambivalent feeling about it.

"It's Bowie. We gotta talk. Not over the phone. Meet me at the Arabica tonight, seven. There's talk on Coventry that you've got to hear."

The voice sounded frantic, but I didn't understand anything he said. Arabica and Coventry were just words to me, though my traitor memory decided to give me an image of the speaker. I saw a thin man in a leather jacket wearing a jet-black ponytail.

The next message was a repeat of the first caller.

"It's Sam again. Where the fuck are you? Call me."

Now I had a name for my policeman friend. I tried to remember him, but my memory seemed to resist it. I couldn't force a memory, they only seemed to come when I wasn't prepared for them.

The next message was like a fist in the gut.

"Dad?" A young woman's voice on the verge of breaking into tears. "Sam gave me this number. Please, talk to me. You're hiding because you think you're responsible for what happened to Mom. Call me. Damn it, I love you. I love you . . . ."

"Gail," I whispered into the phone.

Kate my wife. Gail my daughter. That, my memory would give me. I could feel that something bad had happened, but what I didn't know. I sat there, stomach boiling, wishing that Gail had left her number.

But that would be something I was supposed to know.

The messages ended, and I slammed the receiver down on to the cradle.

* * *

I called Sam's beeper, left my name, and waited.

He called back within ten minutes. I grabbed the receiver before the first ring faded.

"Hello?" I said, my voice wrapped in an asphyxiating uncertainty.

"God damn it, Kane! Where the fuck have you been?" It was the same voice that had left the message. Sam's voice.

"Sam?" I said uncertainly.

"Yes. What the hell were you thinking, falling off the Earth like that? You want everyone to think you're dead? Please, at least tell me you've called Gail."

"I got her message. I had—"

"Christ, and you're just letting her worry about you? After what happened to Kate?"

A flash of a memory hit me, a bad one—blood-red and violent. I saw torn, ragged flesh. I remembered the sickening reek of disinfectant that just failed to cover the smell of blood, the almost subliminal smell of death.

Lo! Death has reared himself a throne . . . .

"Kane? Are you there? Hello?"

I choked back something. The receiver shook in my hand. *Why can't I remember?*

"I had an accident," I said. "I've had some problems." It was an effort to get the words out.

Sam's voice changed. "What happened? Are you all right?"

"I think someone tried to kill me."

The response was silence.

"Hello," I said. It was beginning to sink in that here was someone who knew me, someone who might tell me what happened.

"Who?" Sam said, earnestness replacing the anger in his voice. "Was it Childe?"

Childe. That name again. "I don't know. I can't

remember—" I hesitated. Something inside me didn't want to admit how badly off I was. "We need to meet."

"Where?"

My mind was a blank. I tried to force a image of a place to meet, but forcing my past to the surface was like trying to build a snowman out of water. No memory would come when I wanted a memory.

On impulse I parroted one of the other messages, "How about the Arabica?"

"Which one? Shaker Square, University Circle, Coventry—"

"Coventry," I said. Perhaps I could find Bowie.

"When?" Sam asked.

"Give me three hours or so."

"Okay, 10:30."

I nodded. There was some hope that I would find out what the hell was going on.

"Are you all right? Do I need to send help out there?" Sam asked.

"No, I'll be fine." I said it even though I didn't believe it. "Do me a favor and call Gail and tell her that I'm okay?"

"Sure, but why don't you—"

"Tell her I love her," I said, and hung up the phone, my hand shaking. Somehow, memory or not, I had meant it.

What had happened to my wife? Presumably I was going to find out. However, from the wisps of memory I was getting, I was not sure that I wanted to know.

I needed to find this Arabica before 10:30. I looked at my watch and saw that it was pretty late already. I needed to get going if I was going to find Sam.

I walked up to the window and drew the shades aside. The night was ink-black with solid clouds. The street lamps were globed by halos of wind-whipped snow. It was as if the day had never happened, as if the sun were gone for good.

I looked down and saw the Chevette was still snowed in. It seemed to be my car, but did I want to use it?

I drew the shade and decided to call a taxi.

3

There were a few things I needed to check with the manager here, before I left. I stepped outside and tried not to think of the Eucharist crumbs that dusted the doorway. The idea that I might have been the one to grind the wafer underfoot made me uncomfortable.

The denim jacket I'd found wasn't up to the weather. The wind cut under it, and the snow abrading it made an audible patter. I counted my blessings. I'd been lucky I'd packed more than one jacket. I had, in fact, packed a hell of a lot.

All the signs seemed to indicate that I was running from something, something that had caught up with me at least once. Which made me feel more than lucky that this jacket was large enough to hide the Eagle and its holster.

I trudged through a growing snowstorm to the front of the motel and entered the manager's office. The woman behind the counter was easily sixty-five, wore thick glasses, and had hair the color of FD&C Red # 5. She glanced up at me, then went back to reading the book in her lap.

I walked up to the desk and cleared my throat.

"Can I help you?" she asked in a bored voice.

I opened my mouth, and for a moment I had difficulty speaking. I was suddenly overly conscious of a lot of things: the buzz of the unnaturally white fluorescents, the weight of the gun in my armpit, the smell of

stale coffee from a mug on a counter, melting snow
dripping down my neck. . . .

The sense of hyperawareness passed. "I need to
check how long my room's paid for."

The woman gave a hostile sigh and put the book face
down on the counter, cracking the spine. She looked up,
her eyes magnified grotesquely by the glasses she wore.

"We don't give refunds for—"

"Yes?" I said. Her distorted gaze had made me
realize that I'd still been wearing my sunglasses. I'd
been taking them off when she paused.

"Yes?" I repeated. I was becoming uncomfortably
aware that she was staring into my eyes. It was an
intense and disturbing contact that made me wonder
what she was looking at. Somehow I gained a very
deep feeling of how boring she found her job, of how
lost she felt here. Somehow I knew this woman
regretted missing the chance to be something other
than she was. The wave of empathy was like a blow.

I was drawn, leaning forward. Something pushed at
me, something that wasn't a memory. Something more
like an instinct.

She interrupted me by saying, finally, "What can I
help you with?"

Her entire manner had changed, she wasn't looking
through me any more. I could swear that what I saw in
her eyes was lust, a lust that didn't make me nearly as
uncomfortable as it should have.

"I'm in room 223. I need to know how long I'm paid
up for."

"Yes, certainly." The hesitation in the way she
breathed as she spoke made my interpretation of her
expression unmistakable. So much so that I felt im-
mense relief when she broke eye contact to rummage in
a card file next to the phones.

"Do you have a phone book I could use?"

"By the pay phone, dear."

I glanced around the office looking for the pay phone. I found it back in the hall I'd come through. I left her to search in her files while I stepped outside. The hall was little more than an air lock, with glass doors to the outside and the office. The only things in it were the pay phone and a pair of newspaper machines.

For a few moments I stood there and tried to regain my composure. I was washed by a sense of disorientation. Rationally, I knew that all I had seen and felt about the woman behind the desk had been manufactured by my own mind, but I had to tell myself that none of it was real.

The roiling in my gut was real, though. The feeling of need inside me, a reciprocal and distorted version of what I thought I saw in the woman, that was real. The fact that I stood there with muscles tensed to where they felt as if they'd tear from the bone, that was real, too.

For the first time I truly considered the possibility that I might be psychotic.

My absent memory provided a fragment of a poem;

> *From childhood's hour I have not been*
> *As others were—I have not seen*
> *As others saw—I could not bring*
> *My passions from a common spring—*

The sense of being totally along gripped me again. I clutched the sides of one of the newspaper machines and forced myself to take deep breaths. If nothing else, the effort and concentration that took calmed me. When I felt as if I had rejoined the real world, I picked up the Yellow Pages.

As I called the cab, I started watching outside. Once I'd calmed down my inner world, I began thinking about the threats that might exist in the outer. There were people out there who had left me for dead, and I was beginning to feel much too overexposed behind this wide expanse of glass.

The stretch of Route 322 that I could see was all snow-cloaked shadows. I saw nothing threatening until I'd hung up the phone.

It was a small thing, off in the distance. Out there, by the side of the road, I saw the glow of someone lighting a cigarette. It was far enough away that it shouldn't have concerned me. Except that spot of road had an overview of the motel's entrance, the parking lot, and the door to my room.

I didn't stare. If that distant smoker was watching me, he had a very good view right now, as well-lighted as I was. I didn't want to tip off the guy that I'd seen him, not until I had some idea who he was. For all I knew he could be a cop, or my imagination could be running away with me.

I returned the Yellow Pages, and pulled out the White Pages to try to find an address for an "Arabica," whatever that was. The listing said it was a coffee house, but I couldn't find an address for "Coventry." I had to hope the cabby would know what I was talking about.

I walked back into the manager's office, avoiding obvious glances outside. "Four days, dear," said the woman behind the counter. I jumped at the sound.

"You're paid through Wednesday," she finished.

I realized that I didn't know what day of the week it was. "Wednesday? Morning or evening?"

She returned to her book, but she kept staring at me over the spine. "Morning. Checkout time is at 10:30."

It was Saturday.

The taxi took twenty minutes to show up. Despite the snow, I waited for it outside. I didn't want to spend the time in the office alone with that woman. When the cab came, I was covered with snow, and almost used to the cold.

It was ten minutes toward the city before I was positive the taxi was being shadowed. It wasn't easy for me to make the car. This stretch of highway was without streetlights, and the snow was getting worse. Most of the time the only visible signs of the car were the twin cones of headlamp-stirred snow.

However, not all pairs of headlights are created equal, and my tail was marked by a clump of ice by the right edge of the bumper that warped the lower right corner of its headlight. The car faded behind us two or three times as the cab made its way deeper into the snowbound Cleveland suburbs. But each time headlights reappeared behind us, it was the same car.

I resisted the impulse to have the cab pull over, or to change my destination. I wanted to keep track of these guys as much as they seemed to want to keep track of me.

I wondered if they were the same people who had tried to kill me. That didn't make sense. By all rights, the people who dumped me in the sewer should think I was dead.

I was beginning to have problems with the idea that someone had tried to kill me. If all the blood that had frozen on me was my own, where was the injury that had bled so much? All I had to go on, really, was a gut feeling that didn't even have a memory to support it. From the evidence, it could have been me killing someone and wandering into the sewers to escape . . . .

By the time the cab passed the border into Cleveland Heights, Route 322 had turned into Mayfield and we had passed deep into well-lit suburbia. The general lack of traffic made it hard for my tail to hide. They made a valiant effort, but they only had one car, so no matter what they did, I could eventually pick them out.

The car was a little too old to be totally anonymous. It was a tan Olds that was made prior to the streamlining of the nineties. Mid-eighties was my guess, though they never let me have a good look. Best I could see, there were at least two people in the car, both large males. Nothing much else I could make out through snow and distance.

I finally lost track of them when the cab turned to Coventry. I suspected they'd held back at the intersection of Coventry and Mayfield. By the time the cab went a block, I had lost the intersection beyond a white fog of snow.

It was two blocks to the next tangled intersection when the taxi stopped. It confused me for a moment before I realized that we had made it to my destination. I had to squint past a snow-draped courtyard to see a storefront, but the neon sign was lit up reading "Arabica."

I paid the cabby and stepped out into the snow.

I stood ankle-deep in a snowdrift in the center of the courtyard and stared through the windows into the well-lit shop. Looking in, I felt a nagging sense of familiarity. This place meant something—a lot of teenagers, more punk than anything else. I saw a lot of weird hair and body piercing. I also saw a lot of the bearded-poet type, the kind of folks who wear dirty army jackets, write longhand on yellow legal pads, and quote Nietzsche a lot.

I knew this place.

At one of the tables near the window, a lanky kid with a blond ponytail was having an animated discussion with a shadowy-eyed girl. They both wore abused leather jackets.

I stood there a long time before I walked to the door. The familiarity frightened me, as if this place might make me remember something that I didn't want to remember. But after a few minutes the cold drove me inside.

Stepping from the empty night street into the babble of humanity crowding the coffee shop was a shock. A wave of irrational enmity froze me in the doorway. No one actually looked in my direction, but I felt as if everyone in this place were paying attention to me, weighing me.

I forced myself to walk to the counter. *It's just the crowd. I'm not used to crowds.* That's what I told myself at least.

I was certainly in the midst of the largest group of people I'd seen since walking up *sans* memory. It was only natural to find it disturbing, after what I'd been through.

Of course that was just me bullshitting myself, but it helped to steady my hands as I took a cup of espresso and two horrendously-priced Danishes to one of the few free tables. The table was way in the back, in the smoking section. It was somewhat dark, and smelled like an ashtray, but having my back to a wall helped steady my nerves.

For a while I just sat there, cradling the warm mug in my hands, letting the cold retreat. I forced myself to moderate my paranoia. While some of the patrons gave me some odd looks, I was sure that they were the ones who gave everybody odd looks. I didn't look terribly out of place here, it just felt that way to me.

At the table next to me, two chain-smokers were playing chess. I classified the young clean-shaven one as an eternal grad student, the middle-aged bearded one as another unemployed poet. I didn't know where the assumptions came from, but it reinforced my impression that I had been here before . . . .

It made me wonder if being here was a good idea. If the cops *were* looking for me, and someone here recognized me—

I lowered my gaze. My sunglasses didn't seem much of a disguise.

As if spurred by my thought, someone slapped my

back and said, "Hail Eris, you bastard. How goes the hunt?"

"Huh?" I said. I put down the espresso without drinking from it. I turned around. The speaker wasn't Sam or Bowie, I could tell from the voice.

I looked at him hoping for some twinge of memory. He seemed like someone I should remember. He had wild blond hair and wore at least seven earrings, though his ears were all he had pierced. He wore a denim vest over a linen shirt whose drawstrings left the neck open on a pentagram necklace. He wore a pair of John Lennon glasses with slightly blue lenses. He looked like an avatar of the sixties, though he couldn't be more than nineteen years old.

He awoke no memories. He didn't even awake a sense of dejà vú.

He slid into the chair opposite me, folded his arms on the table, and asked, "Find her yet?"

I was glad for my sunglasses. If he had seen my eyes, he would have seen my confusion. "No, I haven't." I said. "Do you have anything new to tell me?" It was a strange question, but one that came to me automatically—a rote question, something a policeman might ask.

My guest sighed and leaned back. "How'd I know you were going to ask that? Sorry, my friend, nada. I haven't seen them since that open circle I told you about. Not her. Not Childe. But you've been asking around; you know that. Vanished, poof." He flowered open his fingers, "Good riddance."

I nodded.

He held up his hand. "Not the girl, you understand— but that Childe freak. Just gave the fundies and the cops something nasty to have us confused with. Hey, but that's why I like you."

I looked up at the guy, feeling lost. "Why do you like me?"

"You never came in with that Satan-cult bullshit."

"Why would I?" At this point the questions were becoming a defense mechanism, to keep him answering questions so he wouldn't ask me any.

"Hey, man, you're *rare*. Most people, if you say you're a pagan, they think you're out torturing cats somewhere. Take any fundie and talk about any non-Christian spirituality, *boom*, you worship the devil. Somehow pointing out that Satan is a Christian invention doesn't seem to faze them. Childe's as close to the devil as I've ever been."

I still couldn't give him a name. However, as I talked, I got some feeling that I knew his community, that I had brushed against it before. His words held a familiarity that he did not.

And there was that damn name again. "Is there anything else you can tell me about Childe?"

He shrugged. "That I haven't told you already? Not really. English accent, snappy dresser, on a power trip that'd make Alister Crowley and Anton Le Vay look like altruists." He sighed. "Hey, I want you to find this girl. I don't like the idea of anyone stuck with Childe. If there was anything I could do . . . ."

He trailed off.

Behind him, the chess game continued. I heard a slap-ding as the grad student slammed the top of a timer next to the chess board. The poet immediately moved his queen and made his own slap-ding.

"What is it?" I asked. My companion seemed to have lost himself in a thought.

"Are you as open-minded as you seem?"

"I try to be."

He grinned, "Then perhaps I can offer some sort of aid." He fumbled in his pockets and retrieved a bag. Behind him I heard the timer again.

Slap-ding.

From the bag he pulled a stack of cards. Slowly he

began shuffling. "You're not someone who comes believing the oracle, are you?"

I glanced at the cards. "You mean fortune-telling?" What came to my mind when I thought of divination was more con artistry than the supernatural.

The kid shuffled cards and said, "More than that. We attach complex symbols to the cards, manipulate them, arrange them into patterns. The patterns they form are reflections of the patterns around us. This is as much us truly seeing as it is the cards telling us anything." He looked up and gave me a disarming smile. "Sounds pretentious, doesn't it? Just started reading up on chaos theory and emergent behavior." He placed the cards down on the table between us; a slap-ding echoed his motion.

I decided if this kid was about to try a con on me, that would probably tell me more than any oracle. "Go ahead, it can't hurt."

"Form a question in your mind, something for the cards to focus on. Then cut them for me."

I reached over and cut the cards. As I did so, the only question that would come to mind was, *Who am I?*

"Do you want to know the question?" I asked.

To my relief, he shook his head. "Sometimes the reading is more profound if only *you* know what is being asked. At this point I am only helping you to see."

He drew the top card, laying it on the table between us. There was a look on his face I did not like. The card I liked even less. On it a corpse lay facedown, pierced through the back by ten swords. "The Ten of Swords." He swallowed. "This card is the past, the basis for what is to come. You've come through something tragic and unpleasant. Relationships have ended, maybe badly. You've perhaps felt a feeling of abandonment. Things have not gone as you planned or wished them to . . . ."

He took another breath and laid down a card above the first. This one showed a man upon a throne, holding a sword. "This card represents you, and the situation surrounding you. The King of Swords, not a great surprise since he deals with law enforcement. You have a determination to overcome the obstacles that confront you. There is a lot of stress around you, you're fighting your way uphill, but you are fighting."

He laid down a card above the other two; this one showed a woman on a throne, holding a staff in her right hand and a flower in her left. The card was upside down, her flower pointing down at the king's sword. "Ah, this represents your hopes or fears. In a sense, it is what you are looking for. A woman, I suspect that Cecilia that you've been asking about, though the Queen usually has blonde or red hair. The Queen of Wands, reversed. A troublesome woman, vengeful, she may turn on you or others.

"Your immediate past . . . ." He flipped over a card to the king's right. "Whoa."

A skeletal horseman bore a black banner toward the king. Corpses fell across the steed's path. "Death," he said needlessly. "Not necessarily a bad card, but you are in the midst of some change, a major severance with the past. With the swords I see a lot of struggle, but the change is powerful and won't be denied.

"The forces arrayed against you, the obstacles you must overcome . . . ." He turned over a card and laid it across the king. A bat-winged demon squatted on a pillar, raising his hand toward me.

Behind the kid, the chess players went on. Someone hit the timer again. Slap-ding. We sat there, quietly for a moment or two before he went on with the reading. Most of the lightness had gone out of his voice. "The Devil," he said quietly. He placed his cards down and ran his hands through his hair. "Evil forces are blocking your path, and escape from them seems doomed to failure . . . ." He looked up at me and said, "Do you want me to go on with this?"

I nodded, not trusting my voice. His anxiety was infecting me, even though I found it hard to credit the idea that cardboard rectangles could say anything about me.

"The immediate future," he said, slowly picking up the deck. He turned over a card, looking at it for a long time before putting it down. The color drained from his face. I wondered what could be worse than Death or the Devil.

He slowly placed the card down on the other side of the king, opposite Death. "The Tower," he whispered. Lightning struck a lighthouselike structure, people tumbled off the precipice, and flames danced from the windows. "Chaos, disaster. Your upheaval has yet to end, and the tribulations you are about to face will be worse than what you've already endured."

He shook his head. "That's enough, man. I just don't like seeing those cards." He began picking up the spread shoving the cards back into his bag. "Look, I'm sorry. It was a bad idea."

"Don't worry, I don't believe in it," I told him.

He stood up and touched my hand. "Man, I know where you're coming from. But even if I didn't believe it, that kind of spread would freak me."

With that, he left me.

Who am I? I thought.

He was right. Even though I didn't believe it, those cards bothered me. I turned to ask him another question, but he had disappeared into the crowd.

The student and the poet had set up a new game. The poet was busy arranging pawns. Smoke hung low in the air, like fog on a battlefield. *Change, evil, and disaster . . . .*

"Yeah, I have seen her," said the blond pagan. His name is Neil, but he calls himself Sunfox. He hands back the picture I showed him of a dark woman named Cecilia. She is missing, and I've been paid to find her.

"Where did you see her last?" I ask him.

"A week ago last Sunday. She came to a few open circles. She's one of those people who're looking for something, but they're not sure what. The kind of kid that Childe bastard's supposed to prey on."

"Childe?"

"Yeah, that was the last time I saw him, too. A bunch of us got together and asked him to leave . . . ."

The memory evaporated with a slap-ding from the next table.

I tried to hold on to it, but that made it escape all the faster. The young man in my memory was the same one who read my fortune in his cards. Again I was hearing Childe's name, again I was looking for someone . . . .

Am I a cop?

". . . The King of Swords, not a great surprise since he deals with law enforcement . . ."

The poet moved a pawn. Slap-ding.

I cradled my espresso in my hands and thought that Sunfox had given me a lot of information outside of any debatable tarot reading. I looked into my cup and felt a wave of thirst and hunger wash over me, an intense and weakening feeling.

I took a bite of Danish and my first sip of espresso.

Queen takes pawn. Slap-ding.

The coffee slammed into my stomach, constricting my throat. The liquid hit my stomach as if someone had napalmed my abdomen. My gut started spasming violently.

Knight takes queen. Slap-ding.

I managed to drop the mug on the table without spilling it all over myself. I had my hand over my mouth. I knew that I was going to throw up. It felt as if someone were slamming me with an ax handle.

Rook takes pawn, checkmate. Slap-ding.

I stumbled the dozen feet to the rest rooms barely in

time. I could feel the contents of my stomach rising as I pushed open the door. I was kneeling over the bowl before the door had swung shut behind me. It took me ten minutes to expel that single mouthful of coffee; it felt like an hour.

The worst part of all was the steely taste of blood that came with it. I couldn't ignore it, much as I wanted to. Streaking the bowl, swirling with the ugly liquid mass, were trails of bright crimson. The sight of it made me nearly too weak to stand.

As I got unsteadily to my feet, I knew I could no longer pretend that I was okay. Okay people don't vomit blood.

I turned around and leaned over the sink. My eyes refused to meet the mirror, even though I still wore my sunglasses. Despite all the evidence to the contrary, I still felt a perverse thread of denial. It was only a little blood, after all.

I laughed, though I didn't feel at all amused. I was in serious trouble. However well I felt when I woke up, right now I was light-headed from hunger, and probably thirst. My gut was too torn up to handle anything without puking. I needed a doctor.

I ran water into my cupped hands and drank a tiny amount. It washed the taste from my mouth, but from the tightening in my stomach I knew that drinking any more would send me back to the john.

I had a longing thought about the three bucks' worth of pastry sitting back at my table, and almost threw up again. I finally raised my face to look at myself in the mirror.

"Kane," I whispered, "you look like shit."

Part of my face was obscured by a "Silence=Death" bumper sticker. But what I saw showed that, whatever was wrong with me, it must have been getting rapidly worse. I certainly didn't remember looking this pale back at the motel. The stubble on my chin looked black against my skin, and my lips were almost white. Shadows carved out too much of my skull on my face.

I backed out of the bathroom.

Behind me I heard a familiar voice say, "Kane, what the hell happened to you?"

I turned around to face Sam. I was expending what little exhausted effort I had to keep from shaking. I knew him, and the sight of his face inspired a feeling of trust that managed to find its way past my lack of memory. I knew this man was a friend, even though I couldn't remember him.

"Sam," I said. "Get me out of here."

4

Sam helped me out of the coffee shop. I was past embarrassment or any worries about being noticed. He supported me even though he was a head shorter than I was. It wasn't until we were outside and the snow was biting my face that Sam asked again, "What happened to you?"

"Get me to a car," I whispered. "I need to see a doctor."

The whole world felt distorted, *wrong*. I still tasted my own blood, and I felt as if blood tainted my other senses. Colors were too vivid. The street lamps shone like magnesium flares. Each windblown snowflake was a pin piercing my skin. The only warmth I felt was from Sam's neck against my hand.

He lay me against the side of a red Saturn and began fumbling for keys. As he did so, a question came to me, unbidden. "How's Gail doing?"

"She's as well as she can be after losing her mother. We've a car watching her." He pulled the passenger door open and said, "She's worried about her dad, and so am I. What's wrong? This isn't just a missing kid anymore, is it?"

I slipped into the passenger seat and placed my face in my hands. "Kate is dead, isn't she?" My voice had degraded to a whisper. "My wife is dead."

Sam gripped my shoulder. "Christ, what's wrong with you? You identified the body—"

The smell of blood somehow reaches me through the smell of disinfectant and alcohol. She lies on a stainless-steel table like dozens more I've seen before. I haven't had to see this since I left the force. I never wanted to see this place again.

Seeing Kate here is almost unbearable. It would be unbearable even if they hadn't torn at her body. There is an awful stillness, a motionlessness that's perverse and unnatural. Sam is there, holding my arm. He is the only reason I haven't fallen to my knees.

"Kane?" Sam shook me out of the memory. "Are you with me? Are you going to tell me what the problem is?"

I looked up at him. I wiped the blur out of my eyes and said, "I don't know. I can't remember. I can't remember anything."

We sat in his idling car as I told him what had happened. He listened quietly, nodding occasionally. After I finished, Sam said, "This is just great. You know once we get you to the hospital, we're both in the shit. You *know* that?"

I shook my head and said, "No, I don't."

He pulled the Saturn out into the street. The car slid a little. The snow was wet and heavy, the kind that was hell on driving. The wind whipped it into a white wall that erased everything more than half a block distant. Once he'd pulled away from Coventry, and the businesses clustered there, we were the only car on the street.

Sam focused his concentration on the road ahead, "I've been covering your ass when they wanted you in for questioning. You could have been in protective custody by now."

He gritted his teeth, and I could feel his stress at driving in this mess. "Now you've made yourself look

like a suspect, and that makes me look like an acces-
sory—"

"Can you please tell me what's going on?"

He looked at me. I felt the car slide, and he looked
back at the road. "The way you keep things close to the
vest, and you think I know something? God that's what
I hated about you when we were partners." He sighed.
"What I know? Two weeks ago a high-class hood hires
you to find his missing kid. You find some connection
between this kid and a guy, alias 'Childe.' You find
something going on, and you refuse to tell me about it.
They go after your ex-wife, and you insist on going off
on your own after this Childe person—and somehow
you convince me to let you." Sam pumped the brakes
to bring the car to a slow sliding stop at a red light.
"That's 'what's going on.' "

"Am I a cop?"

"Christ, you don't remember anything? Do you?"

I shook my head.

"Damn, I'm glad you asked to go to the hospital. I'd
hate to try and convince you to do anything you didn't
want to. Look, your name is Kane Tyler, you're forty-
five years old. You're the most stubborn man I know.
You were a cop for nearly fifteen years. Since then
you've been freelance, finding people's missing kids."

"Tell me about my family."

The light turned green, and Sam spun the wheels for
a while before the car started moving.

"You have the daughter I should have had. Don't
worry about Gail, I did manage to swing some police
protection for her. I have a detective sitting with her in
Oberlin."

"Oberlin."

"She's eighteen, goes to college there. Is any of this
helping you remember?"

I gritted my teeth and balled my hands into fists. All
of this and no memories surfaced. All I had was one

last lingering image of Kate's corpse. I couldn't even picture my daughter's face. I felt a deep rage for the people who had left me in that sewer. They had taken my life from me, just as surely as if they had killed me.

My gut ached, and I felt very cold. I stared down so all I saw were my pale fists shaking in my lap. "How could this happen? How could I forget everything?"

"The doctors will help you."

I slammed a fist into my thigh. "But *how*?" I looked up at Sam. "There was nothing wrong. All that blood, and I didn't find a wound—"

"Calm down," Sam said. "I don't know what happened to you, but you're frightening me. You could be bleeding inside. You should have gone to a hospital immediately."

"How long has that van been there?" I said, interrupting him. A black van, little more than a shadow, was behind us. It was gaining slowly through the snow. The windows were black, and I saw no sign of a license plate.

"I don't know, two or three blocks?"

"Call for backup," I said, staring at the van. Something else had joined the anger and frustration—fear. I knew that van, even without a memory of it, just as I'd known Sam as a friend the first moment I'd seen him.

"What . . . ?"

"Call! Now!" I could feel that it was nearly too late. The van was accelerating toward us. Something, either my tone of voice or the fact that I drew the Eagle, convinced Sam. He got on the radio and started calling, "Officer needs assistance."

As if in response, the van slid behind us, and thudded against our rear bumper. We blew through the next intersection without even slowing for the red light. Sam's knuckles were whitening on the steering wheel.

"Pull away from them."

"I'm trying—"

The van kept with us, as if it were tied to our bumper. I leveled my gun at the grille of the van, and fired. The sound tore at my ears, so much it seemed that it was the gun's report and not the bullet that shattered the rear window. Gun smoke filled the cab for a moment before it was sucked out by the sharp winter wind.

"What the fuck are you doing?"

I didn't answer. The van was like a wall behind Sam's car. I fired into the grille again. The van didn't slow or pull away. Snow bit my face.

The world began wailing and pulsing red as Sam turned on the siren. With that and the tearing wind, I could bearly hear him yelling into the radio.

Out of the corner of my eye I saw the sliding door on the side of the van open. I tried to shift my aim, but the van rammed the rear of the car, throwing me against my seat. It knocked what little breath I had out of me, and I suddenly had more panicked thoughts about forgetting to breathe.

This is a bad time to start losing it.

I forced those thoughts away and pumped another shot into the front of the van. The shot went wide of the mark and one of the headlights shattered. Without that glare in my eyes, I saw a shadow slip out of the side of the van, out and up.

"What the . . . ."

Something thudded on the roof of the Saturn. I raised the gun and was firing through the roof before I realized what I was doing. Sam jerked, swerving the car toward the left curb. *"What are you doing?"*

I never had a chance to answer him.

The driver's window shattered. I barely had time to see an arm reaching down from the roof to grab the wheel, before the resulting skid threw me against the passenger door. My gun clattered into the foot well.

The car jumped the median, sliding sidewise. Sam fought for control of the wheel and the arm let go just in time for the van to plow into the side of the car. The van stopped, and we kept going, spinning out to crunch into a parked pickup truck, slamming to a halt with a lurch that tried to ram my stomach through my throat.

For a few moments, the world was cloaked in a ghostly quiet. The siren had died, leaving only the crimson strobe of the flasher. The engine had ground to a halt. For a few seconds all I heard was the ticking of cooling metal.

Then I heard a step on the roof.

How could anyone . . . ?

I scrambled to reach my gun. Someone jumped off the roof of the car before I had gotten to where my gun had slid under the passenger seat.

"You?" I heard him say. His voice was harsh and rough, like the grinding of millstones.

I turned to face him and saw a kid; he couldn't be more than eighteen. He wore black, and the only highlights I saw on his clothes were the studs on his leather jacket. There was no sign of the fact he'd been riding on the roof during a near-fatal skid.

He leaped up to squat in the shattered rear window. It was a leap of unnatural dexterity. I kept fumbling under my seat until my hand felt the butt of the Desert Eagle.

The kid looked at me with a monochrome face intermittently tinted red by the oscillating police flasher. He smiled at me with lips that appeared alternately black and soaked with gore. "Aren't you dead, my friend?"

I got my hand around the gun. I pulled it out and leveled it at the kid's chest. Even though I grabbed my wrist to brace it, the tip of the gun still shook.

"Don't. Move." I said. My head throbbed, I felt weak. I felt as if I moved through molasses.

The kid laughed at me. "You really don't want to

shoot me, Mr. Tyler." He leaned forward slowly, looking me in the eyes. The kid had black irises. I couldn't see any pupils, just black, bottomless holes that tried to suck me in. Everything slowed as he reached for something in the back seat. I could feel his breath on my cheek.

My finger felt like lead when I pulled the trigger.

The sound was like a grenade going off in the back seat. The kid flew backward out the rear window, disappearing behind the rear of the car.

The world went quiet again. "Sam?"

I kept looking out the busted rear window, and I saw nothing but flying snow. "Sam?" A note of hysteria leaked into my voice. I turned to look beside me.

"Shit." It was little more than a whisper. The wind tore the words away. Sam was slumped in his seat, unconscious. Blood streamed from his nose and mouth. The sight of it froze me.

So much blood that it steamed.

I reached over and felt for a pulse. It was there. He was alive. My hand came away covered in livid crimson. The heat of it sank into my fingers. I held my hand in front of my face, the blood almost seemed to glow . . . .

The sound of sirens broke me out of whatever trance I was in. I got loose from the seat belt and pushed open the door. Leading with the gun, I inched my way around the wreck. When I rounded the rear fender, I leveled my gun at the pavement—

The kid wasn't there.

I started looking around maniacally until I saw him dimly, through the snow, jumping into the van. He was carrying something. By the time I had the gun steadied in his direction, there wasn't anything to shoot at.

"Missed," I whispered. "Must have missed."

I stumbled around to the driver's side, which was a crumpled mess. Sam was still breathing, but the blood looked even worse on this side. The blood pulsed crimson in time to the light on the dash, like something alive, like a beating heart.

I slid to my knees next to the door, my head level with Sam's. My knees hit the slush, but it felt as if I'd never stopped falling. The world kept spinning and spinning, and I lost all sense of time or space. For a few minutes all I knew was that red pulsing light . . . .

Sam's coughing brought me back to reality. He was on the ground, next to the car, and I was crouched next to him. I had no memory of prying open the wrecked driver's side door, or of pulling him out of the car. My face was barely inches from his.

His eyes fluttered open for a minute and he looked into mine. "Where the fuck did you learn mouth-to-mouth?"

I didn't respond because I was trying too hard to keep the world from spinning out of control. Sam's face was covered with blood. I could taste it on my own lips. I had a horrifying suspicion that I hadn't been trying to resuscitate him.

Sam coughed again, turned away from me, and spat up a mouthful of blood. The sight tightened something inside me. I began nervously wiping the blood from my own face, and sucking if off my hands. I knew it was Sam's blood, but I did it anyway.

I became afraid of what I might do. This man was a friend of mine, and all I could do was watch his life leak out of his body and feel a sick hunger, picture my lips on his, taste the blood again . . . .

I needed to see a doctor. I was having some sort of psychotic episode. What I was feeling was not sane.

Sam had called for backup. Where the fuck were they?

I pushed myself upright, consciously trying to wipe the blood off my hands in the snow. Sam would be fine, fine as long as I didn't do anything more. But all I could think of, all I smelled and saw, was that damn blood.

"Don't think of it," I was almost pleading with myself now. I needed to concentrate on something else, anything else. For once my memory provided something on command.

"Gaily bedight, / A gallant knight, / In sunshine and in shadow, / Had journeyed long, / Singing a song, / In search of Eldorado." I chanted the stanzas like a mantra. With each word I was trying to force the blood away from my sight. "But he grew old— / This knight so bold— / And o'er his heart a shadow / Fell as he found / No spot of ground / That looked like Eldorado."

Minutes it had been, only minutes since the van had forced us off the road. It already felt as if I had spent most of my life here. The taste of blood was still in my mouth as I spoke.

Something about my distorted state of mind made my senses unnaturally sharp. I was aware of everything—the bite of individual snowflakes on my cheek, the crunch of salt under my feet, the rattle of the power lines in the wind, the sound of a car's distant engine, and the noise of its tires crunching the snow.

I looked up and saw headlights in the distance, through a swirling wall of white. The headlights and the emerging silhouette were familiar. It was my tail from the hotel.

I kept chanting, trying to calm myself. "And, as his strength / failed him at length, / He met a pilgrim shadow—"

It was an Olds, and it pulled up next to the wreck. Three people got out of the car. One bent over Sam, the other two walked toward me. My first thought upon seeing them was: *They're dressed like lawyers, not cops. But lawyers don't drive seven-year-old Oldsmobiles.*

A pair of them stopped in front of me. They were

dressed to match, dark suits, wine-red ties, and char-coal-gray trench coats. The one in the lead was tall, black, and completely bald down to his brows. His friend was a weaselish man with a razor mustache and slick hair, who would have looked more at home in a brown shirt and jackboots.

Their hands were empty, but I got the impression that the white guy at least had a shoulder holster under his trench coat.

I whispered, " 'Shadow,' said he, / 'Where can it be— / This land of Eldorado?' "

"Mr. Tyler?" The tall one spoke with a Jamaican accent that was at odds with the snow-whipped land-scape.

I nodded, not trusting myself to speak. My senses sharpened with the tension, my eyes carved razor edges on everything. But my heartbeat, if anything, slowed.

"We represent Mr. Sebastian, your employer."

When I didn't respond, the Jamaican continued, "Mr. Sebastian wants you to come with us. He is very emphatic about police involvement in his daughter's disappearance."

I could feel myself being backed in a corner. "But, Sam, he's—"

"We understand your relationship with him, and granted you some latitude. But Mr. Sebastian does not want you questioned by the police. He does not want official investigations. Especially after what you've unearthed already."

What have I unearthed? "You bastards stole my tapes."

The Jamaican's partner, the one I'd been thinking of as Mr. Gestapo, smiled. His teeth were gray. The Ja-maican nodded slightly, acknowledging my statement but not granting it any importance. "You disappeared," he said.

"You mean I managed to shake your tail and you

panicked." It wasn't time to be lobbing verbal grenades, but anger was welling up and it was hard to contain.

Mr. Gestapo stopped smiling.

"Perhaps," said the Jamaican, "but if you'd been killed, Mr. Sebastian needed to know what you knew."

"So now you know what I know—"

"If you would come with us, please." The Jamaican held a long arm up to the Olds. "Do not worry about your friend. We'll leave a man here to tend to him until an ambulance arrives."

I didn't move. "What if I wish to stay and wait for the ambulance?"

The Jamaican lowered his arm. "Mr. Tyler, we will not force you into the car. But I should remind you that Mr. Sebastian has many friends in the police department. Friends who are quite aware how emphatically he does not want you questioned. If you were to fall into police custody, the consequences would be unpleasant for all concerned." He motioned at the Oldsmobile. "Now, may we please offer you a lift away from here? You do have Mr. Sebastian's daughter to find."

I smiled, shook my head, and got in the car. I felt more and more like the knight in the Poe poem—

"Over the Mountains
Of the Moon
Down the Valley of the Shadow,
Ride, boldly ride,"
The shade replied,
"If you seek for Eldorado!"

5

They put me in the back seat of the Olds, which was good. It gave me some chance to hide how strung out I was. My hands shook, my head throbbed, and my thoughts were racing around in circles, trying to deny that anything odd had happened with Sam.

I needed a doctor more than ever. But some sense of caution kept me from telling my escort.

The Olds pulled away just as the police flashers began emerging from the snow behind us. When the flashers stopped by the wreck, it was a few moments before the snow reclaimed them, turning blank and gray behind us.

"You've caught up with me," I said, forcing my voice to sound more stable than I felt. "Now what?"

"We stay with you, Mr. Tyler. It's because of you that Mr. Sebastian knows what we're dealing with, and he feels very strongly that you should continue—"

"And continue under Mr. Sebastian's leash. I see."

Mr. Gestapo chuckled at that one. "I see you understand. Mr. Sebastian does not wish you to disappear again."

You bastards, my life is falling apart. How the hell can I collect the pieces with you guys riding my tail?

Worse, I was beginning to think I might need a psychiatrist, and not just for my amnesia. There was a less than subtle threat that if I went to the police, I would find it unhealthy. I doubted that Mr. Sebastian would be any more sanguine about me talking to a doctor.

I racked my stumbling brain for questions I could ask that didn't reveal my ignorance. "What exactly does Mr. Sebastian think we're dealing with?" I asked. "What does he know about what's going on here?"

"An old evil, Mr. Tyler. An evil that goes far beyond idolatry and false gods. An evil that threatens his daughter's immortal soul."

I shook my head. That kind of language prompted thoughts I didn't need to be having.

Pumping these guys for information wasn't very effective. The Jamaican was only slightly less laconic than Mr. Gestapo, but his answers were just as uninformative. Hiding my amnesia hampered my questioning. Even so, I got a few solid facts.

It was Saturday the fifteenth, and I'd started this hunt for Sebastian's daughter on the first. My ex-wife had been killed on the eleventh, and Sebastian's people lost track of me on the thirteenth—a full day before I'd opened my eyes in a storm sewer.

I asked them annoying detailed questions about what they were doing when, and most of my solid information I got from the context of their answers. The subtext of their answers, never actually stated, was that I'd been under Sebastian's surveillance nonstop from the point I took his job . . . .

"Where are you taking me?" I asked.

"To Mr. Sebastian. He wishes to hear from you what happened between seven on Thursday and nine this evening."

Great. "Why did you take so long to pick me up?"

"I wasn't certain about your identity until you met with Detective Samuel Weinbaum."

Whatever I had been hired to do, I had to lose my escort and get some help. I felt certain that whatever sickness gripped me was pulling me toward something dark. "I have a meeting," I told him.

"What?"

I removed my sunglasses with a shaking hand. I had been wearing them all night, and removing them flooded the world with light. The Olds seemed to drive through a tunnel of glowing white motes. "I have to meet someone at the Arabica."

I saw him glance at me in the rearview mirror. "You were just leaving there with Detective Weinbaum."

I smiled a little weakly. "I'm not supposed to meet him until closing. He's paranoid about cops, I had to talk to Sam first—"

He kept glancing between the mirror and the road. "I find this sudden revelation somewhat hard to credit, Mr. Tyler."

"The *van* was a sudden revelation. This was just an attempt to get things done with too little time. Or don't you want me to do my job?"

"But why did you and Detective Weinbaum leave—"

"We were going to the hospital to pick up some paperwork."

"What kind of paperwork?"

What kind of paperwork? I was stuck for a moment.

"Mr. Tyler?"

"My wife, damn you," I let my shakiness, frustration, and my anger find my voice. "Blood tests, the contents of her stomach, where they cut into her body . . . ."

I stared at his eyes, and felt my own begin to blur. The frustration and anger were real. I was lying, but my tears were for my wife, and because it hurt not to remember.

He looked away from me. "Forgive me, Mr. Tyler. We'll go to your meeting."

I felt some sense of victory. It was muted because I didn't know what I was going to do when we got there.

* * *

Mr. Gestapo stayed with the Olds, and the Jamaican accompanied me inside. Before we entered, I said, "Take a table near the front. I told you this guy's paranoid. If he sees you with me, he's liable to spook."

He didn't look pleased, but he nodded.

I stepped inside, and the lights were so bright that my eyes watered. I replaced my sunglasses. The smell of coffee made me uncomfortably aware of my stomach. I gave the counter a wide berth.

No one seemed to go out of their way to notice me. The blond pagan who had given me a tarot reading wasn't here. The poet and the grad student had abandoned their chess game. There seemed about half the people here that there'd been when I left.

I had until closing to think of something.

I kept walking farther into the coffee shop, hunting for some sort of inspiration. As I closed on the smoking section, I began to notice that there was more to this place than was visible from the front. The room curled around the bathrooms like the tail of a snake, and I followed it to a smoky alcove that was almost a separate room from the rest of the coffee shop. There was a whole other section back here, dim and smoke-filled.

The walls were dotted with fliers back here: a feminist flier announcing a pro-choice rally, some New Age thing about pagan open circles, a Communist tract about the liberation of Peru; but what captured my attention was a poster for a band called "The Ultraviolet Catastrophe" who were playing at the Euclid Tavern.

The concert poster disturbed me. Most of the $8\frac{1}{2}$ x 11 page was taken up by a black-and-white line drawing. It showed a tanning bed, and on it was a cadaverous man, with smoke rising from his mouth and eyes. In his hand, dangling to the ground, he held a bottle of something that could have been a Molotov cocktail.

The artist's interpretation of the band's name, I supposed. It made me uneasy. It made me feel that Death had walked from his tarot card to sit back here with me.

I turned away from the poster to focus on something more relevant. There was a fire exit all the way to the rear. Dull gray metal with a crash bar labeled "for emergency only." It was obviously wired to an alarm, so my escort would know as soon as I ran for it.

But I walked to the door and considered whether or not I could outrun him. I figured that he wasn't going to give me more than half a minute to think about it before he walked back here to check on me. If I was going to do it, I should do it now.

I put a hand on the crash bar—

"Kane? Is that you?"

I turned, surprised. Two people were sitting at a table next to the fire door, a man and a woman. Somehow I hadn't even noticed them when I'd turned the corner. I was farther gone than I thought.

The man spoke again. "Kane? Christ, what happened to you, man?"

I recognized the voice from the phone. "Bowie?"

He nodded. He was tall, thin, and wore a long black ponytail that hung to the small of his back. He wore a black motorcycle jacket and blue jeans. His only concession to the weather outside was a pair of gray wool gloves, under the fingerless black leather ones that covered his palms.

I looked at him and felt familiarity. Not the sense of trust I'd felt with Sam, but I knew that I had dealt a lot with this person recently.

The woman, a redhead who was between seventeen and twenty-one, brought me no sense of recognition whatsoever. She was looking at me, as if she wasn't quite sure of who I was.

Makes two of us, I thought.

"That is you, Kane?" Bowie asked.

"Yeah," I said.

"You look dead," he said.

"Thanks, that makes me feel better." I took the conversation as a cue to sit. The smoke, and the scent of heavy perfume underneath it, made me feel a little dizzy. I wondered when it would stop being disorienting simply having people recognize me. I glanced around, and, as I expected, my shadow had moved to another table, one in view of the alcove I'd retreated to.

"Let me introduce you," Bowie said. "Kane, this is Leia, Leia this is Kane Tyler."

"Oh, the gentleman who finds missing children." She had a high, slightly breathy voice, with a very distinct English accent. She had a habit of touching the collar of her turtleneck when she spoke. "An admirable pursuit." She held out her hand and I shook it absently. It wasn't until I saw a quarter smile cock her lips that I realized she had meant me to kiss it.

I looked back to the Jamaican. He was still there, pretending to read a newspaper. *At least if nothing else, I have met with someone.*

"So how's it going? Haven't seen you in days." He looked at Leia, and they exchanged an unreadable glance. "And what's with the sunglasses?"

I rubbed my temples. "Light hurts my eyes. Lights and mirrors." I glanced up and both of them were staring at me. "I know how it sounds." It sounded like any number of things, the most probable being that I was stoned out of my mind. I was getting to the point where I was going to start to search my own arms for needle tracks. "I need a doctor," I whispered.

Bowie and Leia exchanged glances again, and Bowie asked me, "Why don't you get one?"

I looked at him and then at the Jamaican. This was a

noisy place, and I was certain that he was out of earshot. "I need to get away from a friend of mine."

Bowie looked off in the direction of the Jamaican. "What, you need some help?" Bowie laughed, and he leaned in conspiratorially and whispered, "Why sure, man."

He was grinning and I felt compelled to say, "This isn't a game, Bowie."

I felt a light touch on my hand. I looked up at Leia. She stared at me in a way that made me realize just how attractive she was. She had a very seductive whisper. "Mr. Tyler, I am certain that Bowie realizes what is a game and what is a not. You need to seek medical attention." She patted my hand. "We will get you to a doctor."

I felt a slight unease in trusting these strangers, but when it came down to it, everyone was a stranger to me. I looked at her and said, "How?" I had the feeling that if I did make it to an emergency room, the police would become involved.

"We know a doctor who can help you." Bowie was still smiling. "Don't we, Leia?"

She looked at him and shook her head. "My grandfather is a physician." She pulled something out of her purse and slid it to Bowie. "I'll page you when my grandfather's ready and I can pick you up."

She stood up to leave and I whispered, "Wait, what about him?" I cocked my head slightly in the direction of the Jamaican. He was still pretending to read the paper.

"I'll take care of him," she said. "Just, whatever you do, stay with Bowie." Leia walked away from the table.

"What is she going to do?"

Bowie chuckled and said, "You see the same ass I do and you can ask that question?"

She walked past the Jamaican's table, leaned over,

and whispered something. I had no idea what she said, but in a matter of a few moments, the Jamaican wasn't paying much attention to our table.

Bowie backed out along the wall, toward the fire door. I saw where he was headed. "What about the alarm?"

He grinned broadly and slipped a tiny pry bar from inside his jacket. "The alarm is set when you push the bar—" He slid up to the door, and I didn't know how the Jamaican could miss him."—not when you jimmy the latch." He put the pry bar between the door and the jamb and said, "That's the theory anyway."

I watched my shadow, back by the entrance to the smoking section. He wasn't looking our way.

There was a small creak as Bowie levered the bar, but no alarm. The door swung out, and I felt a chill wind hit my face. "Come on," Bowie urged.

I didn't need to be told again.

6

We ran, and for once I was happy for the snow. In the whited-out landscape, we were out of sight of the rear of the coffee shop before we had gone two hundred feet. Even if the Jamaican had come after us the instant we'd left, Leia had bought us enough time to get out the door and lose ourselves in the blizzard.

We ran behind buildings, across side streets and through parking lots, until we came to the intersection of Coventry and Mayfield, a couple of blocks north of where we started. We emerged in the parking lot of a Dairy Mart after jumping a chain-link fence.

Bowie led me across the street and away from the intersection, away from the Dairy Mart, away from all the businesses. Coventry Road on the other side of Mayfield was a residential accumulation of apartment buildings. It was also less well lit, cutting down visibility even more.

"Follow me," Bowie said, darting toward a brick apartment building with me following. Once inside, he opened the door to the basement with the explanation, "Lock's broken."

In a few moments it was obvious that this building wasn't our final destination. We passed a pair of apartments, a laundry room, wove our way through ranks of storage lockers, and came out of a door to the rear of the apartment.

Bowie darted across the asphalt behind the apartment, straight for the garage in back. I followed him out a small door in the rear of the garage.

We walked along an unlit path, calf-deep in snow. To our right were garages facing away from us, to our left was an old chain-link fence. After we'd walked passed two or three garages, I finally spoke, "I think we lost him. Where're we going?"

"I know this chick in East Cleveland, she owes me money. We can crash there till Leia calls and picks us up."

"Uh-huh." I assented without letting any of my reservations show. I needed that doctor. I felt a pain in my gut that never quite went away, combined with a hunger bad enough to make me giddy. If I didn't know better, I'd think I was starving to death.

I don't know any better, do I?

"What's over there?" I asked, waving my hand toward the chain-link. It was impossible to see a few feet beyond the fence; whatever was beyond was unlit.

"Lakeview, I think. We passed the rear of the Jewish place a bit back."

Neither explanation helped me, and I kept glancing off to the left. *Golf Course? Country Club? City Park?* Of course, none of those explained having a separate entity for Jews. It stumped me until I caught sight of a shadow on a hill just beyond the fence. An obelisk stood, a darker shadow against the blowing snow.

"A cemetery," I whispered.

"What?" Bowie asked over his shoulder. He was busy navigating himself over a pile of snow covered garbage someone had dumped back here.

"Nothing," I said as he gave me a hand over a dead refrigerator.

"Bowie, you acidhead!" The "chick" Bowie knew was a little upset with him.

We were a few blocks into East Cleveland, and this building was still on the border of Lakeview Cemetery. We had gone up to the third floor, Bowie's friend had opened the door, looked at both of us, and pulled Bowie into the apartment. I had enough of a glimpse to see short black hair, a tank top, and a livid red skull tattooed on her bicep, before she slammed the door in my face, leaving me alone in the hallway.

I was left to listen to their argument through the closed door, feeling less inconspicuous by the moment.

"Christ, Billi, he's my friend—he's in trouble."

"Do I come to your place so *my* drugged-out friends can crash?"

"He isn't—"

"Have you looked at him? It's almost midnight, in a snowstorm, and he's wearing *sunglasses*?"

The only bright spot was the fact that this was only one of two raging arguments going on in this building, and covering the noise of both was a loud party downstairs. I was the only person in the hall, and I did my best not to look like I belonged to Bowie's argument.

"You can't do this to me, Billi. I need to—"

"I don't."

"You owe *me*, Billi."

Any sane person would have made a graceful retreat by now. But I was feeling worse by the minute. The blizzard outside was rattling the windows loud enough to be heard over the chaos in the apartments, and I did not want to go out there again. The cold felt as if it was sucking the marrow out of my bones.

On top of everything else—

I leaned against the wall and stared at the ceiling. If someone showed for me—police, Sebastian, or Childe— I wouldn't put up much of a fight. It was hard for me to believe that when I had gotten out of that bathtub I had felt fine.

What the hell was wrong with me?

"No, Bowie, you're not holding that over me."

"Billi, if it wasn't for me, you'd be out on the street."

"You know I'm going to pay you back—"

"Yeah, right now."

"Bastard."

My view of the rust-spotted ceiling was blurred through the condensation fogging my sunglasses. A bead of melted snow slid across my field of vision as the door to the apartment opened.

I took off the sunglasses to get my first good look at Bowie's friend, Billi. She was as tall as I was, almost as tall as Bowie. But where Bowie was stick-thin, she had an athlete's body. She was wearing sweatpants and black tank top that might have been sexy if she didn't look so pissed.

"Come in," she said.

I stepped through the door, and she quickly slammed it shut behind me. She turned, as if to launch into another high-volume argument. More raised voices I didn't need; my luck was pushed as it was.

"I'm sorry to put you through this," I said. I did my best to sound conciliatory.

She looked at me as if she was about to say something, then shook her head. "Yeah, whatever." She ran both hands through her hair, a gesture of frustration.

We stood there, paused, in the entryway to her apartment. Neither of us wanted me to be here. "All I need is to rest a moment, talk to Bowie— When our ride calls, I'll be out of your hair."

She looked at me with an unbelieving expression. "Don't even talk to me. I'm doing this for your bastard friend."

I nodded and rubbed my temples. On top of everything else, I was beginning to feel feverish. I tried to tell myself that the apartment was just too hot.

I stumbled inside.

I am going to get some medical attention. I'll be fine once I see this doctor. That was becoming as difficult to believe as everything else.

Our hostess left us in the living room. The place was sparsely furnished, a sagging sofa surrounded by shelves made with cinder blocks and milk crates. Spiral notebooks and loose-leaf paper covered every available surface. I took it all in with a glance, then I collapsed on the side of the evil green sofa that wasn't in line with the windows. The cushion sagged halfway to the ground.

Bowie sat on the arm opposite me. He was perched so close to the edge it looked like he was levitating. I closed my eyes, because without the sunglasses the light in here was giving me a headache.

It was hard not to give in to the feeling of helplessness.

"We need to talk," I said.

Bowie shook his head nervously. "Yeah, yeah—You gotta tell me what happened to you." He took a pause, and, very uncertainly, he said, "Was it Childe?"

The pause in his speech made me feel a little sicker. "Damn it, I don't know! I'm barely keeping what's left of my head together. If you're supposed to be my friend, you tell *me* about this Childe guy."

"I don't have a hell of a lot more—"

"Tell me *everything* you know. I need to get it straight in my head. You have no idea how scrambled my mind is."

"Maybe I do . . . ." He looked at me, and our eyes locked briefly. "Maybe I don't." He gave me a funny look then he shrugged. "Okay, everything *I* know about the guy. He showed up about five years ago, hanging around the neo-pagan scene here. He'd just show up at their rituals, circles, whatever you call them. Everyone describes him as tall, bearded, English accent. None of the pagans I talked to liked the guy. He gave everyone the willies—bad karma, smelly aura, or something. Half the people I talked to described him as predatory."

"Childe a real name or an alias?" I asked.

Bowie looked at me as if I should have known that. I probably should've. But I was long past my limit as far as feigning an intact cerebellum was concerned.

"Almost certainly an alias," he stared at me. "The pagan crowd has a thing for renaming themselves. Not that this guy was ever part of the pagan crowd."

I stared back. "Not part of the crowd?" I thought of my errant fortune-teller.

"No. The pagans are a good crowd, throw good parties. Childe wasn't there for the parties."

"What was he there for?" I was getting an odd feeling about the conversation I was having with Bowie. Something was happening.

"He was a predator." Bowie had nearly ceased moving, and a lot of the inflection had gone out of his voice. Looking into his eyes, I could see his pupils dilated nearly all the way. If I hadn't been watching him all this time, I could have sworn he had just taken some heavy drug.

"Predator?" I asked.

"It took a long time for them to notice what Childe was doing. See, they had open rituals, circles, whatnot, where anyone could come and see what they were doing. Childe would pick people, the curiosity seekers. Never one of the regulars, the serious pagans."

"Young teenagers, usually girls?"

"Yes. But boys, too. Anyone who left with Childe never returned to any of the public gatherings. Since these were always strangers to the pagans, it took them a long time to notice."

"But they did notice." I had the eerie feeling of knowing everything Bowie was telling me, and the associations weren't pleasant.

"They barred him from their functions—and he disappeared, along with a large number of confused teenagers."

I rubbed my knees and noticed Bowie imitating my motion. He blinked when I blinked. We were breathing in sync. I had to repress an urge to shudder.

What was happening?

"This is where I came in, isn't it?"

"You were looking for this girl, Cecilia. Childe is still the last person to be seen with her, until you made the tape."

"What tape?"

"The tape you made of the sacrifice—"

Memory slammed into me. A *real* memory, as unexpected and violent as a sledge to the back of my skull.

I stand behind a screen of leafless scrub, calf-deep in frozen mud. Ice cuts into the upper parts of my calves. The night is clear, the air sharp, the moon full. I'm facing a wide clearing, a flat spot bordered by steep, snow-dusted hillsides.

Facing me, a hundred yards away or more, is a flood-control dam, an angled wall of concrete sloping up about a hundred feet into the dark. The runoff forms a creek snaking the left side of the clearing. I'm hidden along the shores of that outflow.

I'm aiming my camcorder at the right side of the clearing, toward a smaller hill nestling by the right corner of the dam. There are structures built into the hill—

That's not what I'm looking at. My camcorder has drifted away from my eye, so there is nothing left between me and what I am looking at.

Between me and the small hill is a semicircle of a dozen people. They stand in a patch of snow darkened far beyond the depths of their bluish shadows. The snow they stand in is black.

The blackness smears what portions of their skin I can see. It dots their jackets, their hair, their jeans. The

*blackness almost completely obliterates the crumpled
form they surround, making it no more than a lump in
the shadow.*

*What they surround used to be human. The
spreading blackness is its blood.*

*One of the circle looks directly at me. The blood
carves a black hollow in his face. He smiles and I
cannot see his teeth for the shadow.*

I jerked out of the involuntary memory as if an icicle
had been shoved into my aorta. The image came with a
legion of emotions: disgust, fear, and—it turned my
stomach to think of it—something akin to lust. I sat
there, shaking, staring into Bowie's dilated impassive
eyes, and decided that I must really be insane.

I ran from that scene, I know I ran from it.

But he had seen me—

"What am I involved in?" I said. My voice was
barely a whisper.

"Something you don't understand. Even the Le Vey
Satanists shy away from these Childe people."

Looking at Bowie scared me. It was almost as if he
had become some sort of automaton. It was hard to tell
if I was really talking to Bowie, someone who knew
me, or if I was talking to some warped part of my own
mind. The sense of knowing what he was about to say
just before he said it didn't help.

It began to sink in that these people had slaughtered
Kate to warn me away. The sick, feverish feeling overcame me again, and I blacked out for a moment.

The next thing I knew was I'd broken eye contact
with Bowie, and I was trying to throw up again. I was
on my knees on the floor, my stomach trying to slam
through my diaphragm, and nothing coming up but a
few bits of sour blackness.

"God, you all right?" Bowie's voice sounded normal
again. I barely noticed.

He dragged me toward the bathroom. I didn't fight

him. As he led me, one bony arm around my waist, he kept talking. "It'll be all right. We're going to get you to that doctor."

The door opened to the bathroom, and suddenly I was faced with a mirror and searing pain. "Lights!" I managed to croak.

Bowie understood me, and hit the light switch, breaking the molten eye contact I had with myself. I turned away from the medicine cabinet and sat on the lid of the john. I waved him away.

His silhouette hovered in the doorway for a moment and he asked, "Are you going to be all right?"

No . . .

"Yes."

He closed the door to the windowless bathroom, leaving me in near-perfect darkness. The only light came from the cracks around the door, filtered through the edge of the hall carpet. It was a dusty, anemic light that carved a thin strip of visibility across the walls.

I was no longer retching, but I felt empty, violated. I felt as if something had been cored out of my being, leaving me with just the husk. I fingered the ring on my finger.

My wife. My daughter. And I couldn't remember . . . .

7

It took me some time before I had gathered the strength to turn on the light. I was careful to keep my back to the mirror until I had replaced my sunglasses. Even with my eyes covered, I winced when I saw my reflection—not from pain, but from the ravages written on my face.

I wasn't looking at the same person who had stepped out of the bathroom of the Woodstar Motel. My face was lined and hollow-looking, worse even than the pale shadowed mask I had seen in the Arabica. My skin wasn't just pale now. It was translucent. The bare bulb above the mirror carved the outline of a skull on my face.

Four hours ago, in the bathroom of the motel, I had looked perfectly fine. An hour ago, maybe less, I had looked in the mirror at the Arabica and saw someone who was ill.

Here I looked like death.

I reached up and touched my cheekbone, under the edge of my sunglasses. My skin felt dry, thin, and cold. As I drew my finger down my face, it left a streak of gray compressed skin behind it. I stared at that strip for a full minute before it returned to the anemic color of the surrounding skin.

Death was a kind word for what I saw in the mirror.

My hands shook, and it began to dawn on me exactly how loose my clothes felt. My jeans were hanging on my hips, the denim jacket I still wore felt like a tent on me, even my holster felt loose. It felt as if I'd lost twenty pounds since the motel room.

I raised my arm so the sleeve fell away from my watch. The watchband—which was snug when I'd donned the watch—was loose on a wrist much bonier than I remembered.

"No way," I whispered. This was an impossibility.

I looked at my hands and saw that my nails had lengthened, just like they were supposed to on a corpse.

I backed away from the mirror and grabbed for the door. My heart felt frozen in my chest. I couldn't sense it beating. And, like during my journey through the storm sewer, every breath I took was a conscious act.

I stepped through the door and into a dim hallway. I took a few steps and leaned on the wall where I could see into the living room. Bowie was there, in a corner, talking on the phone. "Yeah. He's here, locked in the bathroom . . . . Yes, urgent, he looks like shit . . . what? I don't think he's fed at all. Just look at him . . . ."

Hearing him tore at the inside of my head. I wasn't thinking quite right. Whatever help Bowie and his friend were offering, a torn part of my mind was telling me that I was beyond medical attention. Could some doctor who was used to dealing with junkies and over-doses do anything for someone who was turning into a walking corpse?

"Look, just get over here. We'll worry about that when we get him straightened out . . . . Dangerous? . . . When was the last time you were as strung out as he is?"

I was suddenly very afraid of doctors, and what they might find. I needed desperately to get away from Bowie, to get away from the help he was offering. I edged along the wall of the hallway, toward the entranceway, senselessly afraid that Bowie would turn around and see me.

"Yes, that would be easier . . . . If you want me to I will. But all this we've gone through was to avoid that . . . . You know what I mean . . . ."

Somehow I inched all the way to the door. I watched Bowie, and I was frozen for a moment when I saw my reflection in the night-black windows behind the couch. Bowie faced away from me, staring out the glass at the storm.

Either it was the angle, or something he was watching outside, but he didn't notice me. "You didn't tell anyone about him, did you? . . . No, I just noticed this guy standing outsi—"

I stumbled out of the apartment, closing the door on Bowie's conversation.

Even with the sunglasses, the lights in the hallway hurt my eyes. I sagged against a wall, the light a weight on my shoulders. The hall was hot with a heat that didn't reach beneath my bone-dry skin. Cold was deep in the core of my body, as if my chest was packed with snow.

I shook my head and forced myself to walk. I needed to get away. My body was screaming its need at me, and it was a call that was impossible to ignore now.

My eyes refused to focus on the hall ahead of me. My gaze darted to shadowy corners, where the painful light didn't reach. In the darkest corners, the ones of impenetrable black, I could imagine something glistening and wet.

The wall abraded my shoulder like sandpaper, even through the denim, and the sound was like tearing canvas. Snow rattled the windows in the stairwell, like an unwanted visitor scratching to gain entry . . . .

" 'Tis the wind and nothing more,' " I muttered. I almost laughed. I could feel an inappropriate glee surge like a tide, an alien desire to shout the lines from Poe's poem—

"Nevermore," I choked out, grabbing the railing for balance. I was losing it. My mind was as erratic as the

snowstorm, feverish neurons firing at random. My grip on the banister was crushing the skin on my hands.

I stared down the center of the stairwell, all four floors to the ground. The sunglasses slipped off my face and tumbled slowly to the concrete below. They broke when they hit, the lenses fragmenting into a dozen pieces of glittering plastic.

I let go of the railing and jerked back as if I'd been hit. My back slammed into the wall behind me. I heard the plaster crack.

I'd been going *up* the stairs.

I looked up the stairs, where I'd been going, deliriously. Now, listening, I could hear it. The argument upstairs—one I had heard upon arriving here—was continuing, or had renewed itself.

I could just see the door of the apartment up at the next landing. Number 401. The door seemed to swell in my vision. Even with my back to the wall, I was still inching toward it. I could feel it from where I was, a half-flight down. It felt as if it was the open door of a blast furnace. Not heat. Anger. Fear.

"You don't play me like that, *bitch*!"

I could make out the voices now, like a tiny river of lucidity in a feverish desert.

"Please, Tony—" Woman's voice cut short by an impact and the sound of something breaking.

I stood in front of door 401. It was razor sharp in my vision, everything else had blurred away. The entire apartment building melted away, everything but the door.

"You think I'm *stupid*?" Tony was shouting through the door. "You think I ain't got eyes?"

"Please—" a timid, frightened voice, nearly inaudible.

"Do you?"

I tried the doorknob.

"I'm going to kill you if you don't tell me who the fuck he is."

I was breathing again, sucking in hot coppery air. Something in that air shriveled my gut into a hard little knot. The door was locked, but that barely mattered to me. My body was an automaton.

I heard a sound behind the door, a strangled gurgle.

My shoulder slammed into the door. It hit hard enough to break bone. It was the doorjamb that broke. Wood splintered, and the door jerked as the security chain caught it. The chain barely held a fraction of a second—

Then it gave.

I stumbled into the living room. The door crashed into the wall, cracking plaster, and slowly swung back shut.

The room was a mess. Chairs were overturned, a glass coffee table was smashed, blinds had been ripped from the windows, and there was a hole in the drywall where someone had thrown a telephone through.

The only light was from a floor lamp in front of me. Sprawled on the ground, its shade askew, it cast crazy ink-black shadows on the walls.

"What the *fuck*?" Tony was shirtless, wearing only a pair of dirty blue jeans. His girlfriend was naked, and only supported by his hand in her hair. There were bruises across her back, and she was bleeding badly from a broken nose.

Badly.

The smell of blood was rank in the room. I sucked in the smell, and the colors in the room seemed to get deeper, the light brighter.

"This ain't your business, scarecrow. You better leave or I'll have to fuck you up." His hand left the woman's hair, and she slid to the ground, unmoving.

Her bruises shone like crimson flares, her blood was like a river of fire, but where her blood splattered Tony it was like a black taint of leprosy.

Tony stood before me, muscles flexing in a display of intimidation. "You deaf, motherfucker?"

None of this meant much to me at this point. I was quite mad. I was in free fall. The only thing that anchored me to earth was the magnificent flare of emotion standing before me. Looking at Tony right then was like looking at the sun.

And I was cold inside.

"What you staring at?" Tony took another step toward me. His face was reddening, a tide of blood washing over his expression. *"You been fucking with my woman?"*

It began as an angry shout, but it trailed off as I drew the Eagle from its holster.

"Hey, man, don't do something stupid—"

I leveled the gun at Tony's head. "Once upon a midnight dreary—" The poem came unbidden to my lips, some mad urge to taunt the last shred of my sanity.

I was halfway into the stanza when Tony said, "What the fuck are you—"

I whipped him across the face with the overlong barrel of the automatic. His face snapped to the side, his mouth sprayed blood, and he almost fell to his knees. Almost, but not quite. Tony was a strong kid. Strong, and so full of anger that standing in front of him was like standing in front of a bonfire.

His shocked eyes stared into my own, blood streaming down his face. I could tell his blood from hers. His blood burned my eyes with its inner life, while the places where her blood had touched him were dead, dormant, and black.

The shock in his eyes slowly drained away as he looked at me. I whispered, " 'Tis some visiter,' I muttered, 'tapping at my chamber door / Only this and nothing more.' "

Where the woman's blood had been rivers of fire, the blood on Tony's slackening face was the mouth of an open volcano. Heat, where I was so, so cold inside.

I took a step forward, still quoting, whispering,

staring at the transfixed Tony. I lowered the gun because Tony was no longer moving. I was close enough to feel his breath on my face. The only thing separating the two of us was the lamp, a narrow rod on the floor.

Upthrust shadows crossed his face, devouring his eyes, leaving empty wells to stare at me.

"Then this ebony bird beguiling my sad fancy into smiling, / By the grave and stern decorum of the countenance it wore."

I remembered the sacrifice, the memory of a gore-stained face, smiling. Tony's mouth was like that now, blood-covered and black with shadow.

" 'Though thy crest be shorn and shaven, thou,' I said, 'are sure no craven, / Ghastly grim and ancient Raven wandering from the Nightly shore—"

I could feel the same bizarre lust I'd felt during that memory. It struck me full force in the chest, and the groin, an aching hunger that had drawn me to this room even in my delirium. I dropped the gun.

" 'Tell me what thy lordly name is on the Night's Plutonian shore!' "

I raised my arms to embrace Tony. He didn't move.

"Quoth the Raven,"

I stepped on the lightbulb. It popped, plunging the room into darkness.

" 'Nevermore,' " I whispered.

I kissed him, tasting the blood. I felt his heat, and I wanted it. Needed it. The blood that had drawn me here lit a dark fire in my belly. Even as eye contact was broken, and Tony began to move again, I didn't let go.

He bucked and struggled, but from somewhere I found the strength to lift him off the ground. He screamed, but it was muffled by my own mouth. His breath forced life into my own lungs. The fire inside him flared into a nova.

His head whipped from side to side. I felt flesh tear.

Warmth spread across me, inside me. As he thrashed, I bit into the heat, drank it in, absorbed it.

Then my delirium snapped, the fever broke, and I became aware that I was holding a corpse. I dropped Tony, now only so much dead weight, and I could think clearly again.

What I thought was, *I'm a fucking nut. I'm a homicidal maniac. I just killed a man.*

I backed away from the scene, until I felt my back pushing the front door completely closed. The room in front of me was dark, but my eyes had adjusted well enough to see both crumpled bodies. Only one breathed.

I tensed myself, and walked back into the living room, stepping over Tony's body. I checked the woman. Even in the dark I could see that she'd been severely beaten. Even as my mind tried to use her to justify what I did, I felt the same perverse lust when I smelled her blood.

As when I smelled Sam's blood.

I knew that in the state I'd been in, if she'd been the only one in this apartment, she would've been the corpse. Tony had died not for any moral decision on my part, but because he had attracted my attention.

What was happening to me?

I stood by the woman and, thankfully, felt myself in control despite the feelings her blood kindled in me.

At first I thought she was out cold, but when I touched her, she winced and curled up tighter into a fetal position. She was sobbing, but so low that I could barely hear her.

"It's all right," I told her lamely. "It's over."

As I whispered meaningless reassurances, I wondered how much she'd seen. By all rights she should've been running away from me, screaming for the police. Right now I didn't much care. I had a totally selfish desire to get her away from Tony's corpse.

It took a little encouragement to get her to stand up;

fortunately, she didn't stand up facing the door, or Tony. "That's it," I said. "We've got to get you into bed."

She shivered against my arm, which was around her shoulders, supporting her. "I didn't," she whispered. "I don't do things like that."

"I'm sure you didn't." I maneuvered her down the hall toward what I hoped was the bedroom.

"Where's Tony? I have to tell him—"

"Tony left," I said a little abruptly.

She half-turned toward me, as if suddenly realizing I was there. "Who are you?" A note of panic slipped into her voice.

"A friend," I said. I tried to put all the reassurance I could in the word, and it made me feel like a fraud.

She stared at me through a right eye that was swelling shut. The emotion leached out of her voice as she said, "It isn't his fault."

I turned away and kept her moving toward the bedroom.

"He loves me," she said.

I felt sick.

When I laid her out on her bed, she looked up at me and asked, "What's your name?"

Something inside made me say, "Raven."

She smiled, weakly, and I told her to go to sleep. She did as I told her.

By the time I had gotten her—I still didn't know her name, and I didn't really want to—to bed, I was pretty sure that no one in the building had noticed our little disturbance. With what I had broken in on, if anyone had noticed, they'd ignored it.

Flash of a memory, more an amalgam of images and impressions than any single scene from my past. Women all of them, I had met dozens of them, but they all felt like the same woman. Most were clients who wanted help rescuing a child from an abusive runaway spouse. On a few more agonizing occasions, the women were the ones who illegally swiped the kids . . . .

Sometimes the law is a poor parent.

Every time it's the same question. The neighbors hear the yelling, the fights, the beatings—Why don't they ever do anything?

I rubbed my temples. A corpse was a high price for a piece of my past.

But, thanks to the stoic ignorance of the residents here, there were no police, no ambulances, no one even knocking on the broken door to ask what was wrong.

I turned on a still-intact table lamp, to get a good look at Tony. He had collapsed facedown, and I prodded a shoulder with a boot to flip him over.

I took a step back, and almost fell over.

The lower quarter of Tony's face was gone, flesh ripped down to the bone. Torn flesh ran down the right side of his neck to the collarbone. The bite-marks did not come from human teeth.

I raised my hand to my face, and it came away bloody.

I looked down at myself, and Tony's blood covered me, coating the front of my shirt. Tony looked as if he'd bathed in it. I wanted to feel sick, but the sight failed to raise a single twinge of nausea.

I knelt by Tony's head and examined the bites.

I knew I had been the one who savaged Tony's face, I remembered doing it, but there was no way my teeth could have produced the wounds I saw. I traced a line above the worst of it, drawing my finger across the intact skin over Tony's cheekbone. It left a small trail of blood, and the skin beneath turned an even paler white with compression. The color refused to return—

A realization came to me.

I ran to the bathroom, my eyes lowered until I had my hand up to shade my reflection's eyes.

Under the smears of blood, my face looked perfectly normal. There was none of the pallor that I had seen earlier, none of the paleness, none of the desiccation. My body filled out the clothes I wore. The weakness, the disorientation, all the symptoms that had me in a near-panic, they were all gone.

I was more convinced than ever that I had lost my senses. The physical transformation I had seen in myself was flatly impossible, and the only explanation I had was that I'd been in a state of homicidal derangement ever since I had left the bathroom downstairs.

That's a lie. There's at least one other explanation.

I tried to push the thought away.

Lust for blood, an aversion to mirrors . . . .

It was insane.

Someone placed a Eucharist upon my doorway—

It wasn't as if I'd reacted to it.

That sacrifice, the blood—

"Stop it. Stop it. Stop it," I whispered. My mind didn't stop gnawing on the possibility—the impossibility—but I tried to ignore it as I did what I could to clean the blood off myself.

Fortunately, the mess had confined itself to my shirt-front. The shirt was a total loss, but the rest of my clothes had gotten by with only a few minor spatters. My shoes, face, and hands, I washed off. I was hampered by my reflection and my lack of sunglasses, but it was surprising how easily I became used to not looking myself in the eye.

I left the bathroom, and the bedroom door was still closed.

Tony was where I had left him.

I sat, shirtless, on the edge of an askew couch, and considered my options. I had until the woman woke up to do something. The best course—for humanity, if not myself—seemed to be to sit around and wait for the cops, since I appeared to be a psychopath.

For some reason, that option didn't appeal to me.

Neither did just leaving Tony the corpse here. Not only did that woman, whoever she was, have enough to deal with, but if I was serious about avoiding the police, Tony was one hell of a calling card.

So how to dispose of the body? That was the question.

Packing Tony for storage was easier than I expected. It was helped by the fact that, while the corpse was covered by blood, there was none of the spraying I'd have expected from someone missing half his neck—

You know what happened to most of the blood.

—The blood was pretty much confined to Tony and the carpet beneath him. Another lucky break was the fact that the carpet in the entryway was a loose Oriental-style rug resting on the wall-to-wall, and the blood hadn't yet soaked through.

I managed to find duct tape in the kitchen, and rolled Tony and my bloody shirt up in the carpet. It wasn't perfect—his legs stuck out below the knees—but it managed to get most of the evidence in a single package.

I found a garbage bag and stuck that over Tony's dangling feet.

Then I went through the apartment collecting his spoor. It was her apartment, so finding Tony's possessions wasn't too difficult. In a few minutes I'd found his shirt, boots, wallet, keys, and a handful of cheap male jewelry. Most of it was in the bedroom, but the woman slept so deeply that most of my caution in collecting the remains of Tony's life was unwarranted.

Tony's car keys were important. I'd been hoping—praying—for the keys. I couldn't exactly call a cab to pick up me *and* the corpse.

The last thing I retrieved was my gun. Picking it up brought home the complete insanity of what had happened. I had dropped the gun to *bite* the bastard.

What I could make no sense of was that he had *let me*. If he had had any sense at all, he should've dived for the gun the second I'd dropped it. But he had stayed there, fixated on me—

Just like Bowie . . . .

I was avoiding that line of reasoning, so I looked out the kitchen window, searching for Tony's car.

8

It wasn't easy moving Tony by myself. It didn't matter how strong I was, or how strong I thought I was. Carrying a corpse was different than carrying any other two-hundred-pound object. It wasn't just dead weight I was dealing with, but it was loose, jointed, dead weight that insisted on bending and sagging toward the ground. Picking Tony up was like trying to swing a two-hundred-pound sack of wet cement over my shoulder.

I felt incredibly exposed as I descended the fire escape. Even though, by my watch, it was after two in the morning. Even though the snowstorm was still whiting-out everything beyond a hundred feet. Even though I couldn't see another soul. I felt as if I were being watched during every step I took.

It was a harrowing descent. The metal fire-escape had accumulated a layer of snow over a coating of ice. Each step was uncertain and felt as if my foot would slide out from under me. Tony didn't help. Every time a gust rattled through the metal around me, Tony would catch the wind and try to pull me off my feet. Ice motes buffeted my face, but I barely felt them.

In the lot behind the building, everything was blue-tinted monochrome, black, blue-grays, and whites. The cars were hard to discern. A half a dozen sat back here, and all I had to go on were Tony's keys, which went to a Chrysler. Instinct led me to the large, unaerodynamic pile of snow that had no hubcaps.

With one hand, I wiped snow away from the rear of my chosen car, and saw it was a Plymouth Duster. In a final test I fumbled out Tony's keys from my pocket, trying not to let him tumble into the snow.

I shoved the key into the ice-coated lock on the trunk. It slid in, but wouldn't turn. In frustration, I forced it. The key turned and the trunk popped open.

It was Tony's Plymouth.

With a sense of relief, I let Tony's corpse roll off my shoulder and into the trunk. The car was an old model, '76 at the latest, and the cavernous trunk swallowed all of him without complaint. I slammed the trunk shut, thankful that no one had seen me.

My thanks came too soon.

"Sir, you show some instincts that will stand you in good stead."

I whipped away from the trunk, to look for the speaker. I heard him before I saw him. It may have been because of the clothes he wore. It was a few seconds before I saw a white-suited figure emerging from the blowing snow. It was disorienting to watch. I faced the rear of the apartment, and I could see it barely as a shadow within the blue-gray wall of wind-whipped snow.

The speaker appeared between me and the apartment, as if he were emerging from an invisible distance, as if the apartment building had never been there.

"Who are you?" I asked.

"My chosen name is Gabriel." He spoke with a thick Southern accent. He was past middle age; he looked to me to be in his late sixties or early seventies. His hair was white, and blew around his shoulders. He wore a white suit that was more fit for the Bahamas than Cleveland. He walked with a long cane whose shaft was silvered. He had large hands, the hands of a pianist. They completely enveloped the head of the cane when he leaned upon it.

For a long time I stared at him. Then I asked, "What are you doing here?"

Gabriel smiled. "Ah, it has been a long time since any youth had the temerity to question my right to be anywhere. It is my question you ask, sir. One I would be addressing to you—" He motioned to the trunk with his cane. "—if I had not already known your business."

I began to look for a likely escape route. Unfortunately, all of them—the building, the driveway, and the alley opposite the driveway—led past Gabriel. He didn't look threatening, but there was something about his bearing that made me loath to test him. "So you've called the police already?"

Gabriel laughed. "If you were not so obviously ignorant, I should take that question as an aspersion on my honor. I keep my Covenants, sir. Even with those who know no Covenant."

I shook my head; none of this was making any sense to me. "What are you doing here?" I repeated. "What are you talking about? What's going on here?"

Gabriel frowned slightly. "Learn some respect for your elders, Mr. Tyler—"

"You know me?"

He pointed his cane at me. "Keep your peace for a moment and perhaps your questions might be answered. Now, may I speak without interruption?"

I nodded.

"I knew of a man, a man named Kane Tyler. This man was a hunter of children. In time he was hunting one of the Covenant, the one known as Childe. It has come to be that those of the Covenant hunt Childe as well."

He paused for a time and I nodded, still not understanding all of what he was saying. "So you're looking for Childe, too?" After a beat, I added, "Sir?" There was something about him that did command respect.

Gabriel smiled. "Childe has allowed his blood to disregard the Covenant, and for that he must be found and disciplined."

I shook my head. "I don't understand. What's this Covenant that you talk about?"

Gabriel looked at me for a long time. "Who is your master that would send you into the world without that knowledge, at least? Is it Childe that spawned you?"

I stared at him.

"You are ignorant, sir." Gabriel took one step, and suddenly he had closed the distance between us. One of those pianist's hands gripped my chin, cradling my face. He held his face within an inch of my own, staring into my eyes. "Do not feign ignorance that you do not possess. I am lord of my blood, and you may not deny who it is that owns you."

"I don't know what the fuck you're talking about!"

Gabriel grimaced, and I saw anger burn there. It was an anger that never left the eyes, but it was a fury that made Tony's bonfire rage nothing more than a birthday candle.

My feet lifted off the ground before I realized what was happening. "Witless thrall!" Gabriel said as he flung me toward the apartment. I was in the air nearly a full second before my back slammed into the railing of the fire escape. My head snapped back with an impact that felt as if it broke my neck. I tumbled forward, and fell six feet to land face first in the snow. The impact had stunned me so much that I couldn't raise my arms to protect myself. My face slammed into the snow-covered asphalt.

I lay there for a long time, feeling warmth trickle down my cheek.

"Get up." I felt a boot push my shoulder, turning me over.

After that impact, I shouldn't have been able to move, much less get to my feet. To my own surprise, I found myself standing. I stood, shaking, as the wind froze the blood on my face.

Gabriel held his cane in both hands, horizontal at belt height. I could finally see the head of the cane, the head of a serpent or dragon worked in pewter. Set in the serpent's eye was a red stone, a ruby at odds with the blue-gray world around me.

"You have exhausted what license youth and ignorance grant you. I am not here to answer your questions, and you have no leave to challenge me. The only respect due you is the respect due your master." He twisted the head of his cane and slowly withdrew a blade from it. "You *will* tell me who your master is, and your chosen name. If you do not, your master shall find his thrall less than worthy."

I took a step back, toward the building. I reached for my gun, but the holster was empty.

Gabriel shook his head. "You disappoint me. Perhaps I was wrong about your instincts." He kept walking toward me. "Many as young as you would have abandoned the body after such a feeding. I must deal with such violations too often." He raised the blade of his cane to my neck. It felt even colder than the wind. It was sharp enough that I could feel skin part under the pressure. I feared that he would open my jugular.

"Answer me. Do not force me to mark you."

I gasped. "I don't know what to tell you. I don't know what you're asking. My name is Kane Tyler, and if I have a master, I don't know about it."

"If you lie . . ." Gabriel stared at my face, and then at where the blade met my throat. He removed the sword and held it up so that a bead of my blood rolled down its edge. My own blood looked black in the dark, nothing like Tony's.

Gabriel turned the blade, examining the blood. His nostrils flared and he touched the edge briefly to his lips.

He stood there immobile for a moment, looking at me. Then he took a handkerchief from his breast pocket, wiped his mouth and the blade, and replaced the blade within the cane.

He then shocked me by making a low bow. "Sir, it seems the humble servant before you has done you a wrong."

"What . . . ?" The question refused to form itself.

"You are of free blood. I ask your pardon, sir. Such prodigies are rare." He withdrew a card from his breast pocket. "This is not the place for our discussion, and I have withheld you too long. Please come to me. Childe must be found."

He held out the card, and I took it. There was no name on it, only an embossed address, and a single phone number. As I read the card, Gabriel said, "Perhaps then I might answer some of your questions and redeem myself for this unfortunate business."

"Wait, I have some questions now. The first of which—"

I raised my head and Gabriel was gone.

"—why the sudden change of heart . . . ?" I whispered to the snow.

The only sign of Gabriel's presence was the card he had handed me, and a pair of footprints that were already filling with snow. I wiped the snow off my watch and checked the time.

It was 2:30.

I wondered what had happened with Bowie and Leia. I also wondered what their doctor would have found if I'd gone to his office. With all of the reference to blood, insane as the idea was, I was beginning to suspect that the doctor would have found something very unusual.

I pocketed the business card and walked back to

Tony's Plymouth. The keys were still dangling from the trunk. Also sitting on the trunk was my Desert Eagle.

Tony's Plymouth had seen better days. Its left rear fender occupied the back seat. Fortunately, it started. I was nervous as I pulled the Plymouth out onto Coventry. I was the only vehicle on the road. I felt as if I were driving under a follow-spot. All I needed was a bumper sticker, "Body in Trunk."

What now? I asked myself as I drove away from the apartment.

Everything was different now. I'd killed a man. I had little memory of my life before this, but I could feel, in my gut, that I was not a killer. I had carried a badge, carried a gun, but I wasn't a killer . . . .

The first real memory of Kate hit me—

"Are you sure you want to do this?" she asks, massaging the back of my neck. She's using the tone of voice that asks, "You're not just doing this because I want you to, are you?"

I shake my head, massaging the scar on my chest. "I'm getting disability leave now. I think it's time for me to get out."

A guilty silence fills our bedroom. Kate thinks she's driving me to this decision, and I can't do much to dissuade her. Still, I try. I take her hand and turn to face her.

"Look, I know it's what I've done for fifteen years. But I still see that kid's face before I shot him—"

"He tried to kill you," Kate objects. Her mouth is downturned and I know that she could never accept me as a cop again, not after what we've been through. She says that she'll support my decision, but I know if I put my life on the line like that again, she couldn't handle it.

I hug her. "I don't want to face those decisions any

more, I don't want to see any more kids' faces when I sleep."

I gripped the steering wheel hard enough that the whole assembly was shaking. I could remember shooting the kid who put a thirty-two slug through my left lung. I could remember his head snapping back.

Worse, I could picture the funeral. I could picture his mother as clearly as if she were sitting next to me. She hadn't cried, or cursed me. That would have been easy. That must have been what I had been looking for, attending the funeral within days of my own hospitalization. All she had done was sit still, staring straight ahead, blind to everything but her son in that coffin.

Tony's family wouldn't have even that.

My thoughts were jarred when the Plymouth jumped the curb. I had to brake in the middle of a snowdrift. I looked madly around for cops. But any cops were lost far behind the blowing snow. I looked at my watch, and I felt another wave of memory—

"Happy Birthday, Dad." Gail smiles at me. In that moment I see so much of her mother in her, in the long red hair, in the freckles, in the smile. The wrapping falls away from the little crystal box that holds the watch.

"Hey," I said, "are you trying to say something here?"

"Try not to keep so many late nights," Kate says from behind my right shoulder.

"We miss you, Dad," Gail says and hugs me.

—I'd already been driving over an hour.

I cursed my memory. I cursed it for showing me fragments of a life that I could now no longer go back to. The man named Kane Tyler had died in that apartment as surely as Tony had. The man driving Tony's Plymouth was a cipher that I knew nothing about, other than that this man was capable of tearing out the throat of a stranger.

I rocked the Plymouth back and forth, freeing it from the mess I'd put it in. When I got it free, I drove the car west, toward the city.

9

By four in the morning, I'd driven out of the snow and out under a clear sky. The layout of the city was coming back to me, and that gave me some hope—good or ill—for the rest of my memory.

The city slid by me on skids of gray ice. I was surrounded by the deadest part of the night. Tony's Plymouth was the only vehicle on the road other than the occasional snowplow.

The city was an eerie landscape painted in cold colors. White streetlights, bluish snow, purple sky, and buildings made of gray and black shadows. The only warm color I passed came from the traffic lights.

Cold, still, and empty. Even the snow had stopped moving for the night. It gave me a weird sense of superiority to be out at this time of night, as if the city were mine, as if I owned the broad expanse of Euclid unrolling before the Plymouth. It was a spooky feeling, and one that felt as if it came from the same part of my mind that had made me go into apartment 401. That made me nervous, and I turned on the radio.

Some college station was playing an album side from Blue Oyster Cult, *Fire of Unknown Origin.* It fit my mood perfectly. I drove through an empty Downtown accompanied by "Joan Crawford."

I'd spent too much time in this car. I needed to dispose of it and the body. I think I'd only delayed the inevitable for this long because the destruction of the evidence of my crime was as irrevocable as killing Tony in the first place.

At this point there was still some dim possibility that I could argue that Tony's murder was justified, that I was protecting the woman. I did not believe it, but if I turned to the police with that argument, I was still part of human society.

Destroying Tony's body would be an admission that I believed that I'd left that society.

Instead of crossing the Cuyahoga River, I drove Tony's Plymouth down into the Flats. I didn't drive toward the darkened restaurants and bars lining the mouth of the river. I drove away from the development, toward the remains of industry.

I took a turn that carried me under a bridge. Under the snow the tires of the Plymouth left the pavement. I paralleled a rusted chain-link fence that separated what used to be a road from a field dotted with piles of broken asphalt and old tires. I pulled to a stop in a lot dominated by one of the massive pillars supporting the bridge above me. Despite the storm earlier, there was little snow here.

I wiped off the wheel and stepped out of the Plymouth.

Behind the field of debris, a broken hillside rose toward the city. Everywhere down here were piles of concrete, fallen from the bridge above as if it were some gigantic creature shedding old skin.

Further up, where the road finally ended, sat a broken gate in the fence. Just inside was a small brick shack, no more than a shell. The windows were glassless, and it was roofed only by a single girder as ocher as the bricks that supported it.

I stood in a world as dead as a graveyard.

I opened the trunk and searched my pockets for Tony's possessions. I tossed his watch, wallet, and his jewelry into the trunk with Tony, after wiping them for prints. His lighter, a gold Zippo with an eagle engraved upon it, I kept—wrapped in a wad of tissue paper.

" 'Yet if Hope has flown away . . .' "

I left the trunk open, and backed away from the right rear fender of the Plymouth. I gave it a decent clearance, twenty or thirty feet. Then I looked around for anyone observing me. The only witness I saw was a lone crow perched on a metal post by the fence. It seemed to be watching me.

I looked away from the bird and out over the black waters of a river that had once burned. Across the river, a few lone smokestacks released white smoke; one black chimney breathed fire. The sky was black and starless, the only lights red ones—ruby diadems crowning the smokestacks. I stood upon the night's plutonian shore, if I stood anywhere.

The night was quiet, the air still, cold and sharp as a blade. I drew the Desert Eagle out of its holster. I drew the slide, checked the action, and leveled it at a spot behind the right rear tire.

I braced my wrist and fired.

The shot echoed, its flash illuminating the underside of the bridge. I saw there, in an instant, that the girders under the overpass were massed with crows. Hundreds, maybe a thousand, of the birds took wing in response to the gunshot. They exploded out above me, a black cloud cawing a demonic avian chorus.

For a moment I was deafened amid their roar, and by the sound of their wings tormenting the wind. Then, like a dream, the birds were gone, slipping through the girders of the bridge, into the sky, like a handful of sand slipping into the ocean.

When they were gone, I could hear the sound of liquid spilling to the ground. I lowered my gaze. My bullet had torn a hole through the gas tank of the Plymouth. The smell of gasoline sliced though the air toward me. Under the rear fender, a stream of liquid melted the snow. Gas dripped from the bottom of the fender and from the bumper.

The ground sloped in my direction, and a snake of melted snow was weaving its way toward me.

I holstered the Eagle and took out Tony's lighter.

The Zippo's flame was small and blue. It danced weakly in the little wind the night had left. The flame ignited the tissue wrapping the lighter, and I tossed it all into the gasoline. The tissue flew off toward the sky, but the lighter landed in the puddle. The little blue flame escaped and raced to embrace Tony and the Plymouth. When they met, the gas tank unrolled itself toward the sky with a burst of ruddy light and hellish wind.

When the smoke reached the bridge, I was already walking away.

It was after four-thirty when I walked out of the Flats. I was cold, alone, and empty. I had walked all the way to Public Square before I heard the sirens responding to my conflagration. I couldn't feel much of anything other than fatigue and a sense of loss.

Where did I have to go? What was it that I could do?

Everything seemed to be falling apart, slipping away from me. Things had spun out of control. I needed things to stop, to slow down, if only for a while. I wanted to go home, to rest.

I wanted to go home, but I had no idea where home was, or if I still had one.

I needed to find a phone book. The night was leaking away, and I was afraid of the coming dawn. However, I had some little time left. When I reached the intersection central to Public Square, I saw the lights in the lobby of the Terminal Tower. The transit station down there was open, and somewhere inside would be a phone.

By five, I had an address and I had a cab.

* * *

The West Side was more familiar to me than the Heights area. I knew the streets the cab rolled down. I knew when the cab was just around the corner from the house where I had lived the past ten years of my life.

The last five, alone.

I told the cabby to drop me off a fair distance back from the intersection of two one-way streets. I paid him and stepped out into a virgin expanse of snow. The cab continued down the street, its taillights the last thing to vanish as it turned away, looking for a main road.

I stood alone on the street for a long time. The cross street ahead of me was Allan Drive, a three-block-long street that was barely a lane wide. Just looking at it caused tiny flares of memory—

Under the snow, the street is brick and hell on the suspension.

The green house on the corner is home to an old woman with way too many cats.

Kate doesn't like the neighborhood, but she wanted her own house since Gail was born, and she bears it with the same grace that she bears my profession.

Gail caught the bus to the high school on Detroit, three blocks away.

Until Kate left me, that is.

Fragments, disjointed facts. They hit like tiny sparks from an abused piece of machinery. I stared at the wedding band on my finger. Why did I keep it? Did I have some hope of one day coming home and finding Kate there . . . ?

Something is wrong—

I stared at the ring. Kate had left me five years ago. Five long years. I had kept the hope that she'd return. Just like I had kept this ring . . . .

I come home, and I see the house. I know something is wrong—

A memory wanted to come, a memory that filled me with a sick dread. I wanted to call back the taxi. Call

it back and have it take me to someplace else, anywhere else.

But the taxi was gone, and I was committed.

I looked up and down Allen Drive. I couldn't see my
house from here, and every other building was darkened and closed. There was a dim threat I felt, unfo-
cused, trapped within my frozen memory. The feelings
made me cautious, made me worry that my house
might be watched.

There was no reason to stake out my house, but I
worried. If there were police here, they had yet to see
me. I approached from the back. Somewhere a dog
barked at me.

The way the backyards and driveways intercon-
nected on these narrow blocks, it was easy for me to
approach my house from the other side of the block.
The neighborhood became increasingly familiar as I
walked up my neighbor's driveway toward the back of
my house. When I reached my backyard, I froze for a
minute. No footprints marred the snow, no tire tracks
marred the driveway. Everything was still, silent. The
wind had ceased.

Recognition struck like a blow. From the gutter sagging beneath the ice to the too-loose storm windows, I
knew this place. I knew the kitchen window that was
painted shut, and the half-assed addition someone had
tacked to the back porch in the fifties. I knew that the
second-floor window facing me was for the rear stairs,
and if the light were on, I would see the top of the bathroom's door frame. I knew Gail's room overlooked the
driveway, Kate's and mine overlooked the front of the
house and my office was opposite Gail's room. I knew
the glass block on the basement windows was expensive as hell, but necessary since the darkroom equipment in the basement was even more so.

I knew the attic was reached by a trapdoor that stuck

in summer and shouldn't be opened unless you really liked the feel of fiberglass insulation on your skin.

Even as I remembered, I had to revise the memory, correct for the history of the past five years. Nothing was Kate's and mine anymore, except maybe Gail— and she was more Kate's. Gail's room was storage now . . . .

I had walked up on the porch, feeling something wrong. I was on the porch before I realized that all the shades were drawn. I like the light, I almost always leave the shades open. The door—

The memory left me again.

"God," I whispered.

I approached the rear of the house. When I reached the back door, I stopped. Covering the door and the jamb a few inches above the doorknob was a yellow sticker—"Sealed by Order of Cleveland Police Department."

The door was locked, and I didn't like the implications of that sticker. Something *was* wrong here, and not just within my errant memory.

I was about to try breaking in, but I remembered something about the back of the house. I walked away from the door, about ten feet to my left, stopping in front of a mound of snow that sloped against the rear of the house. I started kicking the snow away to reveal a pair of storm-cellar doors. These didn't need a key. The sloping doors were shut with a combination lock.

There was no police seal here, but I had to kick ice away from the lock before I could open it.

While I crouched, I had a few nasty minutes when I couldn't remember the combination. I squatted, fingers numbing on the metal lock, for close to five minutes before I began turning the dial. The numbers finally came, one at a time. With the ice, the lock needed to be forced, but the numbers were right, and I managed to tug it open.

I slipped it off and dropped it into the snow.

The door came open with the grinding sound of breaking ice. The opening revealed concrete steps descending into a darkness the moon didn't reach. At this point, familiarity should have been reassuring, but it wasn't.

The front door is ajar. With the shades drawn, none of the morning light reaches inside the house. I had run here, driven madly, expecting something. I draw my thirty-eight—

I had been driven to come here, driven by fatigue and an aching hole of a memory. But now, as more memories came leaking to the surface, the idea of entering the house filled me with nauseating dread. I felt an urge to run.

I stepped down into the storm cellar.

My eyes quickly adjusted to the feeble light down here. At the bottom of the stair was a flimsy door, unlocked. I stepped through into my basement.

The feeling of familiarity was overwhelming. The past fogged this place, like a choking perfume—a perfume hiding an uglier scent.

I looked around without benefit of the light; the bluish moonlight streaming through the glass block was enough to see by. I found the darkroom I expected, in a walled-off corner of the basement. I stepped in and finally had to turn on a light to see.

I groped in the dark and finally hit a switch that flooded the room with red light, as if the room had been sunk in blood. In addition to the trays, the chemicals, and everything else, there should have been pictures in here. Negatives and prints should have been here. Someone had taken them.

Sebastian's men? The police?

The police, I thought as I found traces of fingerprint powder on one of the trays.

What was on those pictures? Why were the police

dusting here for prints? The ugly feeling grew in my stomach. Something bad was going on here.

I push the front door open with my foot. I sweep the living room with the gun. It's dark and empty. I step in to cover the dining room—

I forced myself to act calmly, to move deliberately. I knew I was nervous about what was going on. If there were important pictures, I knew that I'd stash them somewhere.

I knelt down, almost unconsciously, and pulled a plastic jug of developer out from under the table. Underneath it was a small drain. The grate came up easily. A layer of scummy water sat an inch under the grate. I stuck my fingers in, not quite sure what I was feeling for, but I knew it when I touched plastic.

I pulled a slimy Ziplock bag out of the drain. It came out with a slurp. Inside was a plastic film canister. I had no idea what was inside it, but I peeled open the bag and removed the container. I opened the cap on one and saw what I'd expected to see: rolled-up negatives. I put the cap back on and pocketed it.

I shoved the empty bag back in the drain, and replaced everything else as I'd found it.

I was stalling. Eventually, I killed the light and headed upstairs.

Halfway up the flight, I had to stop. The feeling of dread was like a weight holding me back. By the time I had reached the door to the kitchen, it seemed to take an hour just to reach up and turn the knob.

I could smell it even before the door opened. It tore into me, ripping the shroud from a memory—

"You should not pry into things which are not your business." The voice on the end of the phone had been female, barely. The sound was harsh, violent. There were scratching noises in the background.

I'm remembering the call as I sweep the living room with my revolver. My pants are still muddy. My

*camcorder is back at my car. The call had come on my
cell phone as I'd driven madly away from Lakeview.*

*The voice had said, "You are being punished. Then
you will die." There were moans in the background,
someone in pain, barely conscious.*

*I am remembering the moans as I turn, covering the
dining room. I am remembering the inhuman laugh
that was on the other end of the phone—*

The door to the kitchen sticks on something, but I
keep on pushing. The smell hits full force.

*I remember the noises, wet noises, as my eyes adjust
to the gloom shrouding the dining room—*

The smell is of old blood.

10

I stepped into the kitchen, unable to separate memory from the scene before me.

I stumble into the kitchen, breath ragged and dizzy from the scene in the dining room. I'm frozen at the chaos in here. The overturned dishwasher, the broken table, the dented stove— Everything ignited fragments of my weak memory. *Blood is everywhere. Pooled on the stove, speckling the table, coating the sink. Stab marks*—now dutifully circled by the forensics team—*gouged holes in the walls, as if the house itself were being attacked, bleeding*—central to it all now was the surreal contribution of the police, the strings leading to blood spots on the walls. Their attempt to map flying blood cast the kitchen in a giant spiderweb.

"Kate," I managed to croak out.

I edged away from the kitchen, filled with a sour rage that was nearly as sickening as the carnage in front of me.

I backed all the way into the dining room before I turned away from the scene. When I turned away, the rage burned itself out, blown out by the impact of the full memory, complete and ugly.

Ever since she had left me, I had the dim hope of someday coming home to her. Childe had granted my wish.

* * *

I barely escape that scene in Lakeview. I drive away from the scene of that carnage, numbed. Then the car phone rings. It beeps insistently. I don't want to pick up the phone, but my hand reaches for it.

"Kane," says the ragged voice on the other end of the phone. I don't know who it is—the voice is distorted beyond recognition—but I know what it is, what is represents.

"You killed her," I whisper.

"Hardly," the voice laughs at me. "You should not pry into things which are not your business." The voice on the end of the phone is barely female itself. The sound is harsh, violent. I hear scratching noises in the background.

"You aren't going to get away with this:"

Laughter, endless mocking laughter. Then the voice tells me, "You are being punished. Then you will die."

I hear moans in the background, someone in pain, barely conscious. I can almost recognize the voice.

"Come home, Kane Tyler, someone is waiting for you." She hangs up.

I race the car into the dawn, in a near panic. I know what waits for me, but I keep some desperate hope that I can make it in time. As I drive, I call the police, then I call Sam.

Something is wrong at my house.

I arrive before the police do. I walk up on the porch. All the shades are drawn. The front door is ajar. With the shades drawn, none of the dawn light reaches inside the house.

I draw my thirty-eight, and push the door open with my foot. I sweep the living room with my revolver.

I remember the noises, wet noises, as my eyes adjust to the gloom shrouding the dining room.

The strength goes out of my legs. My breath catches in my throat and I almost drop the revolver. Blood is everywhere. The air is so rank with the smell that my brain doesn't want to identify it.

"Kate," I manage to croak out. Breathing in the blood-tainted air makes me sick. My stomach wants to rebel, but after what I've already seen tonight, all it can do is spasm quietly.

They had crucified her on the dining room table. The violence was so bad that I could not be certain if she had been alive when they had tied her there.

The memory dropped me to my knees. It was so vivid that I almost saw the body on the table there in front of me. Even though Kate had long ago been taken away.

In the moonlight it was hard to make sense of the stains, the strings, the marks left behind by the policemen in their investigation.

The stains formed a vaguely cruciform outline on the table. Markings by the police give it a human shape. The table was scarred, knives perhaps, maybe even claws. I saw wires that could have bound legs and arms. Some of the strings led up to bloodstains on the ceiling.

"No." I whispered again, trying not to see it.

The memory came, in incoherent, unwanted pieces. My gaze fixated on the head of the table, where a single beam of moonlight picked out a shape. I stared at it, trying to make sense of the tiny black knot in the black bloodstain. I edged around the table, irrationally drawn to it.

When my back was to the window, I finally understood what it was. I stared at a finger-sized clump of my wife's hair, glued to the table by her own blood.

I had a memory from after the medics came, when they had finally moved the body out of the tacky blood. I had seen her head nod limply as that knot of hair was tugged from her skull. No one had seemed to notice.

I had loved this woman, loved her past the end of our marriage. How could I grieve for her with my wounded memory? I finally began to cry.

I still have a daughter, I thought.

If anything, that made things worse. Gail had lost her mother because of me, and she was in the process of losing her father. Not only was my memory crippled, but there was blood on my hands. I was a murderer.

A murderer, and maybe something else.

I wanted to see her—desperately—but forcing me upon her after what had happened to me would be needlessly cruel. Better that she should bury me with her mother.

I reached out to touch the table, gripped by a torrent of conflicting emotions—grief, anger, and a hollow sense of failure. My finger brushed a strand of long red hair.

A murderer, and maybe something else.

Why did I insist on maintaining that possibility? Was it some sick way to moderate the guilt of Tony's death? Thinking that was sabotaging my own sanity. Insisting that I was infected by some supernatural entity was insane.

But if it was insane, why did all my feverish symptoms, the delirium, the *hunger*, all vanish when I had killed Tony? I had physical symptoms. I had *needed* that blood. I had needed it when I was in that accident with Sam.

I walked out of the dining room, swamped with fatigue.

Behind the blinds in the living room I could see the sky lightening with the coming dawn. I had a reaction to the light, a visceral fear that I couldn't damp by telling myself it was irrational.

I forced myself to walk to the front windows, and separated the slats of the blinds with a shaking hand.

Through the blind I stared at the sky, which had lightened from purple to a deep aqua.

The fear flared into a barely controlled panic. My hand dropped from the window and I turned away. I faced the dining room and felt a different fear grip me. I had stopped breathing again, just as I had in the sewer. I had no idea when I had stopped. I had suffered too many shocks in the past few minutes for me to pick out one that could have knocked the breath from me.

If that insane possibility were right, if I were somehow the walking dead, did I *need* to breathe?

I ignored the panic, and kept holding my breath. I waited for my chest to tighten, for my body to protest the lack of oxygen. I waited for my vision to darken and for a feeling of giddiness.

Nothing.

I stood, and waited for five minutes, then ten, as the room around me began to lighten slightly with the approaching dawn. The light began to take a yellowish tint.

Something had happened to me. Something that had driven me to tear the throat out of a man and drain his blood. Something that had removed the necessity for breathing.

I had yet to see daylight, ever since I crawled out from underground. I turned to see the predawn glow shining from behind the blinds, and I felt the terror of having to.

I needed to get away from that light.

It was insane to think what I was thinking. But it was either that, or I had lost the ability to trust anything that happened. And, if I had completely lost touch with reality, what difference did it make what I thought? If I had lost touch with reality so completely, I could believe I was a leprechaun for all it mattered.

Of course, no one made movies about leprechauns

bursting into flames and crumbling to dust at the first touch of direct sunlight.

I couldn't leave this house. And there was only one place here I knew the rays of the sun wouldn't reach. I ran through the remains of my dining room and kitchen and took the stairs to the basement two at a time. It was no longer hypothetical. I had stopped playing what-if with myself. I had stopped telling myself that the idea was an insanity.

I dove into the black womb of my darkroom knowing what I had become. As the rush of fatigue crashed over me, I felt the card in my pocket and knew that I was going to talk to Gabriel.

Somewhere in the not-quite-sleep that gripped me, I remembered things. Remembered them, or dreamed them. Maybe both.

The guy I'm talking to is known as Switz. Not his real name. The name has something to do with his excessively Aryan appearance. That's my guess at least. He's blond, blue-eyed, and has a motto in German Gothic tattooed on his bicep. I suspect he's a Nazi, but I don't know and don't ask.

He's not a friend, and I'm not talking to be social.

We're standing in a parking lot somewhere in Richmond Heights. Behind us is a vast expanse of snow-covered Mall, after hours, empty. We're standing behind Switz's car, a brand-new white Mercedes sedan that's at odds with his military-surplus clothing. Switz has just pocketed a large sum of money.

He pulls out the keys and opens the trunk. Inside is an aluminum briefcase covered in black vinyl, which he also opens—

"There she is, Kane. Mother of all handguns, the biggest thing I got."

The gun is massive, a forty-five on steroids. I pick it

up, heft it. It seems almost cartoonishly large in my hands. "Fifty-caliber? You have shells for this?"

"Fifty-cal magnum." Switz nods at the case. "I've enough shells." He smiles. "What you planning to drop with that thing?"

I clear it, check it, put it back in the case. "You don't want to know, even if you'd believe me."

Switz snorts, "Whatever it is, you shoot it with that, it'll drop."

"I hope so." There's a trembling note on my voice. "Is it clean?"

"Clean? Is hasn't even been fired."

"Where's it from?"

"A collector gave himself a 12-gauge lobotomy. His estate got thinned a little. This was still in the packing crate when I got it."

I nod and close the briefcase and take it. "Wish me luck," I whisper.

"With that thing you don't need luck."

Kate and I are having one of our uniquely formal lunches, something that has become a tradition with us since she left me. Dinner was too significant a meal, so it was always lunch at some inexpensive restaurant downtown.

Today we're in the Arcade downtown, sitting at a table next to the mezzanine railing. The light from the glass ceiling is too white with the snow collected up there.

We've just finished discussing Gail's tuition.

Kate reaches out and touches my hand, as physically intimate as we've been for the past five years. "What's wrong?" she asks.

I shake my head.

"Tell me. Something's been bothering you."

I drink some Styrofoam coffee to avoid answering. But there's little coffee left, and it doesn't last long. I stare into the empty cup. "My job," *I finally say in response.*

"What about your job?" *I look up and see the concern in her eyes. I am uncomfortable with the idea that she might still worry about me. She had been the one to leave me. I should be free of her concern—*

Life is never that simple. "I called someone a rotten parent today." *I shake my head at the self-evident hypocrisy of the statement.*

"You deal with rotten parents all the time," *she says.* "Mostly stealing their kids from each other."

"This is different."

"How so?"

"There's this gentleman—I use the term loosely— named Sebastian. I know him from my days in the force. Not as a colleague."

"Uh-huh?"

"He's done well for himself. He was a two-bit punk we'd pick up every other month when I knew him. Since then he's done five years, made some connections inside, and come out a businessman. Now I'm pretty sure he's got a finger in every drug-laced pie in this town."

I crave a cigarette, even though I haven't smoked since I left the police—or, more accurately, since I took a bullet in the lung.

"And he's the rotten parent?"

I nod, "He's got a family now. And a daughter about two years younger than Gail."

"And she's missing."

"Bingo." *I crumble the cup in my hand.* "He's not a man people say no to. But I said I didn't want to touch his money. When he got insistent, I told him that a man who did what he did wasn't fit to be a father—" *My voice chokes off.*

"You were angry—"

"I saw his eyes. I think I'm the first person to have

hurt him, really hurt him, in years. I'm surprised he didn't have one of his bodyguards shoot me there."

Kate looks at me and I can see her read me. It's something she is still too damn good at. "You're nothing like him."

"Then why aren't we still married?" I whisper.

"One of the reasons is you have a tendency to compare yourself to your clients."

"He's not a client."

"Isn't he?"

After five years, she still reads me too well. I find missing kids for a living. Doing that compensates for a lot of moral ambiguity.

"Twenty-five hundred retainer, nonrefundable. Five hundred a day, plus expenses."

The man on the other side of the wide antique desk smiles weakly. "Somewhat mercenary, aren't you?"

"I always quote the price first, Mr. Sebastian." I sit in one of the leather chairs facing the desk. The whole office seems lifted out of the last century, which makes the off-white PC with the rounded corners all the more incongruous. "Too many times the parents know exactly where their kid is, they just don't want to deal with cops or lawyers."

"The money's not a concern. I am somewhat surprised at your change of heart."

"I have a daughter myself, Mr. Sebastian."

"I'm aware of that."

"I find missing kids. That's who I do this for. I deal with a lot of parents I don't approve of. I let our prior relationship get in the way of my job."

Sebastian nods. "I understand." He turns around one of the pictures on his desk and says, "You will find my daughter."

PART TWO

DESCENT INTO THE MAELSTRÖM

Lo! Death has reared himself a throne
In a strange city lying alone
Far down within the dim West,
Where the good and the bad and the worst and the best
Have gone to their eternal rest.
There shrines and palaces and towers
(Time-eaten towers that tremble not!)
Resemble nothing that is ours.
Around, by lifting winds forgot,
Resignedly beneath the sky
The melancholy waters lie.

—"The City in the Sea"

11

I never completely lost consciousness. Even as I was kept company by returning memories, I never lost awareness of the concrete floor I lay upon, or the faint chemical smell of developer. Hours passed, and I never lost those two sensations.

I rested—but I never slept, and I never truly dreamed.

Somehow I knew when I was supposed to rise. It was as if the unseen sun were a weight on my body, a weight that lifted when the sun left the sky.

When I stood, I knew who Kane Tyler was. I had built a mosaic of myself and I could see the broad outlines of the man I used to be. I had been driven, obsessive. Kate had married me, but she had married me when my obsessions had an external focus. I quit the force to save our marriage, and in doing so I had destroyed it.

I knew more about Kane Tyler than I wanted to know.

I knew almost nothing about who I'd become.

There weren't any police in sight out the front. I didn't really expect any. No one had entered the house during my twelve-hour slumber, and the Cleveland police didn't have the manpower to waste staking out my house.

Still, it'd been a stupid risk coming here. I berated myself for not thinking clearly last night. Distressed or not. Memory or not. It was an easy exercise in hindsight to think I should have realized that I'd rented that motel room for *some* reason.

I should have left as soon as I'd seen the blood—if the dawn hadn't trapped me here.

Risk or not, here I was, and no one knew it. Once I left this place, I wasn't going to come back. So I gave myself one more hour, to pretend I still lived here.

Still, I did not turn on any lights, and after checking the front of the house, I avoided windows.

I went upstairs and showered. I did it mechanically, in the dark. I was cloaked in numbness. I'd felt the panic when I'd fallen from the precipice, but I was in free fall now, and a long way from the bottom. Almost everything had been burned out inside me.

Too much had happened to me, too much to absorb, too much to react to. But this was the first true pause in which I had time to think. With my rest, the logical part of my mind started working again.

Childe was central to a cult, a circle of youths that were into dark rituals that offended even people who were into the occult. I remembered only fragments of my investigation, but I could remember that the distaste for Childe was universal throughout the whole neo-pagan community.

I remembered another odd fact now. Within the neo-pagan community, with their elaborate taxonomy of belief systems separating wiccan from druid from followers of the Golden Dawn, and with their disparagement of Satanism as a uniquely Christian perversion, not one of the pagans or fringe-pagans I had talked to had given me even a tentative classification of what Childe actually practiced. They classified *him*: predatory, sadistic, cold, charismatic, and in many cases, evil, but they never classified his belief system. It was as if they never even heard any rumors of what it was he did.

"Childe runs a tight little group," I whispered as I left the bathroom. I said it, but it did not jibe with what Childe's cult seemed to be doing now.

They had killed my ex-wife in a manner almost designed to call attention to itself, killed in a manner that would club the police over the head with its ritualism.

With my healing memory, I was almost certain I could place the leather-clad teenager at last night's collision at the "sacrifice" I had videotaped. His face had been the one to smile at me.

Childe's group was low-key enough to work for years around the fringes of the pagan community without once leaking any hint of its internal structure. That didn't fit with Kate's death or ramming Sam's car.

I had worked with cults before; it goes with the territory. And a true cult is almost always organized around a central charismatic figure. Because of that, because they're an extension of its leader's personality, cults don't change their behavior very often. And if they're inner-directed, they do their best to cut off the outside world almost completely.

I was beginning to understand why I'd been talking to Sam. I had had these thoughts before, and they had led me to the same conclusion. I needed to find out Childe's history.

And now this investigation wasn't just a matter of finding Sebastian's daughter, Cecilia. It was a matter of finding myself.

"Yes," said the voice on the other end of the phone, "We had a Detective Weinbaum here. But his injuries were minor. He was released after twelve hours of observation."

"Thank you," I said to the receptionist, and hung up. University Hospitals had been the second place I'd

called after the Cleveland Clinic. At least they'd given
me good news. It was bad enough that I had Tony on
my conscience, I did not need to find out that I'd
somehow worsened Sam's condition.

I sat on the edge of my bed in a darkened room,
holding a phone on my lap. I could see perfectly well
by the light from the streetlight outside. Everything
was blue-gray and black, a gloom that choked the room
like smoke but somehow didn't obscure my vision.

I'd gotten dressed in the dark, so no one would
notice my house being occupied. I now wore a tie and a
black suit, with shoes to match. Not my first choice,
but it was clean. On the bed next to me lay my gun, my
old clothes, and an old tan trench coat I'd found in the
closet.

An address book sat on a table next to the bed, and I
flipped through it. When I reached my daughter's
phone number, I read it with the strange déjà vú of
seeing a number that I hadn't known I'd memorized. I
wondered again how long things would taunt me with
their familiarity.

I dialed the phone before thinking of what I would
say. It rang four times.

"Please, Gail, answer . . . ."

After the fifth ring I heard Gail's voice. "Hey! You
have reached—*me*. If you're calling for someone else,
you've gotten a wrong number. Otherwise say something at the beep."

The receiver was shaking in my hand. I could see her
face as I heard her voice on the machine. I pictured her
smiling, with her freckles and her mother's long red
hair. So much of her mother in her, except her eyes.
Even as a baby, everyone had said she had her father's
green eyes.

After a long pause, the beep surprised me. I had to
gather myself to leave a message. "Gail? It's Dad. If
you're there, pick up the phone. If not, I'll do what I

can to call you back tomorrow." What could I say to a machine? "When I call you again, it'll probably be late. I'm sorry, I know you have classes, but I can't really avoid it. Good-bye."

I set the receiver back in the cradle. I tried not to feel the press of worry, but it was too late. It wasn't something I'd *ever* been rational about. I had always been overprotective, and every time I had a nasty missing-person's case, even after the divorce, I always had to reassure myself about Gail.

Sam said he had gotten her police protection, and she's in Oberlin, far away from all of this.

But it was 7:30 on a Sunday. Where was she?

I told myself that she was at a movie, or was out with friends, or in the shower . . . .

"Stop doing this to yourself," I whispered to myself. "You do this every time you get her machine—"

I smiled, because I was right, and I could remember it, at least partially. But recognizing it as rote paranoia didn't change the fact that there was a real danger out there—a real danger that I still knew woefully little about.

I had rebuilt some sense of self out of my amnesia, but I was remembering generalities. I still had little or no memory of specific facts or events. Especially frustrating was the gap between the eleventh and the fourteenth, the three days between Kate's death and my waking in the storm sewer—

My God, who's doing the funeral arrangements? Have they done it already? The cops would have to have the body for autopsy, but that'd be done by now . . . .

"Monday, if they haven't held it already. Maybe Tuesday at the latest—"

I realized that I wanted to be there—and if I couldn't face daylight, I couldn't be.

I stood up and walked to the windows, staring out

the blinds at the streetlight. I took deep, unnecessary breaths. My attention was scattering when I needed to think straight. I still carried the phone. I had one call left to make.

I pulled Gabriel's card out of my pocket. Here, at least, I might have some answers to the darkness that had claimed my life. If nothing else, even if he was completely insane, Gabriel knew something of Childe—and Childe was central to everything that had happened to me.

The card had a single gold embossed number upon it, and when I called it I received a nasal computer-generated voice.

"You have reached an automated voice messaging system. At the sound of the beep, speak your own name slowly and clearly. If your response is unclear or unacceptable, you will be disconnected."

The machine beeped at me.

"Kane Tyler," I spoke slowly. I was nonplussed at dealing with a machine, but it did seem to fit with someone who wouldn't put any identification on a business card.

The machine digested my response, and after an electronic pop I heard Gabriel's voice, Southern accent and all. "Greetings, I am pleased you decided to call me—"

"Yes, I—" I started to say, when I realized that this message was as automated as the computer. Gabriel had recorded a message for me. I sighed.

"—assume you wish to meet with me," the recording continued. "At twelve this evening I shall be awaiting you at the address embossed upon the card. If this is inconvenient, please leave a message for me. I await the pleasure of your company, sir."

Midnight, three hours to kill before I talked to him. I sighed again.

The computer voice returned. "To replay this mes-

sage, press one. To reply to this message, press two.
To—" I hung up.

Three hours, which gave me time to find Sam and
ask him a few questions—especially about Childe's
history. I set the phone back on the nightstand, and
pocketed my address book.

Outside I heard a car slow and turn up a driveway.

My driveway.

I grabbed the Eagle from where it lay on the bed,
amidst my old clothes. I heard the engine idle, and I
heard a car door open and slam shut. I edged up to the
bedroom window, but it didn't offer me a view of the
driveway, the roof of the porch was in the way.

I could hear the car, though, almost feel its presence.

I backed out of the bedroom, grabbing the holster
and the trenchcoat with my free arm. It looked as if I
might be leaving fairly shortly. When I'd backed into
the hall, I could hear someone messing with the front
door downstairs.

Who was it? The police?

I slipped into Gail's old room, so I'd have an
overview of the driveway.

A wave of disorientation flooded me, making me
realize I'd been too comfortable with my returning
memory. I had stepped into her room expecting a bed
with a flowered comforter, and shelves of ceramic ani-
mals that she had made. My memory had laid a nasty
trap, I didn't realize I was expecting the little multi-
colored dragons and horses until I had bumped into the
first pile of filing boxes that was stored here.

The box fell with a rustle, spilling 1993 over the
bare hardwood. Dust balls flew away from the impact
like frightened mice.

"Fuck," I whispered. I had to be more careful.
Assuming that I knew something could be more dangerous than ignorance.

I froze, listening for a reaction. Below me, I heard

the front door opening. I heard footsteps. I could almost swear that I could hear someone breathing—

The breathing wasn't me, I had stopped when the car pulled into the driveway.

Whatever else this darkness had done to me— whether it was madness or a supernatural affliction— it did grant me an acuteness of sense that I knew I had not possessed before. I could picture the shoes of the man who tread below me, I heard their rubber soles on the hardwood, and I heard the change when he stepped upon the carpet. I heard his breathing, steady but elevated, the breathing of a man tense but not yet excited.

I heard his footstep upon the stair, and if I concentrated, I could hear the beating of his heart.

The door was closed behind me, but I'd know when my visitor was behind it. I leveled the gun at the doorway and backed next to the window. Outside the window, I could hear a dog barking, and distant traffic. One of my neighbors was watching television. I heard canned laughter.

I glanced down through the blinds. Parked, idling in the driveway, was a familiar tan Oldsmobile.

How did Sebastian find me?

The phone, it had to be the phone. I had been working for this man for two weeks. He was rich, and he was driven. He had hired me and had me followed. I had no trouble believing that he might have tapped my phone as well.

"Damn it, for once we're on the same side," I whispered.

There was one driver. I could see a flash of pale skin and I decided that he was Mr. Gestapo. The one walking up the hallway toward me had to be the Jamaican. They'd cornered me.

I glanced at the window and thought of the teenager

who had somehow landed on top of Sam's car. I drew the blinds on the window, and opened it.

I knew the Jamaican now stood without the door.

My exit was blocked by an old storm window. When I heard the doorknob rattle, I raised my foot and kicked at the bottom of the storm window's wooden frame. The window swung out, hinging at the top where hooks still held it in place. But those fasteners were over forty years old, and I heard metal snap, liberating an explosion of paint flakes.

After that snap, gravity took the window and it slid down like the blade of a guillotine.

Behind me I heard the door burst open and a Jamaican voice said, "Stop, Mr. Tyler—"

I'd already jumped out the window. Below me, the ancient storm window crashed into the hood of the Oldsmobile. The wood splintered, and glass exploded like a crystal grenade. The crash was like an explosion.

It had been Mr. Gestapo's first clue that something was wrong.

My jump ended half a second after the window's impact. Mr. Gestapo had only time to open the door when my feet hit the hood of the Olds. The impact felt as if it had broken both my shins, and had torn every one of my leg muscles from the bone. I should have collapsed and rolled off the hood, but I kept my balance, and I managed to unbend my knees.

I pointed my Eagle through the windshield and said, "Get out."

By now he had a gun out as well, but he looked at me and froze. He stared at me long enough that I had to repeat myself.

"Get out."

Slowly, he backed out of the car. Above me, I heard the Jamaican say, "Stop this, Mr. Tyler!"

I looked up and saw the Jamaican holding his own gun down on me. I stepped off the hood, continuing to cover Mr. Gestapo. I smiled up at the Jamaican. "I'm afraid I am going to have to borrow your car."

"I can't let you do that."

I looked down at Mr. Gestapo and said, "You really want to drop that." He did as he was told.

I looked up at the man covering me. "You have a name?" I asked.

"My name is Bishop, Mr. Tyler." He called down and I could see his breath fog. He didn't seem nervous or out of breath, unlike his partner. "I'm afraid you have to come with us."

"Odd name for one of Sebastian's hoods," I said.

Bishop smiled at the remark, his gun didn't waver. "And you, Mr. Tyler, have an odd name for a policeman."

"What do you mean?"

"Wasn't Cain the first murderer?"

I shook my head. "Well, Bishop, have you thought out the logistics of this situation?"

"What do *you* mean?"

"Your man down here is covered, and you are two stories above me. I see three options open to you. You let me take the car. You shoot me now. Or we stand here for an hour until the police show up and you explain a B&E on *my* property."

"Why do you think I won't shoot you?"

I looked up at him, "Because I'm looking for your boss' daughter, still. I am doing my job, *and I can't do my job if I am attached to you guys at the hip*!"

I could almost feel the options running through Bishop's mind. Eventually, I heard him say, "Go, but don't think this will happen again."

I smiled grimly and walked to the side of the Olds. I told Bishop's friend to get down on the ground, and I took his gun and tossed it in the car with my coat and my holster.

The key was still in the ignition.

It was a pain getting out of the driveway one-handed. But I wasn't putting down the Eagle until I was out of sight of the house.

12

Sam lived on the East Side, so on the way I stopped the Olds at a BP station downtown. I chose my vantage carefully, to be in sight of the approach from the police station and be a short U-turn from the I-90 on-ramp. I didn't want to be cornered again.

The police station was an old sandstone building. Pollution had turned the walls black. If not for the fluorescent lights shining through the windows, it wouldn't be out of place on an English moor.

It was early in the evening, quarter to nine, but it was Sunday and the traffic on St. Clair, between me and the station, was light. I idled next to the pay-phone and rolled down the window. Despite parking myself where I had an easy escape route, the black-and-whites made me nervous.

I dialed Sam's apartment and didn't get an answer, so I dialed the station.

After a couple of rings I heard, "Detective Weinbaum here."

"Hi, Sam. We need to talk."

"Goddamn it," Sam's voice dropped to a harsh whisper. "I told you not to call me here. Where the fuck did you disappear to?"

"My employer offered me a ride. I need what you have on Childe."

Sam's voice lowered. "Are you seriously still in this? After I saw you last time—"

"I'm handling that, Sam."

"Okay. Where are you?"

"Look out your window."

Sam ran across the street, a folder under his arm. I let him in and pulled the Olds in a quick U around the BP parking lot. The green-lit logo was receding down the on-ramp behind us before Sam asked. "What the hell's going on, Kane?"

"I'm trying to find out—"

"No, I mean with you. Yesterday you were a basket case. You were shaking and asking for a doctor. I was scared shitless that you'd wandered off on your own after the accident, the Heights cops have a bulletin to look out for you, and I'm in no end of shit because I have to explain how you were in my car in the first place—" Sam had to stop to breathe.

He didn't sound too good, and I looked at him. His nose was buried under a pound of gauze, his skin was pale, which made the shadows of his bruised eyes even more violent.

"I'm sorry about that. I don't want to get you into trouble."

He shook his head and patted his chest. "No," he coughed. "I can deal with my problems. I do get some slack because Kate's my case. It'll stay that way until you do something that makes me look real stupid."

We rolled onto the Shoreway and Sam asked, "Do you still need a doctor?"

"I said that I was taking care of it."

"That's no answer."

"I know." Before Sam could bring up any more questions, I added, "I have enough of an idea of what's wrong with me to know who to see about it. But it's not something I can tell you about."

"Damn it, I was there when you were shot—"

"I know, but please drop it."

The Oldsmobile plowed east along the Shoreway, streetlights sweeping us like an intermittent strobe. A dusting of snow started to drift down, and I turned on the wipers.

"Okay, but you're worrying me."

I nodded. "Sam, Childe is central to this, so I need to know what you were going to tell me."

He nodded and opened the file on his lap.

For all the effort expended, almost all Sam had on Childe was disappointing. Sam explained that everything they had had come from overseas when he had followed up the suspicion that Childe wasn't native to this country. Indeed, Scotland Yard had a record of Childe's alias, and his addresses and activities in and around London from the late forties.

His passport photo looked much younger than that implied, but I had some suspicions why. Childe's name in London, which remained when he immigrated to this country, was Manuel Deité.

"Five to one it's another alias," Sam said.

"Why?"

"Manual Deity—hand of God—I think our Mr. Childe has a high opinion of himself."

Mr. Deité had been the subject of extensive investigation, mostly under the direction of a Chief Inspector Cross. Why Cross had begun the investigation wasn't in the papers that Sam had ordered from the Yard. However, it was clear that there were three decades of files on Deité and not one scrap of evidence—physical or circumstantial—that tied him to any crime, real or alleged.

The Yard's investigation ceased with Cross' retirement in the mid-eighties. However, with the name, Sam had managed to work forward through immigration and find a passport photo that matched the papers faxed from London. Sam even had an address for Mr. Deité in Cleveland.

Just like London, however, there was no scrap of evidence that connected Childe to any crime here, real or alleged. All I had myself was hearsay evidence placing Childe with Cecilia—and Sebastian had not reported her missing to the police. Considering his desire to keep the police out of things, it was unlikely he ever would.

"That's it?"

Sam nodded. "I've yet to convince a judge that we even have enough to get a warrant for his house."

"You're kidding."

Sam turned to me and said, "Do I look like I kid? What are we looking for? A bunch of missing kids that no one's reported missing? It's a fishing expedition— and even if I got a warrant, what I have is so thin that it'd last about three minutes at the hands of a court-appointed public defender, and wouldn't even get through the door against a lawyer Childe could afford."

"Thank you for reminding me why I don't miss the force."

I pulled off the Shoreway at the tail end of MLK Boulevard and drove around under the highway, pulling into a darkened lot facing the lake. I stopped the car. For a few moments I sat there and listened to the metal knocking.

"I do have something that's unofficial."

"What?" I asked, not very hopeful.

"Manuel Deité seems to be missing."

I sat up, suddenly interested. "What do you mean?"

"I mean that I did some unauthorized snooping in his credit and bank records, and called his house a few times. He hasn't spent a cent since January 26th, when he filled the tank of his car at a Shell station out by the

Metroparks. I can't get hold of him by the phone to his house, or by his two cellular numbers."

"The 26th wouldn't happen to have been a Sunday?" Sam nodded.

That coincided with the last witness I had to see Cecilia. Three weeks ago. All I could think of was that he had gone to ground somewhere when he realized people were looking for him.

But I hadn't been hired until the first.

There *were* other people looking for him. I wasn't sure what Gabriel represented, but it seemed something worth hiding from.

"Okay, what about the van that hit us?" I asked.

Sam shrugged. "I don't know. Hit and run. Some sort of warning."

"What did they take? I thought I saw one kid steal a package out of your back seat."

Sam looked surprised. "Is that what happened to that? I guess that gives us a bit more circumstantial evidence pointing at Childe, then." He shook his head.

"What do you mean?"

"I had a lot more from England on this guy. That's what they took, the bulk of Cross' files from Scotland Yard." Sam nodded to himself. "Yeah, this gives me something on Childe I might be able to use . . . ."

"What?"

"Who else would have motive to swipe them? If I get a judge in a decent mood, I might swing a warrant to search for the van and those files. With that, I might turn up something."

I nodded, wondering. What was in those files? Why take them when all Sam had to do was make another call to Scotland Yard for more copies? The more I learned about what was going on, the less sense it made. I could discern no reasonable motives for what Childe and his people had done in the past three weeks.

That bothered me.

For a while we sat in silence. I stared out, toward the horizon. The sky hung low, its clouds heavy above a black lake frozen into stillness. No moon, no stars, the only lights out there were the small red flashers on the breakwater, and an ice-white spotlight near its end.

Lake Erie was serene, melancholy, and still. It was the kind of stillness that made me wonder what kind of ugliness might lie beneath the surface. If I had not woken when I had, would I have first opened my eyes under that sheet of endless ice?

"Sam?" I whispered.

"Yes?"

"The arrangements for Kate—what are they, who's handling it?"

"I—uh—her sister came in from Chicago to handle it. I've been helping, what I can do."

"When are the services?"

"Tuesday."

A half hour later, the Olds was driving up I-90, back the way we had come. Most of the way, we traveled in silence. It was a long time before I asked, "Gail is coming?"

Sam nodded, sighing. It was as if the statement had released a pressure that had weighed on him ever since we'd left the lake.

"Tomorrow?"

"Evening, yes. We were arranging all this while you were missing. I said she could stay at my place."

"What about police protection?"

Sam looked at me, squinting over the bandage on his nose, "*I'm* a cop, remember?"

I nodded. "You know, if there was any way she could stay with me . . . ."

"Of course I know. You could let *her* know—"

"I tried calling."

"She'll be here tomorrow, and she wants to see you."

I didn't answer. I drove off I-90 filled with conflicting thoughts. I wanted to see my daughter. I needed to see her survive the wound of losing Kate, but I was afraid that she may have already lost me also. How could I talk to her, reassure her, comfort her, when I had passed so far beyond the pale myself?

I felt that if I touched my daughter, some measure of the corruption infecting me would infect her as well. Beside that, the possibility she might reject me for my role in her mother's death was almost comforting.

"Kane?"

"Yes," I said. "I need to see her, don't I?"

"Are you all right?"

"No. You'll be home tomorrow?"

"I sort of have to be, don't I? I plan to be working around the funeral. All day tomorrow, and then after the funeral."

"Sorry this is screwing with your investigation."

"She was my friend, too." Sam looked out the windows at the black sandstone station emerging from the shadows. "Besides, talking to the survivors goes with the territory. You know me, I'd try to be at the funeral even if I didn't know her."

"Yeah, I know." I pulled the Olds to a stop about a block from the station. As Sam stepped out of the car, I asked, "Can you do me a favor?"

He turned and said, "What?"

"Give me twelve hours before you serve that warrant."

"Why?"

"Sometime tonight I want to pay Childe a visit."

"I didn't hear that, Kane." He tossed the file folder on the passenger seat. "Just in case you need that information, those are all copies."

He shut the door. I rolled down the window and shouted after him, "Can I have the time?"

Sam turned around and said, "I didn't get that." He looked at his watch. "I got to get back and wait for a judge to wake up so I can get this Childe warrant issued." He smiled and resumed walking toward the station.

He'd given me my twelve hours. And sitting on the passenger seat was Childe's address. I wanted to go there now, rush in, and demand explanations from whomever I found there—

However, I felt the need for some sense of caution. If there was a possibility of me confronting Childe, I wanted to know something more of his nature.

Also, I had the gnawing suspicion that—Sam's warrant aside—there would be little to find at Childe's residence. I suspected that Gabriel would have information as basic as Childe's address. If Childe was to be found there, I doubted Gabriel would still be searching.

What was at Childe's home would be what was left behind when he disappeared with Cecilia. There might be something there useful to me, but if that was so, it would stay there while I met with Gabriel.

13

Waiting for my midnight conference with Gabriel gave me an hour to think. I drove around trying to reason out the unreasonable, attempting to distill some rational sense out of an irrational situation. The unreason went beyond my search for Childe and Cecilia, and the disintegration of my life—

I forced myself to think the word that was at the core of my dilemma.

Vampire.

The farther Tony's corpse receded in my memory, the more it seemed that all the events I'd experienced, however bizarre and unwarranted, were more than the products of my own derangement. What had happened to me that insisted on that peculiar interpretation?

Fear of the sun, holding my breath . . . .

I was driving the Olds east up Superior, through some of the uglier parts of the East Side. The night turned a blind eye to me, the streets snowbound and empty, the storefronts shuttered in metal or plywood. Ragged men, young ones and old ones, hovered at corners, wrapped in their own secrets.

I felt a need to prove something to myself, before I delved any deeper into something that could just as well be a delusion. I needed some physical proof, some tangible stigmata . . . .

I pulled the Olds over at the corner of E. 55th. At the moment, the only animate things in sight were a few snowflakes dancing in the wind. I stepped out of the car and gathered my coat about myself.

It was closing on eleven, and it felt as if I stood in a world abandoned. In the far distance, I heard a siren. Other than that, the only noise was from the streetlights rocking in the wind.

I crouched and examined the sidewalk. It was a mass of gray slush, but it wasn't too hard to find what I was looking for. The neck of an abandoned beer bottle stuck up from a mound of grime-spotted snow. I withdrew it and upended it, loosing its unfrozen liquid to splatter the slush at my feet.

Stigmata, I thought. If I had truly died, if somehow some supernatural darkness had claimed my soul, my body should not be as it was. It would not act as a living body would. My breathing, my eating, both showed some physical transformation, if they weren't symptoms of some derangement.

I stepped to a storefront, and set down the bottle to roll up the sleeve of my left arm. I made a fist and held out my arm, about half of my forearm exposed.

"Going through with this is not going to argue for my sanity."

I paused a bit after saying that. However, at this point, after all I'd been through, that was no reason not to. The only reason not to was the fear that my hypothesis was wrong, and I *was* delusional.

I knelt down and grabbed the neck of the bottle with my right hand, while I clenched my left. On my exposed forearm, the veins came into relief under too-pale skin.

I shattered the body of the bottle against the metal cage imprisoning the storefront. Before I could reconsider, I drew the jagged end of the glass in a powerful slash across my forearm. I felt its bite as it tore skin. I felt the sour stab of the alcohol contaminating the glass.

The flesh parted across my wrist, the wound deep enough to sever the veins and slash the tendons. My fist shook and opened and I felt as if a brand had been applied to my wrist.

I saw the lips of the wound, ragged and black, before blood oozed to fill the wound. For a moment I felt an exquisite agony, as if the skin had been torn from the wounded area—

And suddenly the pain was no longer there.

My too-black blood no longer seeped from the wound. The blood sat mute, demarking the line where the insult had occurred, little more than would have been there had I suffered a scratch from an angry kitten.

I dropped the neck of the bottle and wiped the blood from my wrist. Beneath it, the skin was whole. No scar, no sign of injury, nothing but the blood on the fingers of my right hand. I no longer had any doubts that something had changed me.

I stumbled back to the Olds, my mind consumed with thoughts of the undead.

I couldn't decide when I had first suspected Childe of vampirism. There was a good chance—I was beginning to think—that I might have started suspecting him and his cult before I had lost my memory. I couldn't be sure of that, because those last days were still one of many black holes in my memory.

But I had seen a blood-drenched ritual, and I had made tapes of it. Damn Sebastian and his people for swiping them.

It was looking more and more as if I had been the one to place the Eucharist upon my own threshold. There seemed to be a peculiar irony to that, since if I was now a member of the undead, the Host seemed singularly ineffective.

I hoped it had at least helped me sleep nights.

Had I had discovered something? The true nature of Childe's cult? Its location? Childe's true identity? Had my investigation unearthed something that had prompted them to violence that, according to the absence of police records, was uncharacteristic?

I still couldn't pin down a motive.

Maybe it's something about their nature that's making me miss something . . . .

Undead. Vampire. Ghoul. Zombie. A thing that survives its own demise, to feed on human flesh and blood. A monster, pure and simple.

Unfortunately, pure and simple monsters didn't accede to logical examination. Pure and simple monsters don't need motivations to act. And if my experience showed anything, if such monsters existed, they were neither pure nor simple.

As far as I could tell, supernatural manifestations or not, the worst blood-drinking fiend still started human, and that meant that I still dealt with human nature. That meant that Childe, and his followers, were still doing things for reasons and were acting in expectation of some result.

The obvious interpretation was that somehow my investigation was getting too close to Childe, and his followers were reacting violently to protect him.

Because that conclusion was obvious, I distrusted it. I also distrusted it, because if shielding Childe were the goal—if that was why they had killed Kate, and why they'd stolen those records from Sam—their effect was exactly opposite what they intended. If anything, they were calling attention to themselves.

As I pulled into Cleveland Heights, I had one more unanswered question to ponder.

Until Cecilia disappeared, Childe had never excited interest from anyone but Chief Inspector Cross at Scotland Yard. Presumably, Childe had been seducing vul-

nerable teenagers into his circle for decades. Until
now, he had never taken anyone that someone missed.

I don't know exactly what I expected from the
address Gabriel gave me. It was in Cleveland Heights,
which I generally thought of as middle suburbia. However, I knew that I wasn't headed to a typical middle
suburban household. Gabriel lived on a street nestled
behind Euclid Heights Boulevard and overlooking University Circle.

When I saw the house, I knew it had been there when
streetcars rode up and down the hill behind me. This
had been here when most of Cleveland Heights had
been a golf course.

The house was a massive structure, the front a forest
of Doric columns two stories tall, giving the facade the
appearance of two Grecian temples set side by side—
the house's entrance set between them. The entrance,
the windows, almost everything else about the house
was dwarfed by the columns.

Like Gabriel's dress, the house was white, and its
nineteenth-century appearance wouldn't have been out
of place on a plantation. At 11:55 I got out of the Olds
and walked up an immaculately shoveled walkway, to
the front door of the house.

When I reached the door, it opened for me. The
action gave me pause for a moment, and I stopped
before I reached the threshold. A figure stood in the
doorway, but not one I expected. Gabriel wouldn't
have surprised me, nor would've a butler or other servant. Instead, I was greeted by a tall, dark woman
dressed in a purple gown that looked as if it could have
been worn in the latter half of the previous century.

She regarded me a moment, and said, "You are
expected."

I stepped through the threshold, still suspecting that

I had somehow mistaken the address. "I'm here to meet with Gabriel," I said.

She shut the door behind me. "I know. Come with me."

The woman was a striking example of exotic beauty, pale as marble and as finely carved as any Grecian Aphrodite—but it was a cold beauty, withdrawn and wary. If anything was out of proportion in the otherwise perfect face, it was her eyes. Even in their half-closed scrutiny of me, her eyes were of startling size, dominating her features. When she turned to lead me, it was her eyes I remembered.

She took me through the house. Despite the high ceilings, the broad corridors, and the lights shining everywhere, the overwhelming impression was one of gloom. There was something oppressive about the decor, and about the placement of light. The disturbing part of it was the elusiveness of the mood the house evoked. I couldn't find a source for the mood that pervaded the house in any particular part. It seemed to be part of the *gestalt*.

My hostess didn't say a word.

"Is this Mr. Gabriel's residence?" I asked to break the silence.

"Just Gabriel," she said.

"Okay. Is this his house?"

"While he is here, it is here he resides." She looked back over her shoulder, and I noticed a small turn at the corner of her upper lip, as if she found my confusion amusing. "This house belongs to Gabriel's circle. This is where he stays when he is in town."

I noted that for future reference. It explained the identityless business card, as well as the voice-mail system. "Circle," was also an interesting word, it implied some sort of societal unit.

"Are you part of Gabriel's circle?"

She laughed. The laugh matched her appearance,

lovely and cruel. "So impertinent." She stopped to turn and brush my face with her hand. She touched me with a heat that didn't quite reach her skin. "So," her eyes stared into mine as she appeared to search for a word. Her eyes drank me in, and it felt as though she pulled something out of me as she stared. "Raw. Yes, so raw you are. So unschooled. Perhaps you need a teacher . . . ."

She drew me toward her, and I felt such a hot rage of desire that it numbed out every other sensation. Everything but those too-large eyes, so violet that they were almost black. She bent and briefly touched her lips to mine.

"Please," I said. Somehow I managed to keep my voice steady.

She released me, a ghost of a smile on her face.

"I'm here to see Gabriel."

"Of course you are." She turned with no explanation or apology, and resumed walking down the hall. "To answer your impertinent question. Of course I am of Gabriel's circle. My chosen name is Rowena, should you care to remember it."

I was still recovering from that near-kiss. I could still feel her lips, as if someone were holding a candle too close to my face. I also felt it in places that I didn't know vampires were supposed to feel anything.

"Why was it an impertinent question?"

"Why is it impertinent for a peasant to interrogate his prince?" She stopped before a large oaken door and knocked. Before she left me she said, "But then you aren't quite a thrall, are you? Pity."

From beyond the door I heard a Southern voice say, "Come on in, Mr. Tyler. Come on in."

I pushed open the door and entered Gabriel's office. I stood for a moment in the threshold. If the rest of the house was designed to have an effect on the mood, that effect was all focused in this one odd-shaped room.

The room was a huge pentagon, the door at one vertex. The entire wall opposite the door was a vast window. Through the window, the city lights were filtered through gnarled trees as old as the house itself. The other walls were of golden wallpaper that fit some garish nineteenth-century motif, embossed so that the shadows formed shifting geometric patterns that changed depending on where I stood relative to the light.

To the left of the great window, an Egyptian sarcophagus stood against the wall, surrounded by a box of glass. On the other wall hung a full-size reproduction of the center panel of Hieronymous Bosch's *The Garden of Earthly Delights*.

My addled memory gave me the name and the artist without telling me where I had learned of him.

"Come in, my friend. Have a seat." Gabriel stood behind a desk of black wood. And motioned me toward a waiting chair.

I sat down, looking at Gabriel. He had a look of wild authority about him, with his cane, his lined face, and his long white hair. Authority and passion that made his gray-blue eyes seem less the color of ice than the color of a gas-jet.

He sat, his long hands enveloping his cane. "Again, I offer my apologies, sir."

I clutched my left hand. "I am still trying to understand what is going on here. No offense, but I don't know who the hell you are or what you have to do with what's happened to me."

"We are here to illuminate each other's ignorance." He leaned forward. "We shall have a fair exchange, question for question. I shall give you the first two as compensation for our prior misunderstanding."

Misunderstanding? This person, who looked to be seventy, had thrown me through the air fifteen feet— one-handed. That had to be one pretty big misunderstanding.

"Let's start there, then," I said. "Exactly what was your misunderstanding? You were threatening me one minute, and the next— What brought on the sudden change of heart?"

"A mistake about your status, Mr. Tyler. I am not infallible. I knew that you were mortal when I first began the search for Childe, and I knew, when I saw you last, that the thirst had claimed you. The thirst could not have been upon you for more than a few days. The possibility that you could have been master-less never occurred to me until I tasted the strength of your blood. You do not have the blood of a thrall, which is what I treated you as."

I didn't feel as if I understood things any better. I shook my head. "You'd better start describing the society I've stepped into, because I don't know anything about masters or thralls, other than what the words usually mean."

"Now that is a broad question, but I did give you two." He paused in thought for a moment.

"We keep a Covenant, sir. That is the first law we hold to. Without the Covenant, our race would swiftly die. There are three things the Covenant holds us to. First, no one who holds to the Covenant may slay another who holds to it. Second, no one who holds to the Covenant may act so as to reveal those of the blood, or allow the revelation of those of the blood. Third, a master is responsible for the actions of all of his blood. Any of the blood who don't hold to the Covenant, even those who are not part of it, forfeit their existence."

I nodded. It made a certain amount of sense, too much sense. It reminded me of the code of a Mafia family: don't kill family, keep your mouth shut about family business, keep your own house in order.

"Our society is larger than the Covenant, but I think of the Covenant as central to it. Within my circle, my duty is to enforce the Covenant—" He looked at me and shook his head. "I suppose I need to explain that as well." He raised a hand and began tracing circles on the desk in front of him. "We are a race of hierarchies . . . ."

14

It seemed that we spent hours in that room. Gabriel spoke of hierarchies, and explained them at length, and I saw the master-thrall relationship mirroring itself throughout the whole society Gabriel described.

A thrall was the lowest someone could be within the society, little more than the animate property of his master. In terms of relationships, a thrall was treated almost as if he were an indivisible part of his master.

The thrall's master was usually the vampire responsible for creating him. According to Gabriel, almost all vampires began as humans chosen by a vampire in search of material for a thrall. Those choices were consciously made; no thrall was ever created by accident.

A thrall remained bonded—physically and psychically enslaved—until his master chose to free him, or until the master was destroyed. From what Gabriel said, I wondered if it was an unusual occurrence for a thrall to end up killing his master. Even if the enslavement was as much mental as physical, I doubted that it could be maintained permanently, or vampire society would stagnate. If there weren't an implicit threat of eventual rebellion, there would be no incentive for any master to ever release a thrall and create a new one.

Though the Covenant forbade masters from slaying one another, a thrall operated under his master's responsibility. If a thrall killed his master, it was the master that was responsible—essentially suicide. I noticed that Gabriel said nothing about any of that. It was probably a touchy subject.

What he talked about, at length, was the web of associations among those of "free blood," as he called it. Just as with any culture, there was a definite pecking order, high to low. The circles that Rowena mentioned were levels of power, or—more accurately—associations of vampires who had roughly the same status. It seemed that individuals could gain status on their own, or the circle as a whole could rise and fall, a combination of a political party and a noble house.

Gabriel explained the relationship between higher and lower, and I began understanding why Rowena would consider my question about her circle impertinent. Vampire society seemed divorced from the material world. The more so the closer to the center you came. In such a society, information was a valued commodity. Information about relationships within the community, especially.

In a way, Gabriel was telling me how grave his mistake was in the way he had first shaken me down, and at the same time telling me how well he was making up for that mistake.

After information, what this society valued was reciprocity—in all its forms. A favor granted meant a favor returned. A wound inflicted meant a wound repaid. It went beyond that, into areas that were hard to understand in one sitting. Favors were exchanged like gifts, but status and power dictated who could initiate such an exchange. Offering something to someone of a level much higher than my own could be seen as a bitter insult, while asking anything of that person could disadvantage me, incurring a social debt that I'd be obliged to repay.

* * *

After he was done with his lengthy description, I was taken by one question that he had not answered. "Where do I fit in this? I've been dropped in here without a script."

Gabriel held up a hand. "This is your third question, sir. You must give me leave to ask you one of my own."

I understood what he was doing now. By allowing me those first two questions, he had expunged a debt between us, a debt that he'd incurred by his "misunderstanding." Now we were in a game of reciprocal questions. I nodded to him, "Fair's fair."

"Who was it that granted you the thirst? Someone must have taken your mortal life, or have fed upon you before your mortal life was taken."

His gaze held me, and I felt the distinct fear of disappointing someone more powerful than I was. "I don't know."

"You don't know?"

"If I do know, it's a memory that's inaccessible to me at the moment."

Gabriel looked at me, and I had the uneasy feeling that those blue-gray eyes could see if I lied. "It is an answer of sorts," he said. "My own answer, to your question: You do *not* 'fit' into our society. You have not pledged yourself to the Covenant. You have taken no name. You are a rogue as outside us as is the human from which you sprang. You are of the blood, which means I must respect you. But you have no status, high or low. I treat you as a peer because I disadvantaged myself to you, but others will treat you as is their fancy."

That disturbed me. It meant I was at a considerable disadvantage in dealing with others of my kind.

"My kind," I whispered, surprised at the form my thoughts had taken.

"Pardon me, sir?"

"No, nothing. This has all been a little much for me. I had a life—"

Gabriel shook his head. "You *have* a life, Mr. Tyler. Don't mistake what has happened for death; those who do taste the true death before long." He leaned back. "But that was not a question."

"No, it wasn't." I sat up a little straighter in my chair. "How *could* I fit into this society?"

"You need to accept the Covenant and choose your Name before us. However, you need one of us to accept you, and such a boon will not be granted lightly or freely. Some measure of responsibility shall attach— not absolute, your sponsor did not create you—but enough that your actions will reflect well or ill upon the one granting you this. Something in return will be asked, and only someone great in his own position would not demand some indenture."

"Someone has to open the door and take responsibility for letting me in."

Gabriel nodded.

"Your turn."

"I presume you've seen Childe's thralls at one point. Describe the last time you saw any of them."

"I can't be certain who his thralls are, but if they are the teenagers he's supposed to be collecting, the last time I dealt with any of them was yesterday. They rammed a van into a car I was in . . . ."

The question game went on for hours. I answered Gabriel's questions truthfully, not because I trusted him—I didn't—but because he never asked anything that was worth it to risk a lie. The only personal questions he asked me were about me becoming a vampire, the sequence of events immediately afterward, and about Tony.

Everything else was about Childe, directly or indirectly.

I learned as much from Gabriel's questions as I did from my own. It was clear that he hunted Childe for some violation of the Covenant. Specifically, Childe bore the responsibility for his thralls' violations. His thralls—apparently the people identified with Childe's cult—had broken the second law of the Covenant, "revealing those of the blood." I had the uncomfortable feeling that I was the one, through my investigation, to whom things were revealed.

Listening to Gabriel, I had the sense that he had some personal stake in finding Childe, beyond the fact that Childe seemed to have violated the Covenant. He seemed to view Childe with the same distaste that the neo-pagans did, and I could not figure out why he would feel that way. However, Gabriel's attitude toward Childe raised my suspicions.

I felt Gabriel was too ready to convict Childe, especially now that I knew the nature of the Covenant. The Covenant now made it even harder for me to fathom what Childe's people—his thralls—were doing. I couldn't account for it even as some sort of mass rebellion, a slave revolt. That wouldn't explain the outward-directed violence. It didn't explain the attention drawn in Childe's name. A thrall rebellion would have at its focus the master.

I wondered what Gabriel gained by dealing with those who violated the Covenant. What did he gain in status and power? I wondered if his gain was roughly proportional to the level of the person he brought down. I didn't question Gabriel about these points. I didn't want to allow him into the routes my own mind was taking.

My questions were more basic to my immediate survival. I kept asking questions about vampirism in general. I didn't want Gabriel to think of me as a fellow investigator. The more he saw me as a neophyte, the safer I thought I was.

So I asked if I had to kill.

Gabriel said it wasn't necessary. Life was the important thing, not death. He explained that I had been in such a diminished state when I had taken Tony that I had no choice but to take all he had to give.

How much blood?

The answer depended on too many things, from innate physical strength to the level of exertion.

Garlic, crosses, and holy water?

He gave me an amused smile and a comment about superstition. "Belief is all you have to fear," he said. "Yours and your adversary's."

Stakes, decapitation, and fire?

Such things would be anathema to any being.

The sun?

Gabriel's expression turned grave as he said, "The light of the sun is insidious. A more spiritual person would say it drives the soul from the flesh where it is bound. From my point of view, it is simple death. Exposed to that light for any length, and you shall become a corpse."

"Speaking of that light," I said, "there are things I must do before dawn."

He nodded at me. "I appreciate all your answers, Mr. Tyler. Your information may yet help me find him, or at least make the case that he must be found." He stood and extended his hand.

I stood and clasped his hand. I didn't know what to make of him now. His comment came uncomfortably close to what Sam had said about getting a warrant. I didn't trust Gabriel, or his motives.

"I apologize for the gaps in my memory," I said, hoping that I had at least gotten as much out of him as he had out of me.

"As I said, what you do know may yet help me." He smiled at me, a smile that managed to condense all the darkness in this house into a single facial expression. "I'm sure you can find your way out."

When I drove away from the house, it was nearly three in the morning. When I arrived at the Lakewood address of Manuel Deité, a.k.a. Childe, it was closer to four. It wasn't that it took an hour to drive from Cleveland Heights to Lakewood. I just needed the time to digest what I had learned—and what I thought I'd learned—when I talked to Gabriel.

Childe had a Edgewater Drive address, and at first I thought that he lived in one of the ranks of ice-tray apartment complexes that claimed the view of the water. However, one look at the address told me that he resided on the other side of Edgewater. The apartment buildings on that side were stone and brick as opposed to concrete, and a few decades ago, these would have had the view of the water—

Now they just had the view of apartments that were more expensive, newer, and uglier.

The building had a parking lot in back. I pulled the Olds up over a hump of snow and looked up at Childe's building. It would have been at home overlooking the Rhine. Most of the buildings on this side of Edgewater would. Childe's building was a Tudor study in stone detailing and leaded glass.

His apartment number was 1000. Probably a place of prominence, tenth floor, facing the front. I left the Olds and walked around the building. When I rounded the front of the building, I saw what *had* to be Childe's apartment. One corner of the building was rounded, almost like a castle turret. On the top floor, the entire outer circumference of that stone curve was fitted with a huge leaded glass window. The window had to be ten feet wide and half again as high. It was hard to tell, since the room beyond was dark, but I had the impression that the inside was hung with heavy drapes.

Now all I had to do was get in.

I continued to circle the apartment building, looking for an entry point. The usual entrances were secure. I could have tried to have someone buzz me in, but I didn't want to announce my presence like that.

When I completed my circuit, I saw my way in.

Above the rear door, overlooking the parking lot, windows looked in on a rear stairwell. The door itself sat within a Gothic arch topped with an elaborate stone shield. I looked around, to assure myself that I was unobserved; then I ran up and jumped at the door. I grabbed hold of the top of the arch, around the projecting shield.

Levering myself up to the window was easier than I expected. I thought of the litany of aches and pains this should have ignited, and now that I was thinking of them, I noticed the lack. I lived in a forty-five-year-old body, but I don't think I could have pulled myself up so easily when I was eighteen.

I remembered jumping out a second-floor window. My body seemed capable of more than healing a slashed wrist.

I stood on a small stone prominence, looking in on the stairwell. The window I faced was locked, but I saw no sign of any alarm system. All that held it shut was a small tab of metal, screwed into the wood of the frame. My first thought was to break the glass, reach in, and unlock the window, but I reconsidered.

If I pulled myself up here so easily, how easily could I force the window?

I grabbed the bottom of the upper frame and started tugging it down. It tried to move, and through the glass I saw the metal of the lock levering upward in response. I saw that it had been painted shut. Paint flaked from the lock.

Then, abruptly, it gave, and the top half of the window slammed down in the sash. A small twisted piece of metal sailed into the stairwell, clattering down the stairs. I stood there for a moment, waiting for someone to react to the noise. No one did.

I climbed though the top of the window, closing it as firmly as I could behind me.

At Childe's door, I wished for some lock picks, or at least a credit card. I was reduced to drawing my gun, looking both ways down the hallway, and kicking it open.

The door blew in after I slammed my foot next to the inner edge of the doorknob. The room beyond was dark. I covered it with the Eagle as the door hit the wall. Even before my eyes adjusted, I knew the apartment was empty. I could *feel* it.

I stepped in, still covering the room with my Eagle. Feelings aside, I wasn't going to let my guard down until I *saw* the place was empty.

I did a quick sweep of all the rooms. All were dark, all were unoccupied. Then I holstered the gun.

I went back to the front and closed the door to the apartment to ward off the curious. By now I could see fairly well, even in the near-complete darkness. Well enough to read titles on the bookshelf across from the grand, draped window. Another of the fringe benefits of vampirism.

I started searching Childe's rooms at the bookshelf. The titles weren't helpful except in confirming Childe's interest in the occult. Many of the books were old, and the majority weren't in English. I noted titles such as *Directorium Inquisitorum, Ordinall of Alchimy, Heaven and Hell, De Quinta Essentia Philosophorum*, and *Iter Subterraneum*. I noted authors from John Dee and Alister Crowley to Thomas Aquinas.

The remainder of the living room, dominated by the great curtained window, was less remarkable. Childe had a predilection for antiques, and I had the feeling that most of his furniture, as his books, must have traveled here from England.

What was striking was what was *not* here. Childe didn't own a television, or a stereo. The only sign that he acknowledged the century he lived in was the presence of electric lights, and a telephone that occupied a table to itself in one corner of the living room.

I examined the phone and found an answering machine. The machine held half a dozen messages.

The first message was a gravelly voice that sounded slightly familiar, though I couldn't place it. "I hear you look for a woman of certain qualities. There will be one at the ritual tonight, I've told her to look for you." There was a computerized date-time stamp on the messages; this one had been left at 6:15 p.m. on Sunday, January twenty-sixth.

The next message had been left over a week later, after I had already begun my search for Cecilia. The voice was unquestionably Gabriel, requesting a meeting.

The next two messages were also from Gabriel, no longer requesting. The last of Gabriel's messages was a virtual demand for Childe to explain himself. The dates of the calls were portentous. One corresponded to Kate's death. The next corresponded to my own disappearance.

The last two were from Sam, leaving a name and number. I noticed that he didn't identify himself as a policeman, and that he left the number of his pager.

I worked through an empty and unused kitchen and a dining room, finding little of Childe left behind. It was as if no one had ever really lived here. The furniture was all in place, but most of the drawers I opened were empty. Nowhere did I find any papers, bank records, checkbook, opened mail, phone bill, anything.

The only sign that this was anything more than a mail drop was in the bedroom. The room was huge, and central to it was a canopied bed, which was curtained with heavy black velvet. The curtains had been drawn aside, revealing that the bed held no mattress, no bedding. The bed frame supported a flat wood panel.

Even though the windows were curtained, I noticed immediately that this room was darker than the others. Dark enough to give my now-exceptional night vision difficulty. It was as dark down here as it had been in the sewer.

When I pulled the curtains on the window aside, I saw why. The glass had been painted so that no light could leak into this room. I backed up to the door, and checked around it. There was a curtain rod mounted just above the door frame, and more heavy curtains hung to the side, ready to be drawn across a closed door—a door that would be held shut by a pair of heavy dead bolts that could not be unlocked from the other side.

Childe was serious about not having his rest disturbed.

However, I had the feeling that there were a number of other places in the city where Childe slept. This one, I felt, was here for the people who were looking for Childe, and the outfitting of the bedroom was secondary, in case Childe needed a dark place to sleep.

It was frustrating, but not unexpected. I knew that there'd be little to find before I'd come here. Childe had been doing what he'd been doing for decades at least. There was no way he could go so long without learning how to cover his tracks.

No papers, no mail . . . .

Now there was a thought. If Childe had truly disappeared with Cecilia, his mail here would have been accumulating for three weeks with no one to pick it up. Even if this was only a front, at the very least, Manuel Deité had to pay a phone bill.

No matter how many places Childe might have, Manuel Deité only had one address in this town.

I slipped out of the apartment and checked the time. I'd been quick, it was only four-thirty. I had some time before I had to worry about the sun.

I descended by the rear stairwell, where I had entered the building. It may have been because I had left Childe's apartment, or because I'd found nothing there, but I let my guard down for a moment when I reached the first floor landing. I began opening the door before looking down the hall. I saw my mistake immediately, but it was too late.

The hall shot the length of the building, from this stairwell across to the front lobby. The mailboxes were set in an alcove about midway down the hall. In front of the boxes stood a beefy man with slate-gray hair, who was busily jimmying one of them open. A younger man stood next to him, watching.

I am no believer in coincidence, and I could pretty much guess which mailbox he was opening.

The younger one saw me, shouted something, and they both started running toward me. I had a split-second to decide if I was running up the stairs or down. I ran up the stairs, hoping that at least one of them would head for the obvious exit. As I rounded the landing where I had broken in, I heard one of them yell, "Police! Freeze!"

15

Time slowed. The thought that I ran from the police might have made me hesitate. But it was too early to be Sam. I never got the chance to stop.

One of them said, slowly and very deliberately, "He's going for a gun."

I heard a gun go off. A bullet struck me, a twenty-pound sledge in the side of my chest. I fell into the window next to me. It shattered as my shoulder smashed against the frame.

"Shit!" One of the cops said, a different voice than the one who said I had gone for a gun.

Another sledgehammer slammed into my shoulder, and the windowframe collapsed around me. The dry wood gave way under my weight, and I felt the bite of winter air as my momentum carried me sidewise and my feet slipped out from under me.

The cop's gun barked a third time, the bullet hammering my gut. I fell across the sill of the window, tumbling forward. There was little I could do to stop my fall.

I pitched out the window before I felt the throb of the first gunshot. Everything felt distant, as if I were watching it all from a remove. I tumbled through space for an endless instant, my body rolling so I faced the sky.

My wounded shoulder plowed into the ground first,

grinding into a mixture of snow and glass. I collapsed into a heap below the window, immobile.

I felt so cold.

I wasn't breathing, and I couldn't feel my own pulse. I could feel the cold, and I could feel the empty holes where bullets had ripped chunks from my body. Oddly, I felt little pain, just an odd pressure in my chest, my stomach, and my shoulder. The wounds were like pits, and I felt as if I was draining myself down into them.

I could almost feel my body shriveling, and my torso tightening in response.

I knew when they came out the rear door, into the parking lot. Not because I could see them, I felt as if I couldn't turn my head, but because I felt a sense of distant warmth. The police radiated an inner warmth that tightened my gut.

"You shot him!" one of them said, the cop who had spouted the profanity. I suspected it was the younger man, though I didn't see him. My eyes were focused on the sky and the wall of the apartment building in front of me. Above me, the window gaped like an open wound.

"Damn straight I shot him."

"Is he dead?"

A face leaned over me, its heat and emotion rippling toward me through the wind-torn air. I could feel parts of my body, inside me, moving in response to the warmth.

The gray-haired cop was ugly and rumpled, and looked at me with an expression of disgust. He still had his gun out as he knelt next to me. I could hear—I could *feel*—the younger one pacing behind me. The old cop placed his fingers on my neck and the feeling of pulsing heat was as intense as an orgasm.

"I put three bullets into him. He'd *better* be dead."

The fingers stayed on my neck for a long time, and my body drew the heat—and something else?—from them. "Fuck," the old cop said, yanking away his fingers. "He's cold already."

With the touch I felt a dreamlike realization that I *could* move if I tried. My anger was building, as if I had to collect the shattered pieces of the emotion and piece it into some coherent whole. The shock was wearing off. This cop had tried to kill me. Hell, this SOB tried to *murder* me. He taken me down without a single hesitation, even down to the lie about me going for a gun.

"This ain't good," the young cop was saying to my right.

"Look, kid, this was a clean shoot. You ever say different, you'll be in shit you don't even know exists." The old cop transferred his revolver to his left hand and felt around my chest until he found my holster. "Bastard doesn't even bleed—" the cop mumbled.

"What?"

"I said, 'Look at this fucking cannon.' " The old cop held up my Desert Eagle with his right hand. Its barrel glinted in the streetlight as he clicked the safety off.

"Just plant the gun so we can call this in," the young cop said in a disgusted tone of voice.

"I ain't planting it. It's *Tyler's* gun." I noticed the old cop was wearing surgical gloves. He began pressing the Eagle in my right palm.

I could see what this was now. These were Sebastian's men. No, that was kind. These were bent cops on Sebastian's payroll. This guy had probably shot me because there was a hefty sum for keeping me out of police custody.

Thinking that allowed the anger to break my paralysis. I screamed. It was an inarticulate, primal scream that sounded as if it were torn from the throat of some wounded animal. My hand clutched the Eagle.

The sound of the gunshot was like an explosion going off in my hand. The old cop cursed, and the young one screamed. I whipped my head to the side to see the young cop collapsing. The wild shot had caught him in the upper right thigh, and the fifty-caliber bullet had shattered his leg.

"Shit!" The old cop's right hand was missing the last three fingers. He was yanking his right hand in toward his body and leveling the revolver at me with his left. Steaming blood stained the snow. Its scent was a dagger into my forebrain.

Something was happening to me.

I got up, and everything I saw seemed to have been carved out with a razor. Blood was glowing fire, turning back at the edges where it soaked into the shimmering violet snow. The old cop scrambled away from me, pointing the gun. His skin glowed, heat and fear and anger rippled off of him, distorting my view.

I could feel my body changing, my bones shifting as I stood. My skin emitted nothing, no heat, no emotion. If anything, it was a gaping *lack* that surrounded me, a desperate hunger.

I dropped the Eagle.

The cop's gun fired, licking a tongue of flame at my abdomen. I felt the bullet as a blow to my midsection, but there was no blood. I could feel the slug pass through my body, tearing its way through, but that was little compared to the tearing my body was doing to itself. I felt muscles ripping and knotting back together; my skin stretched, tightened, gave way, and then regrew; the bones of my face moved of their own accord.

I should have been screaming in pain.

The cop put two more slugs through me before I reached him. I felt a hiccup of fluids as the first bullet shredded my right lung. And, when I was nearly upon him, I was blinded by the flash when he put a bullet through my right cheek. I could feel my jaw cave in with the impact, and I could feel my flesh and bone shred behind me.

All of this happened, and I was only really aware of the hunger.

Still blinded by the muzzle flash, I grabbed for the cop. I could sense where he was, his fear—*his life*—was like a beacon. I felt my hands, fingers much too long, grab the sides of the cop's head. I felt the barrel of the thirty-eight rammed underneath my chin. I heard the click as a hammer fell on an empty chamber.

My vision cleared as I felt the flesh of my face reknitting itself into a new pattern. I felt the sharp curve of new teeth as my jaw rebuilt itself.

The cop looked at me with terrified eyes. "Holy Mother of God."

Nothing was left of my conscious thought. All I had was sensation, and the hunger to posses what this man possessed: heat, blood, life.

I snapped his head back, hearing a crack in his spine. Then I buried my teeth in his exposed neck. My rebuilt jaw easily covered the entire area, and my bite severed both jugulars. None of the blood was spilled on the ground.

When I finally gained control of my actions, I was leaning over the second cop, the young one. He was curled in a fetal position below me, whimpering, "Don't kill me . . . please, don't kill me."

I stood at the edge of a pool of black slush. The snow smelled of blood, a scent like molten iron. Most of the blood came from between the cop's fingers, where he was trying to hold his shattered thigh together.

There was no question in my mind that I was about to kill this cop, just as I'd killed his partner. Then, suddenly, I was in control again. The *need* had receded for the moment. I actually felt warm.

I stood there, paralyzed by what had just happened.

The events had the feverish intensity of a hallucination, but even now, as I felt perfectly lucid, I could feel my body shifting inside.

Bones moved inside me with the persistent pressure of a dull toothache. I stared at my hands.

My hands were inhuman. Their skin was tough, leathery, and nearly black. The fingers ended in curving black nails that were almost talons. As I watched, the fingers shortened, the skin softened and regained its color, and the talons withdrew back into my fingers.

I uttered some profanity, but the word came out as a low slurred whistle because my mouth was rebuilding itself. I put my hands to my face and it was like touching a bony waterbed. I felt what could have been a muzzle retract into my skull.

I turned around to face the other cop.

There was the window, blown open where I had fallen through it. There was the glass, and the remains of the windowframe. There was the imprint in the snow where my body had fallen. An imprint with no blood inside it. There was my fifty-caliber Desert Eagle, dropped on the ground.

And there was the dead cop.

He was sprawled in a half-sitting position, his back to the wall of the apartment building. His right hand was across his waist, fisted into a ball around the missing parts of his fingers. His left hand still clutched the thirty-eight. His face was slack, and as blue as the snow he sat in.

His neck had been torn open down to the bone. Muscle, windpipe, everything between me and the vertebrae had been torn out as if mauled by an animal. The sight should have been gory, but it wasn't. The living cop, next to me, was much worse with his bleeding leg. The dead cop, with the exception of a few trails from his wounded hand, had spilled no blood at all.

My body had stopped changing, and I looked down at myself.

I saw five bullet holes in my shirt, two showing powder burns. I felt underneath, and my chest was intact.

Of course, it's intact, I thought.

"Please don't kill me . . ." the cop behind me whimpered again.

I felt sick over everything that had just happened. I had just killed a cop—a bent cop, but still a cop. The guy with the wounded leg had watched every minute. Shadows moved at windows above me, and in the distance I heard sirens wail.

The man beneath me was the only witness to what had happened. And by Gabriel's Covenant, I had to kill him. He had seen what I had done. If I left him to witness against me, I'd have more than the police after me.

I knelt down and pulled him up to face me. I held the sides of his head like I had his partner. . . .

He was sputtering and tears of fear and pain ran down his cheeks. I felt his terror. Whatever I had become, I couldn't kill him. Not like this, and not in cold blood.

There has to be another way. There had to be, Gabriel had told me that it wasn't necessary to kill for blood. How then did any vampire take blood without revealing his nature?

It was a combination of impulse and memory that made me shout at the terrified cop, "Look at me!"

The memory was of Bowie's reaction when he looked into my eyes. Everyone seemed to have a reaction to my uncovered gaze. The impulse was totally unlike me, possibly inspired by my talk with Gabriel. I remembered thinking, *who is this man—this* human— *to defy my will?*

He looked at me, and when our eyes met, his gaze didn't shift or turn away. He didn't even blink. "You did not see who shot you," I said to him, bludgeoning him with the words. "You saw nothing of what happened. You do not know what happened to your partner. Tell anyone what has happened here, if you even remember it yourself, you shall surely die. . . ."

I felt a flash of memory, someone's stony voice saying, "*. . . if you even remember it yourself, you shall surely die . . .*" I was gripped by the feeling that this had happened before.

I had no time to dwell on it. The sirens were closing on me. The young cop nodded like a zombie, and I let him slide to the ground. I ran back to the building and grabbed my Desert Eagle and its one spent casing. Luckily for me, the cop was using a revolver and I didn't have to go hunting for his brass.

After holstering the Eagle, I grabbed the collar of the dead cop and dragged his corpse to the Oldsmobile. I tossed him in the back seat because I didn't have the time to wrestle with the trunk.

I drove away, relying on whatever psychic impression my will had made upon the young policeman.

16

It was almost five in the morning when I drove out of Lakewood with a corpse in the back seat. I didn't pass any police cars in my escape. I only stopped once, on a side street, to steal a manhole cover. I was caught up in a rush of action which gave me no time to reflect.

The central part of the Cuyahoga River had yet to freeze, and the cop's bloodless corpse found its home in a plunge from the Detroit-Superior Bridge. He slipped under quickly. His legs were bound to the stolen manhole cover with the Olds' jumper cables.

When he had slipped beneath the dark waters of his ultimate dim Thule and I had driven away, my mind was free to think beyond the next five minutes of my future.

I began to appreciate what had happened. I had slaughtered one policeman, and shot out of the leg of another. It had been Tony all over again.

I ran my hand across my face. I was shaking.

"What have I become?" I whispered.

I had no justification for killing the policeman. His bullets could not harm this thing I was. I had been in no danger from him, and I had known it when I had risen from the ground. I couldn't see the circumstances to rationalize dropping my gun and mauling his neck. It was all too much like what had happened with Tony. I had murdered Tony, and I had murdered this cop.

There was one major difference between the cop's

death and Tony's. With this man I didn't even have the excuse that I didn't know what I was doing. I knew what I was, and I had known what I was capable of, and I did not stop myself.

I felt as if, on some level I had killed both of them, Tony and the policeman, because their existence had *offended* me.

I pulled the Olds to the side of Superior, just past Public Square, because I had begun driving erratically, and the last thing I needed was to draw the attention of any more police. Once the car was parked, I put my face in my hands feeling that I had lost Kane Tyler completely.

When I bent over, something small and black tumbled onto the passenger seat.

It was a thirty-eight slug, or the biggest part of one. It was flattened and coated with a thin layer of gore.

I picked up the slug. It looked as if it had struck bone on its way through, a bone that should be broken and splintered. It was covered in my blood, but the only holes were in my clothing, not my body . . .

I had left the human universe, physically as well as morally. I thought of Gabriel's society and wondered how anyone could live like this, live in that world, and remain sane.

Perhaps sanity was only a human concept—

"Stop it," I whispered. "We all come from the same place, all of us." I *was* still Kane Tyler, a Kane Tyler who had undergone a physical transformation of some sort, but I was still the same man.

Thinking that only made the deaths that much worse.

Wind whistled by the car, the sound low and loathsome. Garbage rustled by the car, scuttling across the snow in front of the Olds. I thought of the cop slipping into the black waters of the Cuyahoga and wondered if he had any family. Was there a widow out there, perhaps a son who was trying to understand where his father had gone?

As Gail was trying to understand why her mother had gone?

How could I face my daughter, when I was becoming what I was hunting? I sat in the car a long time, wondering if this life after life was worth what it was eating out of my soul. I sat trembling as I stared at the sky, which had lightened from purple to a deep aqua.

According to Gabriel, all I would need to do was await the transit of the sun, and this would all be over. I would have no more blood on my hands. . . .

The sky ahead of me, to the east, began to take a yellowish tint to the clouds.

I couldn't do this. My life didn't belong to me. I couldn't make Gail an orphan, and I couldn't abandon Cecilia to her fate. If I gave up now, the deaths on my conscience really *would* be pointless.

I revved up the Olds and started down Superior. Now that I'd changed my mind, the coming dawn filled me with a growing fear. I needed to get inside.

I drove through the shadows provided by the buildings downtown, but a furtive glance in the rearview mirror showed me the first molten light washing the tops of the skyscrapers downtown. The eastern faces of the towers were washed in gold, and reflections off the mirrored glass seared my eyes. The sight burned like a brand, scattering purple dead-spots across my field of vision.

I was driving *toward* the sun.

The Olds swerved as I blinked my eyes clear. Twice-reflected dawn sunlight—*Cleveland* dawn sunlight, in *winter*—was as blinding to me as a magnesium flare.

In a matter of minutes, the long shadows of the buildings would crawl across the Olds, leaving me bare to the sun. Worse, something in the ambient light, the light that reached into the shadows, was hot, numbing, and brought with it a crushing fatigue. I felt an urge to pull to the side of the road and go to sleep.

I turned off of Superior to find a darkened bolt-hole. I found an underground parking garage that offered all-day parking for ten bucks. When I pulled into the driveway, the sunlight had reached the second floor of the building. I waited by the gate and peeled off a fifty from the cash I'd liberated from the hotel room.

There was a guy sitting in a booth by the gate, and I waited for him. And waited. And waited.

When the sunlight reached down to the top of the garage's entrance, I laid on the horn. The guy in the booth to my left looked up and gave me a sour look. He didn't move. I laid on the horn again.

He stepped out of the booth and yelled at me, "We ain't open till seven-thirty."

Fuck. I looked at my watch. It was fifteen after.

I rolled the window down the Olds and tried to shout at the guy, but it came out as a wheeze. I panicked for a moment before I realized that I had to consciously start breathing again. As I did so, I tempered my anger. "Come on, I'm only a little early—"

The guy looked peeved, but he stopped yelling, "Look, you have to wait."

"Only fifteen minutes." The dawn was drawing across in front of me, a blinding curtain of light washing across the front of the garage. I could feel my skin tightening. I wanted to shrink into the shadows the Olds provided. But I leaned out the window and flashed the fifty at the guy.

I looked him in the eyes.

The guy squinted as a line of sunlight began crossing his face, "I don't know, my boss'd can me."

I extended the fifty. "For a few extra minutes? Come on, open the gate."

We stared at each other as the sunlight crept toward my hand. I wanted to flinch, but I sensed withdrawing the fifty—or any sudden move—would break whatever spell I was trying to weave.

"I don't know. . . ." Blinding light toughed the edge of the fifty. Light so bright that I was surprised that the bill didn't burst into flame.

It was slow, so damn slow. It seemed an age before he said, "Okay," and grabbed the fifty.

I snatched my hand back, but as I did, I felt the brush of sunlight across its back. The touch of direct sunlight was not as dramatic as I thought it should be. My hand didn't burst into flame, or crumble into dust.

What happened was frightening because it was so subtle in comparison. I felt my entire hand flare with pain, fall asleep, and go numb. It was as if I had plunged my hand into a vat of boiling Novocain.

As the gate opened, I had to drive with one hand. My left hand was limp, paralyzed. I drove into the dark-ened garage as if the gates of hell were behind me.

Whether I was entering or leaving was open to question.

I found a space in the lowest level of the garage, a place that had never even seen reflected sunlight. I maneuvered the Olds into a dark corner, into a space half-concealed by a concrete pillar. I was as far from the elevator as I could get.

Once I parked, I looked at my hand. The skin was white and numb. It could have been an inanimate lump of meat for all I could do with it. I was still staring at my hand when fatigue crashed over me.

More memories, older ones, kept me company as I fell into my not-sleep.

I don't want to be in this man's office, I resent it. Haven't I've been through enough? Dad's dead. What the hell is this guy supposed to do about it?

"Hello, Kane," the doctor says. "I'm pleased to finally meet you."

"I'm glad someone's enjoying this."

"Your mother thinks you need someone to talk to."

I sigh. "You mean she wants me to talk to someone. What if I don't have anything to say?"

"I find that hard to believe," the doctor says. He glances down at the desk in front of him, where he keeps his files. "You seemed to have a lot to say to your classmates—enough to get you suspended."

I shook my head. "That wasn't me talking."

The doctor makes a note in front of him and asks, "It wasn't you? Are you saying that you did not step up on a desk in your physics class and shout poetry?"

"I'm saying that those weren't my words. Mr. Franklin asked what something meant. I quoted something that seemed to apply."

The doctor makes another note. "Mr. Franklin felt you were being disruptive."

"Sometimes the truth is disruptive."

The doctor nodded, but I didn't make the mistake of thinking he agreed with me. I was here because no one seemed to agree with me. Somehow I was wrong. We were all supposed to accept death, and pain, and loss. Give it some higher meaning, and go on.

"So what was it you quoted to Mr. Franklin that got you in so much trouble?"

"It's by Edgar Allan Poe. 'The Conqueror Worm.' It's part of a short story he wrote."

Another note. "How does it go?"

I sigh. I'm surprised that the doctor doesn't have it in his files there in front of him. But then, I am here to perform. Why disappoint him? I stand and recite the poem from "Ligeia," first stanza to last.

" 'Lo! 'tis a gala night / Within the lonesome latter years! / An angel throng, bewinged bedight / In veils, and drowned in tears, / Sit in a theater, to see / A play

*of hopes and fears, / While the orchestra breathes fit-
fully / The music of the spheres.' "*

As I speak, the doctor scribbles, I find that annoying.
He requested this, he should be giving undivided attention to it. I raise my voice a bit.

" *'Mimes, in the form of God on high, / Mutter and
mumble low, / And hither and thither fly— / Mere pup-
pets they, who come and go / At bidding of vast formless
things / That shift the scenery to and fro, / Flapping
from out their Condor wings / Invisible Wo!' "*

Scribble, scribble. He was worse than Mr. Franklin,
who had stood in the midst of his cosmology to stand
looking at me agape. He was worse than the other stu-
dents, who had laughed at things that weren't funny.

" *'That motley drama—oh, be sure / It shall not be
forgot! / With its Phantom chased for evermore, / By a
crowd that seize it not, / Through a circle that ever
returneth in / To the self-same spot, / And much of
Madness, and more of Sin, / And Horror the soul of the
plot.' "*

Damn him. Listen. *Stop that infernal scribbling.* I
climb onto the chair in front of him, as I had in Mr.
Franklin's class. The doctor is like the others. He just
refuses to see.

" *'But see, amid the mimic rout / A crawling shape
intrude! / A blood-red thing that writhes from out / The
scenic solitude! / It writhes!—' "* I begin shouting, " *'it
writhes!—with mortal pangs / The mimes become its
food, / And seraphs sob as vermin fangs / In human
gore imbued."*

I jump upon the doctor's desk to grab his attention. Finally he looks up from that infernal notepad
of his.

" *'Out—' "* I shout. " *'out are the lights—out all! /
And, over each quivering form, / The curtain, a funeral
pall, / Comes down with the rush of a storm, / While the*

*angels, all pallid and wan, / Uprising, unveiling, affirm /
That the play is the tragedy, "Man," / And its hero the
Conqueror Worm.' "*

The doctor looks up at me and asks, "How did you
feel when your father died?"

"Dad!" *she says to me. Her expression shows exas-
peration, as if she doesn't understand.*

"Where the hell were you?"

"With friends—come on, it's only one o'clock."

I'm standing out there, more angry at myself than at
Gail. I'd just gotten home from a bad day, a really bad
day. I look at her, feeling powerless. "I'm sorry, I
overreacted. You weren't here and. . . ."

Gail looks around me and says, "Where's Mom?"

Now I feel guilty as well. "She's upstairs, we had a
fight."

In her face I can see she understands now. I see her
take an unfair share of the weight between me and
Kate. "Oh, Dad—it was about me, wasn't it? I'm
sorry, I should have left a note or something."

"Shh—"

Gail pushes past me, her hands balled into small
fists. "I don't want to give you and Mom something
else to fight about."

"No, no," I reach out and place a hand on her
shoulder. "It's not about you. It's me."

"I'm sorry," she says.

"It's not your fault." I say. "It's never been your
fault."

As I hold my crying daughter, I can't help remembering the girl I'd found today—a girl no older than
Gail, who had slowly died on a filthy mattress in a con-
demned hotel. She had died clutching a dirty needle. In
the end, she had lacked the strength to force the needle
through her paper-thin skin.

I'd been thinking of Gail ever since I'd told the parents.

I look up from my daughter, and I see Kate framed in the stairwell above us. Our eyes meet and I know our marriage has ended.

17

I wasn't going to put Gail through what that dead child had put her parents through. I wasn't going to put Gail through what my father had put me through. I would see her, and somehow I would make some explanation.

I sat up and felt a tug on my left arm.

I looked down.

I'd been slumped against the driver's door allowing my left arm to slip between the door and the seat. My left hand was snow white, and its thumb was caught in the metal under the seat, twisted at an ugly angle. I stared at my hand for a long time, stared at the white, waxy skin.

I didn't feel a damn thing. My thumb was bent back past the wrist, a position that meant a sprain, a dislocation, or even a break, and all I felt was the tension in the muscles of my arm.

The shock of the sight brought back the memory of sunlight on my skin.

I used my other hand to free my thumb from its trap. Touching the skin of my hand was like touching ice. I leaned back in the seat and rested my hands on the wheel, comparing them. I couldn't move my left hand at all; it was only some residual elasticity in the tendons that pulled my thumb back into position.

The skin was dead-looking, slightly puffy and taut. If I hadn't known how it had happened, I would think frostbite. The sight was scary, not just for itself, but because the injury was still there, still affecting me.

Everything else that had happened to me since I had come out of the ground had healed, everything from bullet wounds to the slashes on my wrist put there with a beer bottle. But what the sun had done—that had lasted through the day.

What was I supposed to do? I couldn't quite go into a normal emergency room and tell them what was wrong with me. I doubted anyone at the Cleveland Clinic had vampirism as a specialty. Once again I was forced to drive the Olds one-handed. It made me thankful that it was an automatic.

The sky was still a light azure when I pulled out of the garage. The streetlights were just coming on. It was barely quarter after six, and the city was still wrapped with people. It was Monday afternoon, and the people, and the traffic, made me feel part of the world for a while.

It was too easy to become lost in the night. Too easy to feel alone. I missed the light.

I'd left the downtown area, and was driving past the Cleveland Clinic. Sam lived in University Circle, that's where I was heading. I needed to see Gail, but my hand was becoming harder to ignore.

The base of my thumb had begun to discolor. It was only the color of a bruise, but in contrast to the blank whiteness around it, it was as livid as an open wound. I still felt nothing.

How was I supposed to deal with this? I needed to find out, before it became any worse. I pulled over and got out of the car next to a pay phone. I only knew one source of information who might know how to handle this. I called the number on Gabriel's card.

I stood there, holding the receiver with my shoulder.

It rang a few times, and then I heard the familiar electronic voice. "You have reached an automated voice messaging system. At the sound of the beep, speak your own name slowly and clearly. If your response is unclear or unacceptable, you will be disconnected."

In response to the beep, I said, "Kane Tyler."

Up until then it had gone just as before. But in response to my name, it said, "I am not able to respond to 'Kane Tyler.'" It was my voice, complete with traffic noise in the background. The machine clicked, and I heard a dial tone.

"No . . ." I hung up and tried again. I hoped that I just hadn't spoken clearly enough for the machine to recognize me. I got the same response a second time, and a third.

I slammed the receiver down on the cradle. The bastard had cut me off. Damn Gabriel and his preoccupation with status. I could see his thinking. In his eyes, it wasn't proper to for *me* to initiate a contact with *him*— and that was annoying as hell.

I looked at my hand. Annoying? It might be deadly.

Fuck. I wasn't going to let them lose me that easily. People hung up on me all the time. I had something better. I had an address. That house of Gabriel's held more than Gabriel, and somewhere there was someone who would talk to me.

"What about Gail?" I whispered.

I stood there on the curb staring at my hand. Snow fell, and when the snow touched my left hand it didn't melt. I felt no pain, no cold. My hand didn't even feel part of my body anymore.

I told myself that it had happened twelve hours ago, and the effects hadn't spread beyond my hand. I doubted spending some time with Gail could make things worse; the damage was done.

I shouldered the receiver again and fished out

another quarter. I called Sam's apartment. The phone barely rang once when I heard Sam's voice, "Gail?"

I stood there, frozen by all the possible evils that one word could mean. Gail wasn't at Sam's like she was supposed to be. Sam was worried, I heard it in his voice. That meant . . .

I didn't even want to consider what that meant.

"Hello?" Sam said.

I had to force myself to breathe so I could get the words out. "What's happened, Sam?"

"Christ, Kane, why aren't you at the motel?"

"Gail—" My voice sounded strangled. "Where is she, Sam?" I asked in a hoarse whisper. My breathing was so shallow that my voice didn't even fog the air.

"She was supposed to drive here with the cop—"

"Fuck 'supposed to!' What in hell *did* happen?"

"She took her own car, Kane. I'm sorry."

"My God, what kind of protection is that? How did—Where—"

"She slipped away from her cop. The only word was a message she left on my voice mail; she's coming to see you."

"How? She doesn't know where I am—" I stopped. The phone slipped out of my fingers.

"Kane? Kane?"

"The motel," I whispered. "She's going to the motel." Gail knew where I was *supposed* to be staying.

The receiver swung free as I ran back to the Oldsmobile. She knew about the motel. I needed to get there before she met anyone else who knew about that motel.

I raced back to the motel. I drove with my bad hand, pressing the palm to the wheel and steering by friction. I was making it worse, but I wasn't giving up any of the time it took to drive one-handed. I sped most of the way there, slowing only when I actually saw a cop.

My mind was tumbling with ugly emotions, fear, anger, anticipated grief. I knew that if Gail was harmed, the person responsible would be torn apart at my hands. I tried to tell myself that she would be there, and fine, but Sam's voice . . . he knew I wasn't at the motel, that meant he had been calling. She wasn't there yet. Or she had been there already and—

The shift lever bent in my hand, and I tried to force myself to think of driving.

It was ten after seven when I skidded the Olds into the parking lot of the Woodstar Motel. The Olds threw a shower of snow across the parked cars as if it were a two-ton figure skater. The moment the car stopped moving, I grabbed the keys and dived out into the cold night air.

I looked at the lot, checking the cars. The Chevette, my car, was still there, buried up to the fenders. The Olds blocked it in now, parked cockeyed in the center of the parking lot.

Also here was Gail's car. I knew it the minute I saw it. It was an ancient lemon-yellow Volkswagon Rabbit with an Oberlin College sticker in the rear window.

"Maybe she just got here," I whispered.

I edged up on the Rabbit and placed my right hand on its hood. The hood was cold, and the snow dusted the car evenly. I looked back, up the street. I didn't see Sebastian's men. I looked toward the front of the motel, at the glass-fronted manager's office, and saw no one inside.

There was nowhere left except my room.

I felt my heart beat, much too slowly for how I felt. I fished the motel key out of my pocket one-handed as I ran up the stairs. When I closed on my room, I slowed. I could see lights glowing around the shades in the window.

I inched toward the door, listening.

The TV was on in there.

Gail? Would she've been able to talk her way in? I looked down at the doorknob and saw the fresh scratches of a real amateur jimmying the door open.

When I saw that, I pocketed the motel key and drew the Eagle.

I took a deep breath and kicked the door open, leveling the gun at the room. The door slammed into the room, jingling broken hardware.

There was Bowie, on the bed, beer in his hand, watching the motel's piped-in pornography. He looked at me and said, "And where the fuck did you go?"

I almost shot him right there. Instead I yelled at him, "Where the hell is Gail?"

Bowie looked as innocent as I suppose he was capable of. "Who?"

"My daughter, you bastard!"

He shrugged and sat up, chugging the beer in a way that made me feel sick to my stomach. "Why would I know?"

"Because you're here," I leveled the Eagle at him. "And if you don't explain what you're doing here, I am going to decorate the wall with parts of that skinny torso of yours."

Bowie spread his arms wide and said, "Whoa, whoa, whoa! Hold the phone, I was supposed to be helping you, remember? Doctor and all that."

"What are you doing in my room?"

"Looking for you. You ran out on me and Leia. Where else do I have to look for you, huh?"

"You make a habit of jimmying the doors of people you're trying to help?"

"Fuck it, Kane." Bowie grimaced at the can, crushed it, and tossed it out the door, through my legs. "Did I know what state you were in? You could've been catatonic on the floor for all I knew." He shook his head and said, "Why don't you come in here and put that cannon away?"

I looked at him and decided, even if Bowie weren't completely sincere, he wasn't immediately threatening. I holstered the gun and pushed the door shut with my foot.

The door closed crooked and left in a draft. Luckily, the latch still caught, even after the violence done to it. I leaned against it, and looked at Bowie, keeping my eyes averted from the mirror on the bureau.

Bowie had made himself at home. The remains of a six-pack littered the floor, and he had moved the TV away from the bureau so it sat at the foot of the bed.

"I'm going to ask you again," I said. "Where's my daughter?"

"I'm telling you," Bowie said. "I. Don't. Know."

"Her car's outside—"

"She never came here, man. I been up here almost since you slipped out on me. . . ."

I looked for the phone, it wasn't on the night table anymore. "And you haven't picked up the phone?"

"They're your messages. I was trying to keep a low profile."

"Yeah, right. Where is—" The phone began to ring before I had a chance to ask. The sound was muffled, and it was hard to tell where it was coming from.

"Under the bed," Bowie said.

"Under the—" I knelt and the phone was there, wrapped in a pillow.

"Too many calls, man." Bowie explained. "The noise was distracting."

I grabbed the phone out on the third ring, "Hello."

I was expecting Sam's voice. Instead I heard, "Dad?"

"*Gail?* Christ, baby, where are you? You have no idea how worried I was.

There was a pause as she took a breath.

"What's wrong?" I asked.

"Dad, I'm sorry, I think I've screwed things up."

"Whatever it is, I forgive you. You're all right?"

"Yeah, I think so."

"Now where are you?"

"Bratenahl."

"*Bratenahl?* You're in Bratenahl? How did—" I paused for a while as it sank in. My employer, Mr. Sebastian, had an estate in Bratenhl. "Oh, no," I whispered. "What does he want?"

"He said that you were just supposed to come down here. He wants to talk to you real bad."

"If he hurts you—"

"He's been nice, really."

"*Nice?*" I shouted into the phone. "That bastard's a goddamned drug-dealer. *He kidnapped you!*"

There was a long pause.

"Gail? Gail?"

"Look, Dad, I'm sorry. He didn't kidnap me."

"What?"

"They said that they'd give me a chance to see you. You weren't answering your phone, and you already disappeared once. And you *are* working for him, aren't you?" I could hear the tears in her voice. "I fucked up again, Dad. I'm sorry."

"Shh. It's all right, I'm coming down there, okay?"

I heard her sniff. "Okay. He wants you to come alone, with his car."

"I'll see you soon, baby."

"Yeah, Dad. Love you."

"Love you." I waited to hear the click of a disconnection. Then I slammed the receiver back on its cradle hard enough to explode the phone's plastic shell.

"You bastard, Sebastian!" I yelled at the walls.

"What's going on?" Bowie asked.

"I'm going to see my daughter," I said, yanking the broken door open. I left Bowie to his beer cans and his pornography.

18

The ride gave me time to think, not necessarily a good thing. Feelings washed over me in cycles: first anger, then black depressive guilt, then numbed fear, then rage again. It was very hard to hold my mind together. Whatever I thought about, I kept coming back to Gail, and what I had become.

I kept blaming myself for involving her in this. I had the sick feeling that somehow my job was responsible. I was, or I had been, a private investigator hunting missing children, runaways, parental kidnappings. How could I do that for a living without somehow dragging my own daughter in? I had seen Gail in every case I worked; that had been what destroyed my marriage. . . .

My own obsession blamed itself for her involvement, as if my perpetual worry were a self-fulfilling prophecy.

God, I had entered this line of work because I thought it was *safer.* It was as thankless a job as being a policeman, especially in the custody cases, but it had been supposed to be better. The bullet that pierced my lung made me believe that working on the force was too reckless for a man with a family. So I took a job that destroyed the family that I was trying to protect.

Sebastian had hired me to find his daughter Cecilia. He had put me under surveillance, and I was certain that the cops who had tried to kill me were on *his* payroll. At this point I didn't know what he was capable of. Now he had *my* daughter.

And I *worked* for him.

My vision blurred, fuzzing the streetlights. With all the strangeness going on in my body, I found the tears reassuring.

This had to stop, somehow. It was bad enough that Gail had run into the human part of this travesty. I had to do everything within my power to prevent her from becoming ensnared in the undead half of everything. It was a sick thing to think, but with Childe out there—with his cult out there—maybe being with Sebastian was the safest place for her.

It was nearly eight when I reached Bratenahl, a suburb of walled estates, gatehouses, and garages bigger than my house.

Sebastian lived in a Rockefeller-era mansion of gray stone. The cobbled drive was flanked by a pair of bronze lions gone white with frost. There was no gate barring the Olds as I followed the circular drive to the front of the house, but I noted more than a few anachronistic security cameras panning along the wrought-iron fence surrounding the property. The cameras hung from the eaves, poked out from odd bits of landscaping, and one even nestled in the arms of a century-old oak that dominated the lawn between the mansion and the gatehouse in front.

I pulled the Olds to a stop at the front door. The main entrance was a Gothic stone arch filled with a massive pair of oak doors, and flanked by an acre of leaded glass.

In '77 I was a rookie, and I had busted Sebastian for a dime bag. Somewhere between then and now I had retired, and Sebastian had done five years at Lucasville. Now he lived here, the home of a millionaire with a few zeros to spare.

I opened the door and slid out, shoving my bad hand in the pocket of my jacket.

The massive doors opened, and Bishop and Mr. Gestapo stepped out to greet me. "Welcome, Mr. Tyler," said Bishop. "Mr. Sebastian is eager to meet with you, finally."

I nodded, not trusting myself to say anything that wouldn't sound like a threat. As choked by anger as I was, I still knew I didn't want to antagonize anyone needlessly.

"The weapon, if you please?" Bishop held out his hand. I wasn't in a position to argue. I drew the Eagle and handed it over to him. Bishop took it, gave it an admiring glance, checked the safety, and slipped it into his waistband.

Mr. Gestapo was much less polite. He held out a sweaty palm and said, "Keys."

I looked at him, tempted to toss the keys at his feet. Again, though, there was little profit in antagonizing people right now. I dropped the keys into his hand.

"Come with me," Bishop said. As he led me toward the massive doors, Mr. Gestapo drove the Olds away toward the gatehouse.

Bishop led me through a central hall dominated by a massive staircase. The stairs sat below tall windows that faced north, toward the lake. In daylight it must have been a seven-figure view, but right now the windows were blank, an acre of dead black broken only by the reflection of the chandelier.

Bishop took me along a broad corridor leading off the entry hall. He delivered me into a library that could have comfortably fit most of Childe's apartment inside it. The ceiling was eighteen feet high, and the fireplace, currently roaring away, could have doubled as a garage.

Sebastian stood facing away from me, the fireplace,

and the door. He was looking out a set of French doors that opened up on a slightly lesser darkness than the windows in the entry hall.

"Sit down." Sebastian's voice was a perfect Midwestern null. The voice was at odds with the rest of him. He had dark curly hair, and swarthy Mediterranean features. He had the look of old-world Europe about him.

"Where's my daughter?" I said.

"Where is *my* daughter? *Sit down,* Mr. Tyler."

I sat down on one of two leather chairs facing the fire. I noticed the bullet holes in my shirt. I pulled my coat over to hide them. The damage to my trench coat was less obvious; the bullet's damage was hidden in the midst of all the other damage I'd done to my coat.

"I'm *looking* for Cecilia," I said. "My job, remember?"

I had to half-turn to see Sebastian, who remained staring out the windows. When I turned, I ignited a new ache in my left wrist, still wedged in the pocket of my jacket. I tried to adjust my body to ease the pressure on my hand. I didn't try to remove it from my pocket.

"I've tried very hard to hate you, Tyler," he said. It wasn't what I expected from him. I felt the need to say something, but I had absolutely no idea what it could have been.

Facing out the window, fiddling with his hands, Sebastian talked on as if I weren't quite there. "When you first turned me down, I tried to hate you. Your accusations, 'How could something as evil as I, a drug dealer, be a decent father—' You have no idea of the anger I felt. What I felt because I still *needed* you."

"You're not helping by taking Gail—"

Sebastian raised his head, as if he were talking to a bird perched on the transom of his door. "Am I? I've seen those tapes. Your daughter needs protection, as my own daughter needed protection."

"I appreciate the vote of confidence."

Sebastian didn't seem to hear me. "Hate is not an easy emotion for me, Mr. Tyler. I don't hate the police. We both have jobs, and I accepted the risks of mine, just as they did theirs. Like them, if I have to draw a weapon in my line of work, something's gone wrong. And despite my anger, I can't hate you, Mr. Tyler. I understand you too well."

Sebastian turned to face me, and I saw a rosary in his hands. My throat tightened.

"You hold me guilty of too much. Can you hold that *I* am evil after you've been touched by it yourself?" The firelight carved dancing shadows on his dusky face. The light reflected in his eyes made him look a little mad.

I wanted to tell him exactly what I thought he was guilty of. All I needed to think of were dead-eyed junkies dying of AIDS, or reed-thin teenagers selling what was left of their bodies so they could buy a rock. Something in his eyes kept my mouth shut. The sight of the rosary held my attention.

"If I wasn't a father to my Cecilia, it was because I was kept from her the second five years of her life. And afterward, what could I do after Rosa died?" His eyes welled up and he crossed himself. I had to turn away. It was becoming as difficult to watch Sebastian as it was to see my own eyes a mirror. If I needed any confirmation as to what was happening to me, the uncomfortable proximity of Sebastian's faith was it.

"I didn't know how to be a father. She was lost to me before she was taken."

Sebastian had walked in front of me, but he was staring into the fire. "I have seen those tapes you made. I have seen them too many times. I have seen the—

the—*being* who was once my daughter." Sebastian turned to look at me. "Do you understand?"

I nodded.

"You *made* those tapes. Do you understand the evil I am talking about. The true *evil* here?"

"I think so."

"I do not hate easily. But this Childe, him I hate. He has mortgaged my daughter's *soul*. So she is not only lost to me, but to our Savior as well." Sebastian kissed the rosary and put it in his pocket. I felt better without the beads in view. I felt that I could speak again—

"What about *my* daughter, Sebastian?"

"I need you to lead me to my daughter, and Childe. I need your mind focused, and I need to keep track of you." He stared into the fire and said, "I do not hate easily. But I have hatred for the creatures responsible."

Sebastian's profile, rose-colored in the firelight, appeared as if it were carved out of the shadows around him. "Lately I've had to ask myself, Mr. Tyler, if you are part of the evil that took my daughter."

"What?" My voice was a near-whisper, but the shock in it must have carried to Sebastian. He turned his head to look at me. Half his face ruddy-lit by the dancing flames, the other half a featureless black shadow. But both his eyes locked on my own, and I could see a fire in them that wasn't wholly reflected from the fireplace.

"Are you a part of this evil?"

"No," I said it confidently, but there was a squirming doubt in my gut.

"Perhaps." I saw him fingering the rosary in his pocket. "Only perhaps. If you were to succumb to the evil, though, I would be less a man if I allowed that to harm your daughter. . . ."

There was something in the eye contact, I could tell. The same thing that had drawn Bowie out when I questioned him, the sense that my own words could have some physical effect behind my opponent's eyes. This, however, was different. What was behind Sebastian's eyes was armored by something impenetrable. The light I saw was the reflection of something deep and solid within the man, which could not be moved.

Whatever it was, it was strengthened whenever he fingered the rosary in his pocket. Sebastian shook his head and walked back toward the window. For a long time he stared outside. Finally he said, "Your daughter is lucky, she has her soul."

"What do you want from me?"

"You are going to lead me to Childe, so I can wipe this abomination from the face of the Earth."

"I've been looking—"

"There is no more search. You have what you need. I've listened to your notes. You've known this evil, and you knew enough once to track the evil to its heart. I do not believe your ignorance."

He turned around to face me. He was silhouetted by the reflection of the fireplace in the windows behind him. It looked as if he were walking out of the fire. "I don't know what stays your hand: fear, or something else. But by our Lord, your hand will move. You have no choice."

I stood up and Sebastian looked at me with his hard, fiery eyes and said, "If you are part of the evil that consumed my daughter, I will destroy you." He turned back to the window. "Bishop will lead you to the gatehouse and give you a few hours to think."

19

Bishop locked me in a set of rooms that originally were part of the servant's quarters. These had long since been converted to a set of small apartments on the upper floor of the gatehouse. One of the first things I noted after the door closed behind me was the fact that the iron scrollwork outside the windows was a bit more functional than it looked.

I'd been cornered again.

What had Sebastian done with Gail?

I collapsed on a couch in the living-room area, and felt a renewed ache in my wrist. Not my hand, which was as insensible as ever, but in the area of my wrist that seemed to separate the damaged flesh from the rest of me. The pain was deep into the bone, and made me stand up before I had completely seated myself.

Even without the pocket cutting into it, the ache persisted.

I tried to shake my hand loose of the pocket, but it didn't come free. I had to peel the fabric of my coat away with my right hand as I pulled my hand away. In addition to my hand, I had liberated a smell. A faint overripe smell, some sweet fruit which had just gone a little mushy.

I wrinkled my nose and looked down to my hand. It had changed color. The ugly black at the base of my thumb had spread to the meat of my palm extending into a vague imprint of the Oldsmobile's steering wheel. The back was crossed by a purple-black diagonal stripe where the seams of my jacket pocket had bit. A webwork of coppery-green streaked the white skin. My whole hand had swollen, asymmetrically in some places.

I touched the black area by my thumb. The skin gave with a soft mushy sound and the color seeped a little into the surrounding area—like ink bleeding under my skin. I took my finger away, and a dimple stayed in the blackness, where I had pressed. The smell had grown much stronger in the interim.

"Oh, fuck."

I pushed up my sleeve, and saw the line where the dead flesh—in my gut I now knew it was dead—met my own.

When I joined the force, I had some basic first-aid training. I wasn't a medic, but I could recognize a few basic things; burns, fractures, shock—and when my nose is rubbed in it, I could recognize gangrene.

At the edge of the dead tissue, where the ache in my wrist began, there was a definite line of discoloration. It was reassuring to see the diseased flesh stop at that line.

I walked into the apartment's kitchen and washed my hand off. It was a futile gesture. The smell came from inside the flesh, and when the rot reached the surface of my skin, nothing would stop it. I scrubbed maniacally, my left hand cold, limp, and mushy. I must have washed for five minutes before I came to my senses. Mercifully the mushy fruit smell had receded beneath the lemon scent of the dish soap I was using.

My hand was dead, period. It had to be amputated before the gangrene spread.

"Dad, are you all right—"

I spun around, suds from the dish soap splattering the linoleum of the kitchenette. Gail stood in the middle of the living room, on the other side of the only furniture, a couch and a glass-topped coffee table.

She stared at me. I stood there, gaping a few moments, suds dripping from my dead hand.

"Dad?"

"Where did you come from?" I finally asked. "You startled me." I reached across the sink and grabbed a dishtowel, more to hide my hand than to dry it. It wasn't something Gail needed to see.

She bit her lip as she looked at me. My memory was still playing traitorous games with my mind. When I looked at her, I kept wanting to see a thirteen-year-old who made pottery horses and dragons. Gail wasn't supposed to be an adult. She wasn't supposed to be taller than Kate.

In answer to my question, she gave a halfhearted wave toward an open doorway on the other side of the apartment. Beyond, I saw the corner of a bed. She stood there looking at me for a long time, then she shook her head and whispered, "No. I refuse—" Her voice choked off the words.

"Gail, don't—"

She looked at me and moisture was streaming down her cheeks. "My God, Dad. What's going on here? You're the one who disappeared, and you give me that damn *look*, as if I was some criminal—and, and, and. . . ." She collapsed on to the couch, putting her face in her hands.

"Oh, no, honey." I sat down next to her, putting my good arm around her shoulders. "I never thought that, I just worry about you—"

Gail sat upright and glared at me with her tear-streaked face. "You worry? What about *me*? I'm not allowed to worry about you? You disappeared, Mom dies, and you let me go on thinking the same thing—" Her words caught and she looked away from me, the anger bleeding from her voice. "That the same thing might have happened to you."

I hugged her. In that embrace I felt a profound sense

of loss, perhaps as deep as the loss Sebastian felt. I was here, with Gail, but I had already started down a path that she couldn't follow.

"That isn't going to happen," I said weakly.

"Is there any particular reason I should believe that?" Gail asked. "I have a right to know what's going on here—what happened to Mom."

"I don't want to get you involved in this."

Gail shrugged out from under my arm and stood up. "You're incredible, Dad. Mom's dead. I spent a week with a cop. I'm here because I wanted to see you. Dad, I'm involved whether you want me to be or not."

"You don't know what you're saying."

Gail turned around and yelled at me, *"Whose fault is that?"*

We stared at each other, and, stressed as I felt, I found my gaze searching out her eyes. I wanted to force her away from the subject.

When I realized what I was doing, I turned away. My gaze landed on my reflection in the glass top of the coffee table. The vision brought only a slight twinge; my face was cloaked in shadow, and my eyes were invisible. "I don't want you hurt."

"It's a little late for that."

The words stung worse than the sunlight. They had a similar effect, leaving me numb and dead inside. "I never wanted Kate to—"

Her voice softened. "I never said that." She sat down on the arm of the couch, facing me. "But you've already tried to protect me from what you do. Anytime I ask you details, you close up. It's time you stop it." Gail sighed. "You can't protect me from my own life."

I turned away, nodding. "It would have been better if you didn't have me for a father—"

Gail sighed.

"What?" I asked.

"Nothing. You just always end an argument by blaming yourself. I never could stand that."

Perhaps, but it didn't mean what I said was any less true. Yet Gail was right as well. She had a right to know. But what could I tell her before she decided I was crazy?

"Have you talked to Sebastian about any of this?"

"I asked him what was going on."

I nodded. "What did he tell you?"

"He's crazy. Did you know that?"

I turned back to face her; this time I did look into her eyes. Her eyes were so much like I had remembered my own. "What did he tell you?"

"He told me stories about Gothic paranoia, spirits of evil, and the threat to my immortal soul. He showed me a video." He voice changed tenor. "He *is* crazy. Isn't he?"

"What did he say threatened your immortal soul?"

Gail grimaced and began turning away, but her eyes kept locked on mine. "You, Dad. He said you might threaten me." She reached into her collar and pulled out a rosary she was wearing around her neck.

Strangely, I felt no effect from this rosary—nothing like the one Sebastian had been handling.

"He gave me this thing to protect myself."

I looked at the cross and asked, "What video did he show you?"

Gail described it in hushed tones that sparked my own memory.

The wide expanse of a dam, the circle of figures. . . .

Ten people in the semicircle, facing away from me, toward the structure set in the hillside. The building is stone, its one doorway a shadowed black hole. It looks like a mausoleum.

A woman is led from the mausoleum by a figure cowled in black robes. I feel an awful certainty that the cowled figure is Childe, even though I see none of his features, or much of anything beyond the robe.

The woman, however, I recognize. Her white dress contrasts against the surrounding night and her Mediterranean features. She is Cecilia, Sebastian's daughter.

Something catches in my throat as she opens her arms to the surrounding horde, as if to embrace them.

Childe's people descend upon her—a chaos of motion. I see claws and fangs appear from nowhere. The attackers' bodies distort, backs arch unnaturally, limbs extend. During the frenzy the creatures tearing into Cecilia are no longer human. Cecilia is invisible behind the demonic mass. Only glimpses of her white dress are visible.

And, with each glimpse, over the space of half a minute, her dress darkens. The snow around the attack darkens as well, until the mass breaks off from around her. Cecilia is now only an inert form on a field of black snow.

They appear human again, and then the teenager stares at me with a face covered with night-black blood.

He smiles.

Before I turn and run for my life, I see something else as well.

Childe bends over Cecilia. In the glimpse I see only a pair of pale arms extend out of the sleeves of his robe, over the corpse.

Before I run, I see Cecilia move.

"I made that tape," I whispered. The whole episode could have been staged to drive Sebastian insane. I wondered if it had been.

"Are those bullet holes?" Gail asked. I had leaned back, remembering, and Gail was now leaning forward, staring at my shirt. The rosary now dangled free from her neck. "Dad?"

She looked up at me, and I could see fear in her face. I could feel it welling up from wherever she had hidden it. "He's wrong, isn't he? On the tape those were just shadows right, you're just looking for some nut-cult, right?" She grabbed my shirt and said, *"Right?"*

I shook my head and stood up. I couldn't stand her touching me, touching what might as well be her father's dead body. The dishtowel fell to the ground and I shoved my left hand into the pocket to my coat.

"Your hand, what happened to your hand?"

I stood, back to her, and said, "I caught a little sun."

"No." I heard her voice tremble. "You can't say he's right. You *can't!*" I heard her move, and her hand pulled my shoulder around to face her. "I love you, Dad."

She hugged me, burying her face in my shoulder. I patted her on the back. "I *love* you, too."

"He wants to put a stake through her heart," I heard her whisper into my shoulder. "His own child."

I shook my head. "He's not right about everything," I told her. I felt the rosary digging into my sternum to no ill effect. "He's not right about everything."

"Are you . . . ?"

"Shh."

"And his daughter?"

"I don't know about Cecilia, but it seems that way."

"What happened to you, Dad?"

"I don't know, honey. I'm still figuring it out myself."

There was a long silence as she rested her head on my shoulder. Then she backed up and said, "I have an Ace bandage in my purse. Do you think that would help?"

I knew it was pointless, but I nodded, "Sure, honey."

She ran and fetched her purse, leaving me to wonder

what she must be thinking about me. She returned with the bandage and I told her, "I think I better do this myself."

I turned away and wrapped my hand completely, thumb and fingers together. When I was done, Gail put her hand on my shoulder and asked, "You can't be damned for something you can't control, can you?"

"I don't think—"

I was interrupted by the sound of a gunshot.

Gail broke from me and said, "Dad?"

I grabbed her and dived with her into the kitchenette, flattening myself against her behind the half-wall separating the kitchen area from the living room and the front door. "What?" Gail said.

"I don't know."

The gunfire came from the hall outside. It climaxed with one last, much louder, gunshot. The explosive sound resonated the tile in front of me.

Something slammed against the door hard enough for the walls to shake. One of the pots hanging on the wall clattered to the counter, and fell to the floor. My grip on my daughter tightened.

There was a second or two of silence. I was about to move us from our minimal cover, when the door to the apartment exploded into the room. The force of the door swinging into the apartment scattered yard-long pieces of the doorframe. Pieces of door were immediately followed by Bishop, falling backward with such speed that I doubted his feet touched ground until he landed on the coffee table, blowing glass everywhere.

Bishop held a nine-millimeter Beretta, or something similar, in his right hand. Falling out of his left hand, as he skidded across broken glass, splintered wood, and chrome table legs, was my Desert Eagle.

Bishop was unquestionably unconscious, if not dead. I stepped away from my slight cover, putting distance between me and the door. I held up my hand to prevent Gail from following me into the open.

Following Bishop, walking through the remains of the door, was Bowie. He turned to face me and I saw a large bullet hole in the front of his leather jacket. I stared at him for a second, speechless.

"You waiting for an invitation? Come on, let's move it!"

20

Seeing Bowie here stunned me a moment. Gail stared at me from the corner of the kitchenette, watching me for a reaction. I was still trying to digest the fact that Bowie was a vampire. There wasn't much else that could explain the gaping hole in the front of his shirt, or how he'd taken out Bishop unarmed.

What the hell was happening here?

"Come on," Bowie said. "Before these fucks get their act together!"

Bowie's entrance didn't give me much of a choice. I ran for my gun.

Outside, the night was waking with the sounds of men and dogs. I cursed.

"Come on!" Bowie urged. He shook like a coiled spring.

I holstered the Desert Eagle and held my good hand out to Gail. She hesitated briefly, then took it.

Then Bowie took off down the stairs, out of the gatehouse. I pursued with Gail. "How ... why ..." I began. I stopped when we reached the driveway.

Gail bumped into my side, and stared. Next to the road lay the guy I thought of as Mr. Gestapo. His body was immaculate, and the same blue-white as the snowdrift he'd fallen in. I saw the edges of a wound, but most was hidden because he'd fallen face first into the snow.

"Bowie, damn it! I'm supposed to be working *for* Sebastian!"

"Not since you joined the dance, my friend," Bowie yelled, without turning or slowing.

Behind me, too close, I heard a canine growl and the scrabbling of claws across the driveway. I started running again, pulling Gail along and pushing her ahead of me.

I dropped back a few feet, so the dog reached me just as Gail reached the gate. Bowie was through it, ahead of her, when I heard a growl directly behind me. A Doberman, out of nowhere, clamped its jaws on my right wrist. The sudden pain ignited a flare inside me, a coal of rage I'd been husbanding since Sebastian had taken my daughter.

I growled back.

I turned. For a moment my gaze locked with the animal's. The dog's eyes were empty of everything, like the eyes of a machine. My will burned through those eyes, flashing through the tiny space that was the animal's mind. The dog froze under the onslaught. Something that might have been an abortive whimper died in its throat, behind my arm.

In response, I whipped my right arm toward one of the concrete pillars marking the edge of the gate. The dog's jaws remained attached to my wrist, even as its feet left the ground. It hung on until its back slammed into the pillar. I heard a crack as, about four feet off the ground, the corner of the square pillar put a mortal crease in the Doberman's spine.

All the strength left its jaws, and my wrist ripped free. I ran through the gate as the dog fell to the ground. It hit with a spastic jerk and ceased moving.

Gail wasn't running; she had turned and was staring at me.

I grabbed her as I passed and I heard her whisper, "The world's gone crazy."

I silently agreed with her.

My car, the Chevette, was sitting at the curb, idling, the door open. Bowie was already behind the wheel. He began shifting gears as I shoved Gail in the back seat. Bowie floored the accelerator as soon as most of my own body was in the vehicle.

A Chevette wasn't meant to attempt screaming acceleration on icy pavement, but somehow Bowie managed it. I had to hook my left arm over the passenger seat to keep from tumbling out of the car. My legs dangled over the curb, and the door tried to slam shut on them without quite succeeding.

I managed to lever my legs inside. "What the hell are you doing? Sebastian is—"

"I know, I know." Bowie kept staring ahead, as the Chevette swerved. The passenger door swung widely, but I had my hands full holding myself in place. I kept staring behind us, waiting for the Olds, or some other car, to slide out of Sebastian's estate after us.

"Shut the door, no one's following us."

"How do you know?"

There was a snick next to me. I turned to see Bowie holding an illegally long knife. "Hard to drive with four flats." With a flip of the wrist the knife disappeared.

"What's going on?" Gail finally said with all the angry confusion I felt. "Who is this guy?"

"Friend of your father, sweet-cakes." Bowie said.

I slammed the door shut. "That remains to be seen. This is one hell of a bonehead stunt. I should throttle you for endangering my daughter."

"It's my life, Dad." Gail said. "*I'll* throttle him."

"Hey, man, it's *your* skin you should worry about. You were in there with the man most likely to drive a stake through your heart." Bowie looked at me. I stayed quiet. "You're damn lucky I followed you."

"Was that man dead?" Gail asked.

"What man?" Bowie asked.

"The man, back there, in the snow."

Bowie laughed. "Of all the— Of course he's dead."

"Why did you have to kill him?"

"He was an asshole, he shot me, and I was hungry. That's two more reason than I needed."

"What about the Covenant?" I asked.

Bowie gave me another look, as if he was measuring me. "What about it?"

"You know what about it. The second law, 'No one who holds to the Covenant may reveal those of the blood.' " Bowie smiled. "You been talking to people, ain't you?"

"Damn it, you've left corpses all over the place and you're blabbing all . . ."

"All this in front of your all-too-human daughter? Tsk, tsk."

I looked back and saw Gail shrink back a little in the seat. She was pressed all the way behind my seat, as far away from Bowie as she could be within the Chevette.

"Look man, first off, I am not leaving 'bodies.' I left one body for Sebastian, who is already too aware of what's going on, and who certainly isn't going to anyone else with the corpse. He'll probably decapitate it, stake it, burn it, or something. Second, you got the abridged version of the Covenant."

"Abridged?"

"Fuck, yeah. Three lines are easy to remember. But we're talking about something older and longer than the Magna Carta. Whoever enlightened you probably saw no profit in describing all the exceptions."

"Like?"

"Like, humans can join the Covenant. Hell they have to if you don't want them to have one hell of a shock when you bring one over."

"Lord, you have no idea," I whispered.

"I knew what you were going through when you

stumbled into the Arabica. The doctor I was going to take you to, he's Leia's grandfather."

"Why?" Gail said from behind me.

"Why what?" Bowie asked.

"Why are you helping my dad?"

"Kane's hunting down a guy named Childe." Bowie's face got a serious cast then. "Got my own thing with Childe."

"What?" I asked.

"Personal," Bowie said flatly. "You find him, so would I."

I rubbed my forehead. We were rolling out of Bratenahl, and back toward Cleveland Heights.

After a long pause, Bowie asked, very gravely, "What do you remember about being brought over? Who did it?"

"I don't know."

"You don't know," Bowie repeated slowly.

"You said you knew a doctor?" Gail asked.

Bowie nodded, still looking askance at me, as if he didn't trust my answers.

"Then you've got to take Dad there, he needs help. His hand is injured."

"What?" Bowie asked. When I pulled my bandaged hand out of my pocket, Bowie added, "What the fuck is that smell?"

I noticed it as well. A sweet-rancid odor was suddenly very noticeable. It was thickening in the air, and when I looked down, I could see a damp stain spreading on the elastic bandage covering my left hand.

Gail started coughing.

"My hand," I said. Breathing in the odor made me gag.

Bowie rolled down the window and leaned away from me. I stared at my hand. It was swollen and misshapen under the loose bandage, except where the stain centered around the base of my thumb, where it appeared the flesh had collapsed.

"What happened?" Bowie shouted into the wind.

"Sun?" Gail said, speaking through her hand.

I rolled down the passenger window.

"Of all the idiot things—" Bowie coughed. "Yeah, sweet-cakes, we're going to see the doctor."

Bowie drove through Cleveland Heights, and into Shaker. He pulled us to a stop in front of a large brick house set about thirty feet back into its lot. It had large windows and a Tudor design that reminded me of Childe's—or Deité's—apartment building. Even though it was a common style—a lot of the buildings in Shaker and Cleveland Heights wouldn't be out of place in Lakewood, a lot of them built around the same time—the similarity put me on edge.

Bowie parked my car on the curb. He piled out as soon as he killed the engine. I could smell why. Without the constant wind through the open window, the reek from my dead hand was overpowering. The bandage was crusted with seepage and the form underneath was only barely hand-shaped.

I stumbled out, and Gail followed with her hand over her face. "My God, Dad." She looked on the verge of throwing up, and the tears in her eyes had to be as much from the smell as from sympathy.

The ache in my wrist had gotten worse, and I was rubbing it unconsciously. I could feel an ugly give to my skin, even though the sleeve of my jacket.

"Come on," Bowie said. "Got to fix that hand." He made a face when he said it.

He walked up to the house, and I was disturbed when I realized that the place was familiar. More than the accidental similarity to Childe's apartment. The place in Lakewood was just another building. I felt as if I had been here. However, with the holes in my memory, I had no idea if the familiarity was significant. I didn't know if it represented something that had happened in the last two weeks, or if the feeling came from some fragment of the prior four-and-a-half decades that I had yet to remember fully.

"What kind of doctor?" Gail asked. He voice was muffled under the handkerchief she held to her face.

Bowie chuckled, "Someone with an interest in our kind."

I wondered what kind of medial school someone went to, to specialize in "our kind."

My unease was becoming difficult to ignore. What did I know about this place? What was I trying to remember? I felt my good hand moving toward my holster as Bowie leaned on the doorbell. After a minute or so the door inched open. A redheaded woman looked at Bowie through the crack, Leia.

"Yes?" she said in her high, breathy, English voice.

"Leia? Could you get your grandfather for me?" Bowie nodded back toward where I stood back from the doorway. I stopped reaching for the gun.

She looked past Bowie, at me. "You found him!" Her accent made me think about Childe again, redoubling my sense of nervousness. She looked about the age Childe was supposed to prey upon. My hand found the butt of my gun. "Who's the girl?"

"His daughter— Look, we got to do something about his hand."

She looked at me, and I saw something alive in her eyes. Not the fires I felt in Sebastian's, or the machinery I felt behind the Doberman's, but something moving, living, and writhing in pain. When she spoke, her hand went to the collar of the black turtleneck she wore. A single blocky earring glinted from underneath a tumble of red hair. "What happened to his hand?"

"Bad dose of sun," Bowie said.

She nodded, and I lost sight of those pained eyes. I felt no desire to see whatever those eyes had seen. "I'll get Grandfather. Wait here," she said, closing the door.

As we waited, Bowie said, "Good looking babe, ain't she?"

"Hadn't noticed." That wasn't quite a lie. I repeated Gail's question, "So what kind of doctor is Leia's grandfather?"

"He was a medic in World War Two, when he got involved in—"

The door opened again. Standing there was a broad, white-haired man in a blue bathrobe. "This better be good, I was—"

He had begun by addressing Bowie but as he spoke he slowly turned, and I could see his nose wrinkle. "God," he said. "How much tissue is affected?"

He addressed the question to me. "My hand," I said. "About six inches up the wrist."

He shook his head. "Come around back. I don't want that smell infecting my house."

PART THREE

THE CONQUEROR
WORM

> By a route obscured and lonely,
> Haunted by ill angels only,
> Where an Eidolon, named NIGHT,
> On a black throne reigns upright,
> I have reached these lands but newly
> From an ultimate dim Thule—
> From a wild weird clime that lieth, sublime,
> Out of SPACE—out of TIME.
>   —"Dream-Land"

21

Bowie nodded and waved us along. I followed. As we walked up the driveway, we passed a black BMW with vanity plates, "Ryan 1."

"Ryan's a first or last name?" I asked Bowie.

"Last, I think. Always call him Doc Ryan."

We came up on a patio around back, and stopped at a pair of storm-cellar doors abutting the house. The doors were new and set in fresh cinder block that appeared to have been built in the past two years or so. Bowie stopped by the doors, which—conspicuously—had no external handles.

"Come here often?" I asked.

"Doc's been practicing a lot longer than I've been nocturnal."

Not a real answer, I thought. "So how long have you been 'nocturnal?' "

"Half a year or so."

"Who 'brought you over'?"

Bowie looked at me askance again. "If we get the time, I'll tell you the story."

Gail spoke up from behind us. "Is this doctor Ryan one of . . . one of you?" she asked Bowie.

Bowie shook his head. "No, the Doc ain't one of us. I thought I mentioned that."

"He's not?" I said.

Bowie shrugged.

"He knows what he's doing?" Gail asked.

"I suppose so," Bowie said. "The gentry pay him enough for services rendered."

Gail squeezed my shoulder. I felt her concern. But, it was *my* hand and I couldn't help feeling that it was wrong for her to be here. Even if there was some family exemption, some loophole in the Covenant that let her be here, it was wrong to drag her along—

But what choice did I have? Did either of us have?

With Bowie's little asides, I felt my daughter being ensnared by the same nocturnal society that had ensnared me. Bowie, with nearly every sentence, was dropping references to a culture I barely knew and Gail was totally ignorant of.

Ignorant of, and already trapped within. Just the fact that she knew meant she was ensnared in the web of relationships Gabriel had disclosed to me.

Which made me wonder where Bowie fit within that web. With the easy way he talked about the Covenant, he must have a role within that society. Being only six months a vampire meant he was almost certainly a thrall to some older vampire. Which meant that, when I dealt with him I wasn't dealing with Bowie. As far as the social rules were concerned, I was dealing with Bowie's unknown master.

A master whose name he'd avoided mentioning.

I had an awful thought. What if Bowie belonged to Childe?

Before I could worry any further, a short buzzing sound escaped from the doors. Then, after about two seconds, they swung outward. The wood exterior panels were only veneer. On the inside, the doors were thick, plastic and metal, with a rubber gasket surrounding the edges—airtight and soundproof.

At the foot of the concrete stairs stood Doctor Ryan. He had dispensed with the bathrobe. He now wore jeans, a flannel shirt, and a long white lab coat. He still wore a pair of slippers.

His hand rested on a metal box mounted on the wall, pressing a green button. Bowie led us down the stairs and once we all cleared the doors, Ryan pressed a red button and the buzz repeated itself, louder this time. The doors shut behind us with a hydraulic whisper of air.

It wasn't any warmer down here than it was outside. Combined with the white tile walls and the stark fluorescent lighting, the place felt like a morgue. *If he treats vampires, maybe that's what this is.*

"What's your name, son?" Ryan asked with a puff of visible breath.

"Kane," I said.

Ryan looked a little disappointed with my name. "And you, miss?"

"Gail—can you help my dad?" She was still talking through a handkerchief.

"I'm certain I can." To Bowie he said, "You go upstairs, I don't need company while I work."

"Sure, Doc. Maybe Leia can get me something to eat." Bowie grinned and left before Ryan could answer him.

To Gail, Ryan said, "You should go with him."

Before I could raise an objection, Gail straightened up and said, "I'm not leaving my father."

Ryan looked at her and said, rather gravely, "This is not going to be pleasant." When she showed no sign of backing down, Ryan said, "Well, stay out of my way."

He led us down halls that were all concrete and white tile. Every ten feet or so we passed a blank stainless steel door, like the door to a commercial-sized freezer.

"Quite a setup," I said, cradling my hand and trying not to inhale the smell.

Ryan seemed preoccupied. "What I do can be quite lucrative with the right patient." We stopped in front of a door like the others. "Now I need to see that hand."

He opened the door. I expected to see lines of meat-hooks, hanging slabs of beef, or the like. Instead the room looked fairly normal, if stark. It was populated by stainless steel cabinets, chromed fixtures and spigots set into the walls, carts of medial equipment I couldn't identify, and an examination table under an intricate-looking set of operating lights.

"Sit down," Ryan said, motioning to a chair in the corner of the room, also fitted with lights and equipment. I sat.

"You," he said to Gail. "Come with me."

While I did my best to get comfortable without touching my hand to anything, Ryan went to the wall and began flipping switches. Gail stood next to him and cast nervous glances back over her shoulder at me.

Lights came on around my end of the room, and the whir of a ventilation fan started up. That was good, because once we'd stopped moving, the odor from my hand had quickly built to intolerable levels.

Ryan handed Gail a surgical mask and said, "Tie this on and stand over there." He indicated the far corner, away from the chair where I sat.

Gail tied on the mask and backed over to the corner that Ryan had indicated. Ryan laid out an equipment tray on one of the carts, tied on a mask, and began scrubbing at a sink across the room from me.

"Are germs really a problem?" I asked, thinking of alleged vampiric immortality.

Ryan laughed softly, with an ironic lilt to it. "Depends on the germ. I can tell without looking, for instance, that under that rag on your hand, a herd of anaerobic bacteria are having a festival."

"Ugh," Gail said. From here I could see some of the color going out of her face.

" 'Ugh,' is right." Ryan shut the faucet off with his elbows and began the delicate procedure of retrieving a pair of surgical gloves from a tray near the sink. "You're new, aren't you."

"Why do you say that?" I asked.

"Experienced vampires do not go around nursing advanced cases of solar necrosis. They usually have enough sense to feed right after the initial injury, before circulation shuts down completely." He pushed a cart toward me with his foot. It bore an ugly selection of surgical instruments. "Take off your jacket and roll up your sleeve for me, would you?"

I did as I was asked, doing my best not to smear the contaminated Ace bandage against my clothes. The bandage itself was now stained, streaked with red and black, and every time my hand brushed something I could hear an ugly liquid sound.

" 'Feeding' would have stopped this?" I asked as I manhandled my jacket. I left the holster and gun in place, and the Doctor didn't comment on them.

"Most of the time, if you survived the sun in the first place. Fire's a different story," Ryan nodded.

I noticed Gail edging across the room to get a better look at what was going on. Ryan paid no attention to her. He kept talking, "But, you see, after the bacteria has a chance to do gross damage to the tissue, that's something else. Would you place your hand over here?"

I did as he asked, placing my bandage-covered hand on the examination tray he indicated. He picked up a pair of scissors from his pile of instruments and began cutting away the bandage. "Don't move."

"I can't." My hand was an inanimate lump of meat.

Ryan talked as he worked. "If I had been doing my work in a research hospital, I'd know more than I do. Forty years as an individual doesn't match ten in a well-equipped—This is bad."

Gail's eyes widened, and her hand went up to cover her nose and mouth.

Ryan had just peeled away a length of bandage with a pair of forceps. Beneath, my hand was pockmarked by greenish-black lesions that swelled up under the skin. The skin had broken in places, weeping thick noxious fluid. The meat where my thumb met my palm was entirely eaten away, leaving a moist ragged crater where the flesh had liquefied down to the bone.

"A human would've probably died of blood poisoning by now." Ryan paused a moment, arrested by something other than the sight of the wound. The pause only lasted a minute before he began rambling again. "Now I was going to explain this to you, without getting into the spiritual gibberish—"

Ryan carefully removed the remains of the bandage as he spoke, dropping them into a stainless steel tray. He then retrieved another tray, slipped it under my hand, and used a bottle of clear liquid to wash the discharge erupting from the sores in my hand. I felt nothing.

"Aren't you just going to cut it off?" I asked.

Gail made a strangled noise and turned away from the scene. I could hear her sucking deep breaths through her mouth.

When I looked down again at my hand, I couldn't take my eyes off of what Ryan was doing. He would rinse a fleshy crater, then attack it with a small sponge clamped in his forceps. Each sponge only lasted a dozen seconds before he'd toss it in with the scraps of my bandage.

"Again, if you were human." A sponge tossed. "The infection that created you—I was about to explain—has some pseudo-regenerative capabilities." More rinsing.

"Infection?"

Fresh sponge. "Vampirism is a result of, or a complex related to, an infectious entity somewhat akin to a virus." Swab. "Unlike a virus, it doesn't destroy the cells it infects, quite the opposite in fact—it can infect dead tissue and revive it. I've never had the resources to analyze it properly, I don't even know if it is alive, or simply some extremely exotic collection of proteins." Toss. "But this entity infects every cell of your body now, and every cell needs it to survive." Wash.

"That caused this?" I still stared at my hand. It looked as if I'd run it through a garbage disposal. It was puffy, discolored, and perforated by sores that sank though flesh, muscle and bone.

"The dissolution of that pseudovirus caused it." Ryan said. "This thing is photoreactive. UV B breaks it down fairly quickly, and direct sunlight can trigger a chain reaction from the surface all the way down to the bone. All tissue along the way dies off, and the natural decay process starts."

He dried parts of my hand with a final sponge. He retrieved a scalpel. "It's medieval to do this without a local, but I've never found an anesthetic that works properly."

"I don't feel anything in my hand."

"Not yet," Ryan said, and began cutting. He cut around the worst of the lesions, slicing ragged black flesh away from the lips of the wounds. I finally looked away, toward Gail.

She was facing away from us, leaning on the examination table. I felt a wave of empathy for her; she shouldn't have had to be here for this. As I watched, she turned around and waved weakly at me, as if to say she was all right. I noticed that she kept her gaze locked on my face, never looking down toward my hand.

Doctor Ryan never stopped talking. "What I have to do now is isolate whatever tissue in your hand that hasn't had its gross physical structure destroyed. That tissue can be revitalized back to something like life."

"Something like life?" I asked and looked back at him. I caught sight of the bones in the base of my thumb. They appeared to be eroded. I turned away again.

"Infected cells are hardier—survive everything but destruction of the cell membrane—they can radically alter their own function, but they don't reproduce."

"How can my body replace tissue that dies off—" I was about to say "naturally," but there was nothing natural about this.

I suspected the answer before Ryan provided it. "Human blood, living whole human blood. You ingest it, the blood itself is infected and incorporates itself into your own tissue. Blood's the only medium that's readily absorbed, but any properly suspended solution of intact human cellular material could do as well."

"Has to be human?"

"Nonhuman cellular material can be infected, but can't be absorbed. There are a few species that can be carriers, but none are suitable for feeding from. And as far as I know, the infection results in vampirism only in humans—and then only in select cases."

He kept cutting as he talked. I felt nothing but the occasional twinge along my wrist where the living tissue stopped. I kept glancing back to see him removing ragged strips of red-black, unrecognizable as flesh, and dropping them into the waste tray. The smell was beyond belief. I had to cease asking questions because breathing made my eyes water.

I kept looking back at Gail, occasionally forcing a smile. By now she had backed away from the smell herself, back to the corner Ryan had put her in.

Somehow, Ryan managed to stand the smell, talking all the while. "With no intervention, the infection only thrives in a particular type of host—and then only after death. And *then* only if death follows swiftly after infection. In most humans this entity can't survive the first twenty-four hours in a living host. Though, if another infection weakens the immune system, the entity can survive much longer." Ryan's voice took on the same distant tone it had had when he'd mentioned blood poisoning. I had the feeling he was remembering something specific.

He turned my hand over, resting the perforated back on a gauze pad. He began working to excise the rot from the meat of my palm. "If a susceptible host does die while infected, the infection spreads like a brushfire through the whole body. Much faster than the normal decay process. Often too fast for rigor, or even lividity, to set in. The infection actually reanimates the tissue."

I looked up at him as he set down the instruments. He looked at my palm. He nodded to himself and looked back at me. "So far so good."

I lowered my gaze to what was left of my hand. I had trouble accepting it as part of my body. Large patches of flesh had been eaten away down to the bone, as if it had melted. The edges of the wounds were now razor-sharp, thanks to Ryan's scalpel. There wasn't nearly enough blood, and my remaining skin was now snow-white with occasional streaks of discoloration.

"The structure of the remaining tissue should be intact enough to allow reinfection. If all goes well, your hand should reform itself and expel the remaining damaged tissue."

Ryan took the tray of waste and dumped it into a metal door set into the wall. An incinerator, I supposed. He stripped off his gloves and tossed them in after the waste. That done, he returned to the sink and scrubbed again, and replaced his gloves.

"This is where this may begin to hurt," he said as he picked up a large hypodermic needle.

He swabbed my right arm, and sank the needle into a vein. "I have to use fresh, infected blood," Ryan said. "The patient's own is always the best to use when the damage is this grave." Then, slowly, he withdrew blood from my arm. The blood didn't look quite right to me. It seemed thicker and darker than it should've.

That wasn't the part that hurt.

What hurt was when he began injecting the blood into the remaining flesh of my dead hand. I felt nothing at first, as he slid the needle through the edges of the largest wounds. But at the third injection, the permanent ache in my wrist began traveling down toward my fingers. Sensation began returning, a pins-and-needles sensation of restricted circulation.

Then, as the hypo was emptied of its blood sample, leaving white trails of flesh pock-marked with needle tracks, I began to feel the raw ends of the nerves.

"God," I gasped, breathing again.

"Dad," I heard Gail say. She ran toward me.

My hand twitched. It was on fire. I could feel it burning everywhere Ryan's scalpel had cut. I could feel the blood he'd injected, rivulets of lava running under my skin.

I stared at my hand, teeth clenched, and watched as Ryan's miracle happened. Pink color began to creep down my arm, past my wrist, and to the strips of flesh still connected to my hand. My wounds began to bleed.

I felt the now-familiar sensation of skin tightening and flesh flowing. The lips of the wounds stretched and flowed across naked bone and tendon, knitting together with their neighbors. It felt as if my skin were being torn off my hand, and then stapled back into place. If I hadn't been riveted by the sight of newly vital flesh, the pain might have made me black out.

But, after a subjective eternity, I sat, exhausted, with an intact hand resting on a gauze pad soaked with blood and plasma. I stared in disbelief as I clenched it into a fist.

"Good Lord," Gail said from my side. She had seen the entire process.

Ryan leaned over and swabbed off my hand. "Let me see," he said.

I let him take my hand and prod it. As he did I marveled at the sensation of feeling in my hand again.

22

Doctor Ryan's treatment, and his nonstop dialog, answered many of the physical questions about blood and regeneration. Even so, for all his scientific jargon, his explanations seemed incomplete. I was a vampire because I was a susceptible host for the vampiric pseudovirus, and had "died" shortly after being infected with it.

But what made Kane Tyler a host susceptible to vampirism? Ryan could offer me no clear answer beyond the fact that it involved the time since infection, the physical state of the host, and environmental factors up to and including the state of mind at the time of death. A susceptible host was a rare phenomenon, and that was how the vampiric pseudovirus could evolve, and propagate without destroying the host population.

At least until social forces overwhelmed the evolutionary ones. Ryan mentioned, almost off-hand, that most vampires were now made as the result of a conscious decision by their creator. Apparently, any human, susceptible or not, would become a vampire with a sufficient infusion of infected blood.

Ryan indirectly answered a few of my more obvious questions. Regeneration or not, "dead" or not, most of the organs in my body performed the same functions as they did before, only at a much lower level of activity. The infection impregnating my flesh took up most of the slack of a slowed metabolism, and my blood now had the duty not just of oxygenating tissue, but of replacing it as well.

A stake through the heart, as long as it remained in place preventing regeneration, would pretty surely kill me. Same for decapitation. My body could withstand an extreme amount of purely mechanical damage—a gunshot, stab wound, a broken arm—and rebuild itself. But anything that destroyed large masses of tissue— fire, acid, or sunlight—would cause my body no end of grief.

To hear Ryan speak, the whole subject of vampirism had no claim on the supernatural. Ryan had a ready answer for all the physical stigmata, and what he said fit well with what Gabriel had deigned to explain about the subject.

But there were things that Doctor Ryan did not explain and, with his point of view, things I doubted he *could* explain. He didn't explain how I could look into someone's eyes and push his or her mind in a particular direction. He didn't explain the fire I had seen behind Sebastian's eyes, or why I felt an unease around his rosary and not my daughter's. He didn't explain why I couldn't look at myself in the mirror. He didn't explain why I could see blood as a luminescent fire that turned slowly black as it died.

He did not explain why I could sometimes feel the emotions of people around me, like ripples carried upon the wind.

After all the poking and prodding, Ryan released my hand. "I've done all I can tonight. Nerves take more time to regenerate than other tissue. If you could stay here the night, I'd like to look at it in the morning."

I took my hand off the tray and clenched it a few times. There were a few aches deep in the bones, and it trembled when I moved. It was gaunt and skeletal, but a miraculous achievement all the same.

"You might want to wash that off," Ryan waved over to the sink. He yawned. "I'll tell my grand-daughter to set up the guest rooms for both of you."

I looked at Gail and said, "Just for me. My daughter won't be staying."

"Dad," Gail said at me in a harsh stage whisper. I looked at her and shook my head aggressively. "No."

Ryan didn't seem to notice the exchange between me and Gail. He yawned again and nodded. "I'm too old to keep these hours," he muttered.

He waited for me to wash my hands before he led us up. He locked the door to the basement after we emerged. "I'll let you see your daughter out yourself. I must see Leia and get some sleep."

Once Ryan was out of earshot, Gail glared at me. "I go through all this to see you, and you're sending me away? How can you do that?"

I put my arm around her shoulders and started walking her to the door. "I don't know if you're safe here."

"I thought you were friends with that guy."

"Please, Gail, I don't know everything that's going on here." I took her out the front door and led her up the walk to the Chevette. "But I do know that I've been mixed up with people who've killed your mom, and who would've killed me but for some fluke, and I'm no longer sure who those people are."

When we reached the Chevette, she looked at me and said, "Then come *with* me, Dad. We can both leave here, get away from Sebastian and everyone else."

I shook my head.

"Why? Why are you going to stay here? He fixed your hand. It's all right now—"

I kissed her on the firehead. "I need to find Cecilia, and Childe."

"But her dad wants to put a stake through her heart."

"Then I have to find her before Sebastian does, don't I?"

We stood there for a long time. Her breath trailed off into the night. The air from my own lungs was nearly invisible. She reached down and took my left hand in her own. "You're so cold, Dad."

"I've been colder."

"I don't think I believed it until I saw your hand. Whatever I said, it wasn't *real* until that happened." Her grip was tight, as if she were afraid I might run away. "They did this to you, the same people who killed Mom?" She looked at me with shiny eyes.

"I think so," I said. "I don't remember what happened. The . . . *transition* left some gaps in my memory."

"God can't damn you for this, can He? You didn't have a choice."

It wasn't a question I expected from her. I didn't know how to answer her; there were times in the past three days that I felt my soul descended to near-irredeemable depths. "If we're damned, it is for our actions, not some opportunistic infection."

Gail didn't let go. "What have you done, Dad?"

"I don't know what you mean."

"Yes, you do," Gail said. "I can see the weight in your face, the way you look at me. You can carry guilt like a badge."

Silence stretched for a long time. The only sound was the wind crying through the branches of the naked trees. Somewhere above, a crow cawed after something.

How could I lie to her?

"I've killed two people."

She stared into my eyes, and I saw in there a glowing warmth. It was both like and unlike the fire I had seen in Sebastian's eyes. The light in her eyes had the heat and intensity of Sebastian's, but not the fearful violence. Instead of a barrier, it was a welcome.

"Were they innocent?" she asked me.

"What?" I was drawn back by the question, enough that my hand pulled free of her grip. "What kind of question is that?"

"You killed two people because you were a vampire?" Gail asked, looking at me with a warmth that seemed to melt down her face with her tears.

I nodded, two deaths that should have never happened.

"Were they innocent?"

I stood aghast at the question. What the hell did it matter? I had two people's deaths on my hands. "My God, Gail, they didn't deserve to die. You can't play God with human lives."

She grabbed me, "Damn it, Dad! You're not an evil person. I know you. Who were these people? What were they doing? Why did you . . . ?"

I looked into her eyes. Had I turned into a monster or not? I had made the difficult admission already, hadn't I? "I—"

"Who, Dad? How did it happen?"

"Tony," I finally said. "The man's name was Tony. I broke into his girlfriend's apartment. He was. . . ."

"He was what?"

I shook my head. "You can't justify this."

"He was what?"

"Beating her, okay? That's not the point."

"Damn it, it *is!* If you were still a cop, could you have shot him?"

"Maybe, I don't know . . . just drive to Sam's, would you? Use the cellular to call ahead and give him some warning."

Gail backed up and wiped her eyes. "Okay. What should I tell Sam?"

"As little as possible."

She opened the door to the Chevette. "You're not going to be at Mom's funeral, are you?"

I shook my head. "Not unless they have it after sundown."

She took my hand again. "I forgive you."

"Thanks." I started to walk back to the house, but she kept hold of my hand.

"For everything," she said.

I took my hand back and said, "I love you, Gail."

"I love you, still," she said.

I began walking back to the house. Behind me I heard the Chevette start up. Over the engine I heard Gail shout at me, "I still loved you, even when you shot back." Then the engine revved and started to fade in the distance.

I rubbed the spot where the bullet had emerged from my lung, back when I was still a cop. I stood in front of the door for a long time before I could wipe my eyes and enter.

I took refuge in Ryan's den, trying not to think about Gail, and Kate, and trying to keep from going into an emotional tailspin. I stood in front of the French doors, staring at the snow beyond. My own gaunt face stared back at me out of the glass. Shadows made my eyes invisible, a pair of black holes in my face that caused me no pain.

"Can I get you something to drink?" came an English-accented voice from behind me. I turned around to see Leia, Ryan's granddaughter. I didn't hear any irony in her voice.

I shook my head, suppressing an internal shudder. Ryan had told me that the drain my injury caused to my body's resources would require me to feed pretty soon. Ryan had said I could eat and drink normal foods. However, I couldn't digest them, since acid production in my stomach was now about nil. My stomach lining would become more and more sensitive the longer between real feedings.

However, I didn't want to think about blood, or real feedings, not with my last two victims fresh in my mind.

"No, thank you," I said. "Your name's Leia, right?"

She nodded and I caught the scent of a strong perfume. The perfume was the only thing about her that was overstated. "Yes." she said. "Did—" there was a slight pause as she bit her lip. "Did Grandfather help you?"

"Very much," I said. I flexed my intact left hand, still skeletal and trembling. "He saved me from a rather stupid accident."

"Good. I'm glad he could help you." She smiled, but it didn't reach her eyes. Something deep in there told me that she was very unnerved by my presence. I'd be unnerved, too, considering her grandfather's clientele.

"You don't need to be afraid of me." Fear didn't seem the right word, but whatever empathy I had wasn't providing me with convenient labels. I sensed confusion, wariness, caution, expectation—some or all of which may have been me rather than her.

"I'm not afraid." Her smile faded with a sharp feeling of a nerve being brushed. My comment had struck a chord, what one I didn't know. Almost as if she'd seen me notice, she resurrected her smile and said, "What's there to be afraid of?"

I nodded. "Indeed. What?" I turned my gaze back out the French doors. She had caught me within my own fears.

" 'For, alas, alas! with me,' " I whispered, not really aware that I was quoting aloud, " 'The Light of Life is o'er.' "

"What's that from?" Leia asked.

I cleared my throat, embarrassed at having quoted the verse aloud. "Edgar Allan Poe, a poem. It's about death." I lowered my head. "Everything he wrote was about death."

I heard her moving around behind me. "You don't seem the type to spontaneously quote poetry."

I turned around to face her; she had taken a seat in a recliner facing the hearth. She sat, legs crossed, looking at me intently. The low fire brought out livid copper highlights in her red hair.

"I read a lot of Poe in high school. It comes back to me every once in a while." Once in a *bad* while. Ever since my father died. Poe came back when death was near.

"How does it go?" she asked.

"Hm?"

"The poem, how does it go?" There was something in her eyes that drew the poem to the surface.

"It's called, 'To One in Paradise,' " I said. " 'Thou wast that all to me, love, / For which my soul did pine— / A green isle in the sea love, / A fountain and a shrine, / All wreathed with fairy fruits and flowers, / And all the flowers were mine.' "

I paced as I recited the poem from memory. I had to stop and catch my breath, because my throat was tightening up.

" 'Ah, dream too bright to last! / Ah, starry Hope! that didst arise / But be overcast!' "

I turned away from Leia to face the French doors again.

" 'A voice from out the Future cries, / "On! On!"— but o'er the Past / (Dim gulf!) my spirit hovering lies / Mute, motionless, aghast!

" 'For alas! alas! with me / The light of Life is o'er! / No more—no more—no more—

" '(Such language holds the solemn sea / To the sands upon the shore) / Shall bloom the thunder-blasted tree, / Or the stricken eagle soar!' "

I leaned on the windowsill and whispered the final stanza.

" 'And all my days are trances, / And all my nightly

dreams / Are where thy gray eye glances, / And where thy footstep gleams— / In what ethereal dances, / By what eternal streams.' "

I ended with my forehead touching the glass and the sensation that everything behind my chest had fallen away.

A long silence followed before Leia said, "I'm sorry."

I collected my thoughts enough to say, "What for?"

"That poem's difficult for you, isn't it?"

I tried to dry my eyes as subtly as possible as I turned around. "It's not the poem."

She stared at me, and I got the feeling she was seeing into an uncomfortable depth. "No," she agreed. "It's not."

"So you live here," I said to change the subject. "With your grandfather?"

She nodded.

"What about your parents?"

"They died, a long time ago."

"Sorry."

She shrugged.

"Are you friends with Bowie?" She looked to be about Bowie's age.

She laughed. "Hardly what you'd call our relationship. Let's just say I associate with him. Are *you* friends with him?"

"I don't know. Where is he? There are a few questions I have to ask him."

Leia shrugged. "Bowie has gone, to do the things that Bowie does. Are you sure about me getting you something?"

I felt an unnatural clarity in the air, as if every sense had been honed to a scalpel edge and was cutting into my brain. Brushfire emotion had consumed everything inside me, and sensory input rushed in the fill the void. The light burned my eyes, Leia's perfume stung my nose, and the ebb and flow of my own blood was a hammer in my ear.

Hunger was suddenly a deep ache inside me. Leia stared at me knowingly and said, "Are you *sure*?"

The offer violated me, as if a stranger were viewing my own private perversion. She looked at me and I felt the thirst swell inside me—

I felt a wary sense of self-preservation. I did not fully trust this place, and Gabriel had impressed upon me that everything freely offered carried a price along with it. I shook my head. "No. Thanks."

She frowned briefly, as if something was wrong. I didn't know what. I was able to push the sudden wave of hunger away. The need wasn't yet strong enough to make me lose control. From talking to Ryan, who opined much more freely than Gabriel, after two victims I should have at least a week—if it hadn't been for the drain because of my injury. As it was, I could go one or two days before I reached the state where I became uncontrollable.

I pushed the urge away, but the taste lingered in my mouth and the light was still bothersome. I walked over and dimmed the lamps to a tolerable level, where they barely competed with the glow from the fireplace.

I looked at Leia, seated in the recliner, looking at me with a faintly curious expression. Who was she? Why had she been seated with Bowie the first time I'd seen her?

Like Bowie, she was young enough to be recruited by Childe's cult. . . .

"Do you happen to know anything about a man calling himself Childe?" I asked.

Her face darkened, but she showed no surprise at the question. "He is not a man."

"You know him, then."

She stood. "Evil. Pure distilled evil. Everything he touches turns to rot sooner or later." She walked until she was nearly touching me. The smell of her perfume was overpowering. She ran a finger under the collar of her turtleneck as she spoke. "You should leave Childe be while you still own yourself."

I shook my head. I couldn't back away now, even if I wanted to, even though the farther along I came, the less certain I was of what was happening.

She stepped back. "Don't think your losses make you special, my poetic friend. Revenge is not a happy pursuit." Leia stepped around me and out the door. "The guest room is upstairs and to the right."

I stood in the doorway and watched her ascend the stairs, a spectral figure. The black sweater and pants soaked up the darkness, with only her flowing red hair to mark her humanity.

Revenge is not a happy pursuit.

That woman had been hurt by Childe. I wondered how her parents had died, and how her grandfather had gotten into the business of treating the undead.

23

I didn't go to the guest room. I didn't think I could sleep normally now if I tried, despite feeling the burden from Ryan's ministrations. My hand had drained me, and dark thoughts had drained me even more. More than my hand, the events of the past three days wearied me. I had been pulled along this path nonstop, and more than my body, my mind was tired.

I needed to relax, if only for a few hours. So, after Leia's departure, I rummaged through Doctor Ryan's bookshelves. Ryan's library was a much lesser and more pedestrian affair than Childe's, but in it I found something familiar: a small cloth-bound volume entitled simply, *Tales and Poems*. Under the title was the name, "Poe."

The memories it sparked were melancholy, but so were the tales, so were the poems. Right now I needed the familiarity, the feeling that something of myself was still mine, unchanged. As always with Poe, I needed the feeling that I had company in the darkness.

I pulled a drape across the French doors, shutting out the rest of the world, and settled in the recliner, which still held a whisper of Leia's perfume. I opened the book at random. The first line my eyes fell upon were within the opening paragraph of "The Masque of the Red Death."

"No pestilence had ever been so fatal, or so hideous.

Blood was its Avatar and its seal—the redness and the horror of blood."

It was as if the two decades since my father's death had never happened, and Poe's words were still talking directly to me. I let myself be taken to Poe's realm because, somehow, it vindicated my own. . . .

In a few hours I had passed from the Prospero of the Masque to the Fortunato of the Cask—from Doom to Revenge. I had passed into a blackness now wholly literary, and therefore a little lighter.

The first tier of masonry had but been laid within the text when a noise drew me out of the story. I looked up, not sure what I had heard. The winter night was deathly silent, a blanket of snow soaking up stray sounds.

I convinced myself that it had been the house creaking, or something popping within the hearth—a few shadowy embers still glowed there, the last ghost of a fire.

Just when I returned to reading, I heard the noise repeating. I heard it, again—a very distinct knocking coming from in front of me. Something about the rapping frightened me.

Lightly tapping, the noise repeated itself.

I told myself it was nothing, the wind . . . But there wasn't any wind.

I slowly placed the book on an end table. A Raven, embossed in gold leaf, looked up from the cover.

I stood up and walked toward the heavy purple curtains I'd drawn across the French doors. It was those doors from which the sound came. Someone gently rapping on the panes to gain admittance.

"Bowie?" I asked, even though I knew it wasn't him. Bowie would not cause me such dread.

The rapping continued. I felt certain that whatever was outside those doors represented death. The sense was so strong that, as I reached for the curtain, I felt as if it could be Kate beyond, risen from the stainless steel cart from which I'd last seen her.

I flung open the curtain.

The feeling of fear and present death did not cease when I saw the man who had been knocking at the door. If anything, my feelings deepened.

The man did not have the appearance to inspire terror. He was, in fact, attractive in an androgynous fashion. He was dark-skinned, but any attempt to put his face in a set racial category was doomed to failure. His nose was European, his eyes could be Asian, his hair was Indian, his skin African—but none of the terms fit him. He was not a marriage of separate races. He was of a race of himself.

"Come with me," he said. His voice did not fog the air. I doubt it was even audible inside the house, beyond the glass, so softly was it spoken. I heard it nonetheless, and I found myself unable to refuse.

I opened the door with the feeling that this was a particularly vivid dream. The cold and my feet sinking into the snow only slightly dispelled the illusion.

I never felt so much power tied into a single entity. Standing next to him was like standing next to volcano that was about to erupt. There was nothing about his appearance, absolutely nothing, that gave that impression. Physically he was less imposing than I was.

"You will walk with me," he said.

I didn't have much choice. Even if I had felt able to refuse, this man's bearing and his sudden appearance would have demanded some sort of attention in spite of the intimidating presence around him.

I followed him away from Doctor Ryan's house, and into the night-emptied streets of Shaker Heights. Once out of sight of the house, he addressed me again, "Ask your questions."

"Who are you?"

He glanced at the sky and said, "Another spirit

bound in chains of flesh. No names for me, Mr. Tyler, I am not here."

The denial of one in power. I could feel the tug of secrecy behind this visit.

"You know me," I said, half-question, half-statement.

"I have an interest in what you are involved in." We stopped and he gave me a searing look. "You are an outsider."

"I know. Why are you here?"

"You question my presence?" His stare became a holocaust, I could feel his gaze stripping layers from inside me. I knew now what Gabriel had told me about power, and status. I was standing in front of a vampire as far beyond Gabriel as Gabriel was above a Thrall.

Still, under that invisible assault, I managed to whisper, "Yes, I am."

The first trace of expression crossed his face, a slight upturn at the corners of the mouth. "Strength," he said to himself. He turned and continued walking along the sidewalk.

"Perhaps I'm here to offer you Indenture."

"Indenture?"

He turned around and extended his right arm beyond the sleeve of his jacket. It extended for an unnatural length. "You feel the hunger upon you, don't you?"

In response, I felt the ache begin in my stomach, in my brain. The raw need consumed every vein in my body. A death chill frosted every nerve. The night focused into razor clarity, every angle slicing into my brain. Every sense amplified a dozen times, including the ethereal sense that told me of the power this creature before me held.

This creature, now, burned like a pillar of divine fire. I saw within him a heat, a power to take away the hunger, the need, the pain. More than enough. More than I could take in a dozen lifetimes. His life burned infinitely brighter than that of the human souls I had seen.

And before me was his extended arm, the life within nearly too bright for me to look at, the heat within burning the frozen skin of my face. The skin of his arm was bare before my face, and as I watched, the skin laid itself open to me. A slit appeared between the bones of the wrist, above the vein, traveling up the arm and pulling apart.

Blood spilled out of the wound, fire-red, leaking on to the ground. The smell drew me, and my lips were almost upon the spilling wound before I whispered, "No."

I knew what drinking would mean, I knew there was a tie in the blood beyond what Ryan suspected. No one had to tell me that, I could feel it. I felt it rippling from the blood that spilled from his arm—its life, powerful, seductive, and not my own. Accepting this from him would form a bond that I did not want to make.

I was still leaning forward, the need, the lust, pushing me. I repeated, "No," and pushed the arm away. The blood drew a black arc in the snow. It was the hardest thing I had ever done.

When I turned away, everything returned to a sense of normalcy. I expected him to be angry, at the very least. But, from behind me, I heard the whispered word again, "Strength."

I turned to face him. He was no longer a god offering communion. He was a figure of purely temporal power.

"Who are you?" I asked, my voice unsteady.

"No one to trifle with." He extended a now normal-looking arm ahead of him. "You have some strength. Do not confuse it with power."

He began walking, and I had no choice but to follow him. I began to think that, had he wished me to drink, I would have drunk. My victory had only been over myself, my own desire. Apparently that was enough for now.

"What did I refuse?" I asked.

"Security," he said. "Comfort. No small bit of power. That, and slavery."

It was the blood. Ryan's pseudovirus transmitted itself through blood, taking over the flesh, controlling the flesh. Somehow the mind controlled Ryan's bug—

"You think you understand." His words made me feel naked, as if my thoughts were exposed in his presence.

He laughed and it was terrifying to listen to. More terrible because I knew what he was laughing at. "Such desperate clinging, Tyler." His eyes burned when he said it, heated from the internal fire that had nearly consumed me before. "The doctor has buried himself in the flesh, as have you."

He reached over and gently touched the edge of my chin. "Do not think describing the Mystery, in whatever detail, will explain it."

I was frozen, staring at him. I almost wanted to believe I was held in place by some mental power, but I knew that it was awe that held me there. His face was a fusion of the angelic and the diabolical, shaped like a man's face, but no longer remotely human.

It stroked my cheek as if comforting a child.

"Blood is All. But the All is not simply blood. It is Life, Spirit, Soul. *Our* Mind, *our* Soul, everything *us* that transcends the physical is chained within us, has become part of the flesh chaining us to this world. It lives with the flesh, dies with the flesh. It controls the flesh and is controlled by the flesh. Ryan is not of *us*. He does not see the mind within the blood, the soul within the blood. He cannot see what we see, or understand that there is anything unphysical about us." He looked deeply into me and said, "You have seen the soul within the blood, tasted it."

I couldn't bring myself to speak, so I nodded.

"You have seen the maelstrom of faith within a righteous man."

I thought of Sebastian and nodded again.

"You cannot look into the daemon within your own eyes."

I nodded again.

"You have left the world of men. The human being you once were is dead, and the remnant spirit has remolded your flesh. You must set aside the beliefs you once had; such things can only hurt you now."

"But—"

A stern edge crept into his voice. He dropped his hand. "You think like a human and you will die like one."

I backed away. "Why are you here?"

"Because of your ignorance, your novelty, your potential importance. Because you are a rogue. The first such born to us in half a century to survive the day of his creation. Because you are of use to me."

The sense of otherworldliness seemed to recede. The cold I felt was real, and the colors I saw belonged to Shaker Heights, not a higher, or lower, realm.

"What use?"

"You have no master. No one has given you what I offered you." He gestured with the arm he had brandished earlier. It was intact, no sign of wounding now. "You have a freedom that few have until centuries after their birth."

I was glad of that, at least. I didn't relish having a master, of any sort.

"No Master. No Teacher," he said. "A rogue is dangerous, especially to himself. You have no status, no role, no protection. You honor no kin. You have no Name."

"This makes me useful to you?" I asked.

"Yes, Kane Tyler. It does." He steepled his hands in front of him, as if consciously withdrawing all the intense impressions I had felt around him, as if he folded his sprit back within his body. "I am older than you can imagine, and my power is such that even a thrall to me is a force few would contend with. But I cannot move incautiously, my acts bear too much weight for me to make an ill move."

"Are you asking something of me?"

He laughed, "I am offering something."

"Something with a price."

"All things have their price. Can you accept the Covenant?"

Could I? Perhaps, more importantly, could I reject it? Gabriel had labeled me an outcast because I had not accepted the Covenant, and had said that someone would want much for "granting me that boon."

"What do you want in return?"

"The conclusion of the troubles that have come to this city."

"Childe?"

He laughed softly, "It is not for me to accuse. For me to express myself, rightly or wrongly, in this matter would do worse damage than is being done now."

"Then what do you want from me?"

"Those who search for the truth in this are blinded. I wish your eyes. I wish to commend upon you the duty of vengeance."

"I thought that was Gabriel's job."

"Such it is. But I shall not wrongly demean his status if he is blameless. You shall be my agent, but you shall not be me. Shall you accept the Covenant and provide this for me?"

That gave me all sorts of questions about Gabriel's role in all of this. I found myself nodding even before I had decided to do so.

"Again, shall you do this, refusing the option to turn back?"

"Yes."

He placed a hand on my forehead, and I felt a

. burning there. "Between me and the night," he said, "name yourself."

The word was pulled immediately from my lips, as if it wasn't me talking, but something speaking though me. "Raven," I heard myself say.

"Raven it is, and shall ever be. As Jaguar, I am witness to your entrance to the Covenant, speak your name now, and it will be known of what you are a part."

I opened my mouth to ask a question, one of a tumult of questions about Childe, and Gabriel, and even Bowie. However, before I had taken breath to speak, he had removed his hand and had stepped backward into a shadow. Though my eyes never left him, I could not see where he went. When I looked down, I only saw my own set of footprints.

"Jaguar," I whispered, naming the apparition.

He had been right. Neither Ryan nor I had come close to the mystery. Or the Mystery.

24

I took my vampiric nonsleep in Ryan's windless guest-
room. For once I wasn't tormented by memory. I
simply rested, barely aware of my surroundings or the
passage of time. The sunlit hours of Tuesday passed
without me.

I came to full consciousness with someone knocking
on my door. I felt a weird sense that the day had not
fully passed, and that I had just laid down upon the
bed. A glance at my watch told me that the day had
indeed passed. It was nearly seven.

I sat up feeling fatigued and hungry. I rubbed the
sleep from my face as the knocking continued.
"Coming," I said.

I stood up, feeling as rumpled as my clothes looked.
I picked up my holster and put it back on before I
unlocked the door. I opened it to found Leia standing
outside. She'd traded her black turtleneck for a navy
blue one, and her perfume was as strong as ever.
"Grandfather wants to see you in his office, to look at
your hand."

I nodded. "I'll be down in a few minutes."

I had a memory flash, and as she turned to leave, I
asked, "How long have you been here?"

"Here? With my Grandfather? All my life."

I shook my head, "No, in Cleveland."

She shrugged. "Six months or so, why?"

"Just curious. I've noticed your accent."

"Oh," she said.

Still thinking of England, I asked, "Does the name Cross mean anything to you?"

"Should it?" she asked.

"I don't know."

"You enjoy asking questions, don't you?"

"It's my job."

She gave me a half-smile and said, "In my experience questions are often far more interesting than answers. Pardon me, but I have errands to run."

She left me abruptly enough for me to feel that I had hit something significant. What, I didn't know. However, I was too much a detective to discount Leia and Childe's common nationality as coincidence.

I met with Ryan in his office downstairs. It was a study in whitewash and stainless steel. However, it was aboveground and a much more pleasant environment then the morgue in the basement. The room felt as if a person worked and lived there. There were pictures on the wall, a reassuring clutter on his desk, and a spider plant hanging in one corner of the room.

I sat for the doctor as he poked and prodded my left hand, which now bore no sign of yesterday's gangrene. There was, in fact, little now to distinguish it from my right hand.

Ryan, as he'd shown last night, was a talker. As he flexed my hand and dragged little pointed implements across it, he'd talk all about what he thought was going on inside me. He talked about how much resources my body had used up during the night. How it had expelled or reabsorbed the dead tissue. He talked about a lot of chemical esoterica that I couldn't understand.

Most important to me was the fact that he talked. It wasn't very hard to change the thread of his conversation.

"So," I asked as he tested the reflexes of my pinkie, "how'd you get into treating vampires anyway?"

"The war," he said without missing a beat. "I was a volunteer medic. I was in London, treating civilians during the Blitz." He nodded absently to some pictures on the wall, many were black and white, showing a young Doctor Ryan. "During the worst part of the bombing, there was an epidemic of unexplained deaths. All in a single ward, all in the middle of the night. We weren't equipped for autopsies, not to mention the lack of personnel." He rolled up my sleeve and began prodding my wrist. "So I stayed up to watch the men in the ward. That night I saw my first vampire. The creature must have been caught in the bombing, much of the soft tissue had been burned away. The face was little more than a charred skull."

He paused for a while, looking my hand over. "Sunlight is bad, but fire is worse. Destroys the tissue immediately. This thing's skin was like charcoal. It rustled like dry leaves when it moved. And when it moved, its skin cracked, showing livid red tissue." Ryan shook his head. "The mass of blood it would have needed to repair that damage would have been twenty or thirty full grown men. As it was, with me and the orderlies there, once we overcame our shock and saw it begin feeding, we restrained it—and inadvertently killed it."

Ryan put down my hand and pronounced, "Your hand is fine, Mr. Tyler. My suggestion is to feed, rest, and build up your strength. You should be as good as new."

"Thank you. What can I do to repay you?"

Ryan smiled. "Money usually suffices. If you're low on funds, a blood sample once you've fully recovered."

"More research?"

Ryan nodded. "Feel free to remain my guest here as long as necessary."

"I appreciate the offer." I also had the suspicion that

it was too generous. "Do you think you could answer a few of my nonmedical questions."

"I'll do my best, Mr. Tyler," he folded his hands. "It's actually refreshing when one of my patients has an interest in what I have to say."

"That's unusual?"

Ryan chuckled. "Very. What do you want to know?"

"I was interested in what you could tell me about some vampires I'm interested in."

"What about them?"

"What you've heard, what they're like—"

"I suppose I'll be more forthcoming than your kinsmen, for what little I know about the figures in your society."

You're part of that society as well, I thought, *you have to be to do your work.* "Tell me what you know about one named Childe."

Ryan shook his head. "He is old. He came out of central Europe about four hundred years ago. Childe is very—" He wrung his hands as if groping for a word. "Inner directed, I suppose you could say. He uses people. Uses them up."

"You know him, then?"

"No," Ryan said quickly. "I know *of* him."

"From England?" I asked.

Ryan gave me a blank look and then he nodded. "Yes, from England."

I nodded. "Your granddaughter said you left England about six months ago. Why did you leave?"

"Huh?"

"You were there since the war?"

Ryan nodded.

"Why return to the States now?"

"Oh. The last of my wife's family passed away. There was nothing left to hold us there." He glanced up at the wall and said, "I thought you wanted to know about vampires?"

"Do you know of a gentleman named Gabriel?"

"Gentleman," Ryan smiled. "Appropriate word. He's one of those Americans that become so enamored of aristocracy that they become more class-conscious than the British. He's pre-Civil War, and he slipped into the society as if it were made for him. He would hate Childe."

"Why?"

"Because Childe has no use for any rules of society, human or otherwise. He's fond of quoting Alister Crowley, 'Do what thou wilt shall be the whole of the law . . .' The fact that Childe is older, more powerful, and has more status than Gabriel does would be almost a perpetual insult."

Ryan stood up. "Now, if you please, I have business to attend to."

I stood and extended my hand. "Thank you for your help, and for fixing my hand."

"It's my job." Ryan shook my hand. "As I said, feel free to use our guest room."

"Thank you, but I think I should be moving on soon."

Ryan got up to leave, and I asked, "How come you're still human?"

"What?"

I stood up myself. "You must have been tempted, doing all this research, to become one of us." The phrase, "one of us," came much too easily to me.

Ryan shook his head. "Never."

"You could, though, couldn't you?"

He nodded. "Yes, I could infect anyone I wished to, viable specimen or not. But I have never been tempted. I've seen what it can do."

Ryan, somewhat hurried, left me there. I could tell that I had hit a nerve or two. I also could tell he was lying through his teeth about not ever meeting Childe.

I glanced at the wall with all the pictures. Many

shots—wartime England, a primitive-looking hospital, Ryan doing this, Ryan doing that, Ryan with the hospital staff, a color picture of Ryan and his granddaughter with a modern London background. I took a step back from the wall and was struck by a feeling that something was wrong here.

The sound of someone clearing his throat interrupted me. I turned to see Ryan standing at the door, waiting. "I'd like to lock up, Mr. Tyler."

I nodded. "Sure," I said, slipping out the door past him. I still felt something was not quite right about that office. I just wished I could figure out what it was.

I called Sam's number once Ryan and I were through with each other. Gail answered the phone. "Hello, Weinbaum residence."

"Gail?"

"Dad?"

"Yes. What are you doing answering Sam's phone?"

There was a pause before she said, "Hoping you'd call. How're you doing?"

"Hand's mostly better," I locked my lips because a hunger was nagging at me as well, something I needed to take care of soon. I never again wanted to push myself to the point where something like my attack on Tony became inevitable. "How did things go at . . . how'd things go?"

She paused for a long while before she answered. When she spoke, I could hear the stress in her voice, "It went well, I guess." I could tell she'd been crying.

"I wish I could have been there."

"So do I." She sucked in a deep breath. "I'm going to miss Mom."

"I miss her, too." *I've been missing her for five years.* "Is Sam around?"

"Sleeping," she said somewhat abruptly.

"He's asleep?"

"You make it sound like an accusation."

"He's supposed to be protecting you."

"It's not his fault."

She seemed on the verge of tears again. "I'm sorry," I said. "Look, I'm going to take a cab down there—"

"You don't have to do that."

"I need the car."

"Oh. I'll be here, I guess."

The strange conversation lasted a few more minutes, talking about nothing in particular, and I hung up the phone and realized that I still had a family. Despite everything else, they hadn't taken *that* from me. When I called for the cab, I rummaged through my pockets for what was left of money I had liberated from my hotel room.

In fishing for cash, I found something that I had totally forgotten about—a small black film canister with a gray cap. I hadn't slowed down long enough to look over the negatives I had found in my house. What-ever was on them still belonged to one of the black absences in my memory.

As I gave the dispatcher Ryan's address, I popped the gray cap and withdrew the negatives. There were a half-dozen strips of various lengths, all high-quality black and white, 35 millimeter. When I hung up, I uncurled them and held them, one at a time, up to the light.

The stills were from long-distance surveillance. They weren't unusual in themselves, documenting people and places. What was unusual was the sense of menace that pervaded the images, images that were otherwise mundane. It was a visceral response that had little to do with what was actually in the pictures.

Without a magnifying glass, some of the pictures were indecipherable. However I had very clear pictures of a number of cars, most focusing on the license plates.

One was of a dark van with no plate that could have been the same vehicle that'd slammed into Sam's car.

Another was a dark BMW with a vanity plate, "RYAN 1."

I had also taken pictures of Ryan's house. There were other houses I'd photographed, some of which seemed run-down and abandoned, but the only place that I *knew* was the doctor's.

I had also photographed people, young people for the most part. I suspected they were either members or candidates for Childe's little cult. In addition to faces that I could not remember, there were three faces that I did know. I had a picture that was recognizably Leia, and on a separate roll I had a picture of the same leather-clad teenager that had jumped onto Sam's car.

My short-circuited memory made a series of connections—

In front of a mausoleum, standing upon a field of black snow, a teenager smiles at me with a mouth invisible under night-black blood . . .

With a millstone voice, the same teenager speaks from the shattered window of Sam's car, "Aren't you dead, my friend?" Washed by the car's flasher, he smiles at me with lips that appear alternately black and soaked with gore.

That same gravelly voice speaks from Childe's answering machine. "I hear you look for a woman of certain qualities," it says. "There will be one at the ritual tonight, I've told her to look for you."

A van plunges out of the darkness and sideswipes me. I'm thrown into a drift.

I'm dragged into the van, and the same stony voice says, ". . . if you remember us, this, anything, you shall surely die . . ." After which I smell rusty leather, and hear a heavy wet sound. . . .

The fragments wrapped within my memory to place this teenage vampire in a role as the leader of Childe's thralls. Childe's lieutenant, I thought. He was at the right hand of the black-cowled Childe at the mausoleum. He had called Childe to deliver Cecilia. He had led the attack on Sam's car. Somewhere in my black memory, he had attacked me, made me what I was.

All that made it even more troubling to me that, in the picture, this kid was clearly talking to Bowie.

25

Outside, the cab honked its horn for my attention. During the wait I had searched for any sign of Bowie, and had found none. When I went out to the cab, I was still racked with contradictory memories. I still recalled little of the time between Kate's death and my own subterranean waking. However, I now remembered the first time I had talked to Bowie.

I told the cab to go to University Circle. I sat in the back, staring at the lightly snowing evening.

"I've seen you talking to Childe's people," I tell him over a cup of Arabica coffee.

"And you think?" He shakes his head at me. "You don't know how wrong you are, man."

"Why are you talking to these people then?"

"You're supposed to know your enemy, ain't you?"

"Childe's your enemy?"

"He fucked with someone I care about. . . ."

Even as I remembered it, I found that I wasn't so ready to believe him now as I had been then. Though, if he was Childe's tool, why had he helped me as far as he had? If he wasn't, why did I now have the impression that his message on my voice mail had set me up?

Thralls did occasionally kill their masters. Perhaps Bowie *was* Childe's, and had killed him off. Loss of a leader could do strange things to a cult, perhaps even spark a flaring of atypical violence.

That didn't explain why Kate and I had been targets. Had I been close to finding out something? If they had been trying to conceal their vampire nature, they'd done a lousy job of it.

"Maybe Childe's still around, and they're setting him up," I whispered. His own thrall had picked out Cecilia as a potential victim. As far as I could see, she was the first of Childe's people to have disappeared with someone to miss them. Everything since seemed to have been designed to draw Sebastian's attention.

The taxi pulled up in front of Sam's building, and I paid the cabby off with the little cash I had left. I entered Sam's building, thinking that I had almost figured out what was going on.

Gail opened the door a crack to talk to me. The funeral had been hard on her, I thought. Her face was pale and drawn. "Hi, Dad," she said through the crack in the door.

"How are you dong?"

"Not too great," she said, shaking her head.

"I'm sorry."

"It's not your fault."

"Can I come in?"

Gail looked back into the apartment and paused. "We should let Sam sleep."

"Is there something wrong?"

She looked at me and said, in a voice thick with irony, "I don't know, Dad, Mom was buried today, what should be wrong?"

I felt sick at what I said. The new sense of empathy I had—the sense of a psychic wind carrying emotional heat and cold through the aether—carried ripples of confusion, of grief, and of sadness from Gail. I had a sense of clarity beyond anything I'd felt before, and with it came a feeling of loss from my daughter beyond any I had felt myself. "Forgive me, it was a stupid thing to say."

She stared at me, and I felt a sense of something that Gail wanted to say, and wasn't saying. "Whatever happens, I love you, Dad. It isn't your fault . . ." I stood there, waiting for some revelation. Instead she said, "I forgive you."

"Okay."

"The Chevette's in the lot out back. Go find what you're looking for, okay?"

"Okay?"

She closed the door leaving me with a feeling of unease. I was unsure where my normal parental concern ended, and my paranoia began. I wanted to break in the door and ask her what the problem was, but I told myself that I'd seen her, and she was all right, and she was safe with Sam.

When I left, the press of my hunger was bad enough that I could almost smell blood.

I was sick for blood, and I didn't want any more lives on my hands. I needed to take care of it immediately. I had an idea I wanted to test, so I drove by University Hospitals. I parked the Chevette on the street, straightened my jacket to cover the holster and the bullet holes in my shirt, and headed for the emergency entrance.

I walked in, past a reception desk and into the hospital proper, concentrating on projecting an aura of belonging there. I don't know if it was my attitude, any vampiric powers, or simply that the nurses running the desk were too overworked to notice me, but I slipped in without hearing any comment or objection.

A security guard paced the halls, but he faced away from me, and I followed the corridor in the opposite direction from him.

So far so good, but I soon found that at least one part of my plan was ill-conceived. I had intended to slip into the hospital and steal some of their whole blood supply. That was easy to say in the abstract, but now, as I wandered the night-emptied corridors of the hospital, I found it a little difficult to follow through on the premise when I had no idea where anything was. I could feel hunger eating away inside me, making it harder for me to think clearly.

I ran across a few directory maps, but none had a convenient label saying "find blood here."

After about half an hour of random searching, all I had succeeded in discovering was that I could do a pretty good job of mentally convincing inattentive humans that I wasn't there. That was useful, but it didn't help my hunger, which had grown even worse with my mental effort. The hunger was an ache in my joints, a pressure at the back of my skull, a fire searing behind my eyes.

I wandered deep into the hospital complex, away from the constant activity around the emergency room. This corridor was empty enough that I must have let my guard down for a moment, because, just as I was washed with a stunning wave of hunger that near-doubled me over, a tall woman stepped in front of me.

"Pardon me, but can I help you?"

The woman confronting me was thin, and maybe an inch shy of six feet tall. That, combined with her intense gray eyes, invested her with a quiet authority. I glanced down to her name tag, stitched on her white coat over her left breast. "Dr. Nicholson."

I felt warmth, heat, and life inside her. I knew—I could feel—that what she carried within her could fill the void that was eating a hole inside me. We were separated by six feet, but I already felt the strength of her pulse under my fingers. Something savage inside me told me I wanted to grab her right there and sink my teeth into a vein.

She was becoming impatient with me, I could sense irritation rippling within her. "Can I help you find something?" There was a note of demand in her voice that almost hid the subliminal fear. She knew I wasn't supposed to be here, and the strength of my hunger was so intense that even she had to feel it on some level.

I took a few steps forward, and she said, "Sir, I'm going to have to ask you to leave."

I took another step.

"Do I have to call Security?" The fear was reaching her voice now. I felt a tidal pull toward her.

I stared into her eyes and felt my words push into the deep gray pools I saw there. "That won't be necessary."

I felt a spike of fear accompany her answer. "No, it isn't."

"Don't be afraid."

I heard her swallow. "I'll try." I felt the emotion dim somewhat, but it didn't disappear. That was interesting. What exactly was I doing? If it was control, it wasn't absolute.

She kept staring at me, as if fascinated. *I can take her here,* I thought, *and she won't resist. She'll feel panic, and fear, but she won't stop me.*

I almost reached for her—

Then I heard Gail's words, *"Were they innocent?"*

Instead of grabbing her, I spoke. "I need whole blood. Take me to where you keep it."

She nodded. "Follow me."

As she led me off, I tried to imagine what was going on inside Dr. Nicholson's mind. I still fought the frightening impulse inside me that made me want to take all of what she had inside her. When she finally took me into a darkened lab and opened a refrigerator for me, I got a nasty surprise.

Of the bags of whole blood I saw filling the refrigerator, none of them bore the heat of life. I was desperate in my hunger, and I grabbed one of the bags. The fluid inside seemed black and dead to me, I gently bit into it, to taste the contents.

I heard a sharp intake of breath from the doctor, who still held the refrigerator door open.

The taste of the blood made me gag—like bile in my mouth, like death. I threw the bag down in frustration, and a tiny stream leaked out of the hole my tooth had made. It made a black trail on the linoleum floor.

I looked up at the doctor, and the sense of the life within her was overpowering. As was her fear. "I'm sorry," I said.

There was no way around it, I had to drink from a living person. All I could hope for was, as Gabriel had said, it didn't have to be fatal.

"What are you going to do?" she asked.

We stood apart, the light from the refrigerator the only barrier between us. I could feel the pull of her blood, and I could feel the skin begin to tighten around my jaw. "I won't hurt you," I said, with difficulty. I hoped it wasn't a lie.

I stepped forward, and she let go of the refrigerator door. It closed neatly all the way, leaving only a sliver of light between us.

I touched her neck, and felt the shiver of a racing pulse. "Please calm down," I said, as gently as I could manage.

"I can't," she said.

I felt for her, for her vulnerability. She didn't deserve this, but my own remade nature insisted that nether of us had a choice. I leaned forward.

My lips almost brushed her neck, but I held myself back. I didn't want to injure her. "You take blood, show me the vein you use."

In the ghost-dim light I saw her shake her head. Her

arms were folded across her in a protective gesture. My will was holding her here, but she was afraid. I didn't blame her.

I took her hand, gently, and drew it out in front of her. "Show me. Please." The heat this close to her body was intoxicating. I could smell the life, and every vibration of her pulse sent a tremor through my own body.

After a long pause, she reached down and rolled up her sleeve.

"Forgive me," I said. I leaned over and kissed the crook of her arm, the vein a hot brand against my tongue. My remade teeth bit into the skin almost on their own. Her life, her warmth, filled my mouth. I heard her breath come in shuddering gasps as I drank.

The blood filled weaknesses I hadn't been aware I'd been feeling, the nagging pain evaporated, the fatigue drained away. As soon as I realized that the thirst no longer was a weight within me, I forced myself to stop. It took an effort to pull myself away from her arm, but I managed it. I had refused temptation on a much grander scale last night.

As I pulled away, I was grateful to find that my victim was still standing. As I broke, she sighed and collapsed against me. I had to scramble to keep her upright.

I was beginning to worry when I heard her whisper in my ear. "Who are you?"

"No one important," I said, walking her into the light out in the hall. I looked down at her arm. It was pale and still bleeding, but not badly. I sat her down on the first chair we came to.

She was conscious and seemed to be all right. She looked at me with a wistful expression that made me nervous. "Who are you?" she repeated.

We were out in a corridor, apparently alone. "Just a random nut," I told her. "You should forget about me."

She nodded. She had her arm bent upward, and was putting pressure on the wound. Whatever I was doing mentally, this woman was still in possession of all her faculties. Again, I wondered what was going on inside her mind.

She looked up at me and nodded. "But will I see you again?"

I was stunned by the question for a moment. In response I just shook my head and said, "I don't know." Then I got out of there as quickly as I could.

I wasn't thinking about much of anything as I wove my way back out of the hospital. I wasn't concentrating on not being seen. I passed a small alcove of vending machines, and shortly afterward I heard feet running after me. "Kane? Kane Tyler? Is that you?"

It was a female voice that I barely noticed as familiar. I had conflicting urges to draw my weapon or run, but I turned to face the person.

My first thought was, *what is* she *doing here?*

She slowed to a stop, still holding a Styrofoam cup of hospital coffee. "I thought that was you. If you're here to see him, you missed visiting hours. He's asleep anyway."

I stood there blankly staring at the woman. I knew her, though I could not remember her name. She was in her early thirties, blonde, and wore a dark flowered print dress that was at odds with the weather outside.

She was Sam's girlfriend. Seeing her here gave me a sick feeling of who she was talking about. "What happened?"

"Oh," she looked surprised. "You didn't know? Well, don't worry, the doctors say he'll be fine. They managed to deal with the blood loss in time."

I wanted to shake her. "What blood loss?"

"From the accident. They let him go home and one of the sutures burst open while he slept."

I shuddered. *"When?* When did this happen?"

"Sometime last night—"

I was running for the car before she finished her sentence.

Gail wasn't there to buzz open Sam's apartment. At this point I had lost all concern for subtlety. When she didn't answer, I kicked in the door to the lobby. I ran up the three flights to Sam's apartment, cursing my own stupidity. I had known something was wrong, I had felt it, and I had left her there.

I had even smelled the goddamned blood.

I pounded on Sam's door and received no response. I drew the Eagle and tried the doorknob. It was unlocked. I felt the copper taste of fear in my mouth, a taste that reminded me of blood.

I pushed the door open with my foot, covering the apartment with the Eagle. The living room was empty, but the smell of blood was there—ferric and sharp-tasting.

"Gail!"

I received no answer as I swept the apartment with my gun: living room, kitchen, bathroom. . . .

The blood-smell came from the bedroom. I stood in front of that door a long time before I had the courage to open it. I couldn't take it, not if Gail. . . .

I kicked in the door to Sam's bedroom. It was dark and motionless in there, but my night eyes quickly adjusted. The bed was soaked with blood, blood that was cold, dead, and black.

Gail wasn't here.

"You bastards!" I yelled at the walls. "Where is she? What are you doing?" My voice spent, I whispered, "Why did she lie to me?"

Looking around, I could see the chaos made by the paramedics when they'd grabbed Sam. From the bloodstains on the bed, I could picture the opening of the wounds in his face, spilling across the pillow.

I couldn't picture it as accidental.

I tore the place apart, looking for some clue to where Gail had gone, but I found nothing of hers in Sam's apartment. The only thing I did find was on the floor next to the bed. It was a dirty, folded, piece of paper that looked as if it had spent a long time in someone's pocket, only to slip out when its owner knelt over Sam's bed.

I unfolded it. It was a map of Lakeview Cemetery.

26

I drove away from Sam's apartment building knowing that to find Gail, I had to find Childe's people, his thralls. A knot of rage burned through my gut, at myself, and at them. I had to get to them before they harmed her—

I couldn't complete the thought. The emotion made it hard to think clearly, and I needed to think clearly. I only had two things to act on. I had a map of Lakeview, and I had a memory of dams and mausoleums. I had a memory of running from the teenager with the blood-black smile, of Cecilia's animate body on the blackened snow, of the mausoleum from which she emerged, and of the flood-control dam that had hovered over the whole scene like some gigantic memorial.

Clearly marked, on the map of Lakeview, was the location of that dam. At the moment, that was all I had.

As I drove up Mayfield from University Circle, I passed a large wrought-iron gate that said, "Lakeview Cemetery." My destination.

I felt pressed for time, and parked opposite the gate as soon as I saw it. The cemetery was shut up and dark, long past closing. The sidewalk on that side of Mayfield was deserted. The dark quiet beyond the fence seemed to have reached out to claim Mayfield as part of itself.

As I got out of the car, I glanced up toward the

well-lit intersection of Coventry and Mayfield, with its BP station, its bars, and its people. All of it bustled in the distance. From where I was, cloaked in the silence next to the cemetery, it looked like another world. They even seemed to have less snow up there.

I dashed across Mayfield, and up Lakeview's driveway, stopping at the gate. The gate was large and wrought iron, flanked by shorter fences. I walked to the right of the main gate, staring into the darkened foliage beyond the fence, and waited for the traffic on Mayfield to die off for a moment.

During a pause in the traffic, I took a step up and vaulted over the fence. The ease with which I did it—the fence was seven feet tall—surprised me. Somehow I was exploiting both the energy of my anger and of the fresh feeding.

God help anyone who harmed my daughter.

I came crashing down in the snow-covered mulch on the other side of the fence. I stood still for a time, listening for signs that someone had seen me cross the fence. I heard nothing. The snow absorbed the sounds of traffic.

I slipped through the naked winter bushes and into the cemetery. The sense of entering another world was complete. I stepped out into a word of naked trees, rolling snow-blanketed hills, and a total absence of people.

There were footprints here and there, where people had visited, or tended a grave. But, like the graves themselves—mostly marked only by blank humps of snow—the signs of people seemed distant and irrelevant when weighed against the omnipresent stillness.

The silence allowed it to sink in, what had happened. The worst of my fears, the fear that one day I would be hunting down someone's child only to discover the child was my own. My fears *had* been a self-fulfilling prophecy. I had brought all of this down upon us, and it wasn't hard to believe that my own anger was the only thing keeping the guilt from paralyzing me.

I followed the map as well as possible in the darkened cemetery. More than once my haste threw me down on an ice-slicked road. In my blind rush, when I did see a ghostly figure emerge from the woods, I had drawn my gun and almost shot before I realized who it was.

I held my gun upon the white-clad figure and stared for a moment before speaking.

"Gabriel," I said in a puff of fog.

"Indeed, sir. Now, Mr. Tyler, would you put aside that weapon."

"Give me a good reason."

"You try my good graces, sir. You're in no position to test me."

"Am I not?" My hand was shaking. "I had the impression I left whatever grace there was between us when I stepped out of your house."

"You try my patience, Mr. Tyler—"

I steadied my gun with both hands. "You pedantic, pretentious—You have about five seconds to explain why you're here or you'll feel what it's like to have a fifty-caliber bullet pass through that smug expression."

"You're threatening *me*?"

"It won't kill you, but I'm curious about what might happen to your motor skills."

"Mr. Tyler!"

I took a step forward, staring into Gabriel's eyes. They were closed and dead to me, almost opaque. Even so, I looked into them and poured all my anger into my words. "You're so fond of form. My chosen name is Raven."

Gabriel shook his head, "I don't believe I can accept you as a peer, sir."

"Fuck what you believe. Tell me what you're doing here, *now!*"

I don't know if it was the force of my anger, the threat of the gun, or the blessings of Jaguar, but Gabriel backed up.

"Don't you *dare* move," I shouted at him.

His glare raged with a fury mirroring my own, cold where mine was hot. "All right, Raven, ask me what you will."

"What are you doing here?"

"The same as I was doing when first I crossed your path. I felt the intensity of a feeding. I came to investigate."

"Looking for Childe?"

"Looking for Childe."

"Why?"

"Because he breaks the Covenant—"

I shook my head and felt a glare colder than the snow that soaked into my shoes. "Everyone looks for Childe. He's convenient, isn't he? No one seems to pay attention to the radical change in behavior his thralls have undergone. Or that he disappeared with his last recruit, the first person he's taken that anyone seems to have missed. Childe's been around too long for all this to happen at his hand."

"What are you implying?"

"Isn't it obvious? Childe's being set up. And at the very least you're looking the other way. At worst—"

"Mind your accusations. You do not know what you're dealing with."

I closed the distance between us and pressed the gun barrel to his temple as he had placed a sword against my neck. "You don't know who you're dealing with. My daughter is in the hands of those people. Childe, or the people who're scapegoating him. If I find you're involved, I will tear out your heart. What's down the hill?"

"Nothing you should concern yourself with." His face was remarkably calm.

"Let me be the judge of that."

"There's a young woman down there with a tale to tell."

Those words were enough to send me scrambling down the hillside, toward a fenced-off access road that led to my destination. "Don't pursue this," Gabriel called down after me. "Let Childe sink under the weight of his excesses."

I ignored him as I jumped over the gate blocking the snow-covered road. I didn't know what Gabriel was, but at the very least he acted like a cop who simply ignored inconvenient evidence. He disgusted me.

"You've made an enemy today," he called after me at last. I couldn't have cared less.

I ran down the road to a large bowl-shaped valley close to the center of Lakeview. I emerged on the floor of that valley. Towering to my left was the wide concrete face of the dam.

It was just as surreal as I remembered it, a wide slope of concrete hovering over a flat field of snow marred only by one paired set of footprints.

Near the base of the dam, opposite a tiny, snaking river escaping from its base, huddled a small hill next to the wall of the valley. The footprints pointed me directly at that hill.

As I'd remembered, mausoleums were set into the side of that hill. As I ran out onto the dam's flood-plain, following Gabriel's steps, I noticed no sign of graves on the field between me and the hill. The mausoleums down here had to predate the construction of the dam.

My memory of Cecilia's sacrifice kept replaying itself in my mind. I received no new insights, only more and more vivid shots of adrenaline. Little had changed down here, down to the blue-tinted moonlight.

I had to stop between a pair of barren trees, because it was the spot where I had seen Sebastian's daughter die—and perhaps be reborn. I was directly in front of the tomb from which I'd seen her emerge. Gabriel's footsteps led directly to the tomb's door. And so did others.

It was hard to tell, but where the flood-plain had been virgin except for Gabriel's footprints. Here, by the hill, there were signs of two, or maybe three other people walking around the site. I felt even more unease when I remembered why Gabriel said he had come here.

A feeding.

More footprints led to the mausoleum than left it.

This mausoleum seemed typical of the other half-dozen granite boxes set into the hillside around it. It had the same peaked temple roof supported by two polished granite pillars flanking the single door. The door was gated by a latticework of eroded green bronze. The only decorative carving on the tomb was an Egyptian sun-disk on the lintel above the door. I was certain that this was the place from which I'd seen Sebastian's daughter emerge.

What disturbed me was the fact that this tomb bore no name.

I glanced to the tombs to the left and to the right, "Forbes," on the one, and another name, illegible in shadow, on the other. The place I faced was unique. It must have been built just before the dam, just before they stopped using this place where the dearly departed could be washed away the next time they opened the sluice.

I glanced at the dam. Close as I was, it filled half the world, ground to sky, at an oblique angle. I felt as if I had fallen into a surrealist painting. Some element didn't belong here, the dam, the hill, the nameless tomb, myself. . . .

Not a place I'd chose to be buried. Not a place I'd choose to die.

I stared at the footprints leading to the door of the nameless mausoleum. I felt the same dread that I had felt when approaching Sam's bedroom.

It seemed an eternity before I had gathered the courage to walk up to the gate in front of the door. I stared in, past the green metal scrollwork, trying to see through the one window in the door beyond. The darkness was impenetrable, even to my sensitive eyes. The little windows set into the recessed door seemed to be painted black.

Just like the bedroom in Childe's apartment. Perhaps for the same reasons. It was easy to believe that all my answers lay beyond the bronze scrollwork in front of me. I listened for a few moments, trying to sense if anyone was here.

I let the silence hover a little longer than was comfortable. I felt alone. I hooked my fingers into the cold metal scrollwork, next to the lock, and pulled.

The gate flung open, unlocked. I expected the mechanism to protest more upon opening, but it glided open on well-oiled hinges.

I now faced a heavy, studded, wooden door.

I looked around and listened again. This time I heard something—

I backed, slightly, and began raising my gun. I wasn't quick enough. The door was yanked open from inside. A stench of rotting death billowed out, piercing the cold, worse than anything my gangrenous hand had emitted—the warm, wet smell of decayed meat.

The smell pushed me back like a fist. I saw the source of the smell and wondered if the gun was going to do me any good.

I saw its clothes first, maybe because I didn't want to see the rest of it. What I saw was typical teenage Gothic-punk. Black jeans, black T-shirt, black leather, black everything. At least everything *used* to be black.

Everything was torn, ragged, splattered with mud and darker filth.

It emerged into the moonlight, following its smell, a first-hand example of someone who did not wear vampirism well. Its hair was gone except for a few random patches. Feral red eyes burned inside sockets sunk into craters of tattered white flesh. Black sores pockmarked its skin. I saw tendons working through holes in its cheek and the backs of its hands. Fingernails and teeth were absurdly long.

It hissed like an angry cat.

I leveled my gun and tried to stare it down—a move that had been successful lately. But, behind those bloody eyes I didn't see much I could influence. And what was there was dedicated to being permanently pissed off.

The thing leaped at me, screaming something shrill and inarticulate. I ducked to the side just in time to avoid having a bite taken out of my left shoulder. I felt its hand brush by me. Its touch felt unclean.

Before I'd turned fully around, I felt claws rake across my left hip. I backpedaled and saw the thing trailing bloody pieces of my shirt and my jacket. It was fast.

It advanced toward me, a moving corruption.

I fired the Eagle. The zombie and I were connected for a microsecond by a tongue of flame, then it fell backward into the snow, a ragged hole kicked into its chest. Of course, it started getting up again. I walked closer and fired again, this time into his head. Its face caved in and chunks of skull blew into the snow. It stopped moving.

I knew, despite appearances, that I hadn't finished it off. Looks weren't anything. It had looked dead *before* I shot it, and I'd survived a bullet in the face myself.

Though, looking at the mess in the snow, I realized that the bullet *I'd* taken was not into the brain-case, and hadn't been fifty-caliber. From the look of things, at the very least I'd slowed it down a bit.

The mausoleum still hung open, behind me. I ran back up to it.

The first thing I saw, as my eyes adjusted to the gloom, was that Sebastian had left his spoor here, in the form of two dead soldiers. The two crumpled bodies cluttering the marble floor, dressed and armed as they were, were unlikely to have come from another source.

As Gabriel had said, a woman sat here. In the darkness I was allowed one momentary illusion. I almost whispered, "Gail!"

Then I saw through the shadows and saw the face of Cecilia, Sebastian's daughter. She didn't look as bad as the thing I'd pumped lead into—the corpses on the floor didn't look *that* bad—but she didn't look good.

She sat at the far end of the tomb, one of the corpses crumpled at her feet. She glared at me and demanded, "Who the fuck are you?"

Nice Catholic girl, I thought. I glanced at the bodies on the ground and said, "Someone who isn't working for your father." Saying that severed whatever ties I had left with Sebastian. It felt better than it should've.

"Like the last guy?"

I heard a rattle and as I stepped forward, over the first corpse. She was handcuffed to a wrought-iron bench set into the narrow far wall.

"Are you a cop?" she asked. "I told everything to the guy with the cane."

I bent over and rolled one of the dead men onto his back. I didn't know him, but the wound was familiar. His neck was half gone, the wound a black crater in the darkness. In one hand he clutched a rosary, in the other a thirty-eight. Neither appeared to have helped him much.

I picked up the rosary, which didn't seem to hold any special power. Maybe he hadn't gone to church enough.

"Who are you?" she repeated.

"Where're Childe's people? Where're the rest of his thralls?"

She shook her head. "I don't know what you're talking about."

I rolled over the second body, whose wounds were less severe, smaller, and just as fatal as the first's. Two generic hoods with the job of scouting locations for Dad. "How long ago?" I asked.

"What?"

"How long since you and the zombie feasted on these two?"

"I didn't—"

I knelt down in front of her. "No games. I know what you are. This guy has most of his neck, unlike the zombie's dinner. That, and you're pretty damn fresh for someone who hasn't had a drink for a long time. How long have you been here? Since Childe's little ritual? You should be starving."

"Stop it! Stop it!" She was crying, and I backed off. She looked down at her feet and whispered, "I was insane with it. Dominic—" she indicated the corpse "—was dead before I realized I knew him." She sobbed. "I've had to sit here with him for a whole day."

Sebastian had had over twenty-four hours to realize his hoods were missing. I looked back out the door. I could see the bloodless zombie out there on the ground, looking even more cadaverous and thin even though his chest had reconstructed itself.

In the distance I heard sirens. My gunshots had not gone unnoticed.

"You have a choice, Cecilia. I can leave you here for the cops, or I can take you, and you tell me what I want to know." I stared into her eyes, and I didn't know if it was vampiric persuasion or the unambiguous options that made her say, "Take me."

I holstered the Eagle, reached down, and pulled the handcuff chain apart.

27

Fortunately, I was able to lock the mausoleum shut on the corpses. I collected my brass and left zombie-boy where he was. I pulled Cecilia along, through the cemetery, without running across Gabriel again. And, despite the sirens, we reached the gate before any police showed themselves.

I pulled her over the fence and we dashed across Mayfield to the Chevette.

"Who was that he left guarding you?" I asked. I wanted her talking.

"Joey," she said. There was a long pause. "At least I think he's still Joey." Her voice was small and leeched of any of the earlier bravado. I suddenly felt for everything she was going through.

Despite the wave of empathy I felt, I had to remind myself that she was one of Childe's thralls now, which meant she was involved in whatever happened to my daughter. "How did Gabriel get by him?"

"Who?"

"The man with the cane."

"I don't know. He just looked at Joey, and Joey didn't move."

Rank hath its privileges. Apparently Gabriel had better luck staring down the opposition than I did. "I need you to tell me about him, and Childe's people."

She looked up at me, and I stopped next to the Chevette. I wanted her in the car. Her dress was gore-stained, black with dried blood, and I didn't want anyone to see her. "They have my daughter."

"I'm sorry," she said.

I opened the passenger door and set her in the car. "Talk to me."

"I met Joey once, before. . . ." She shivered. "I had no idea that would happen to him. He wasn't happy, even before all this. He thought he was a bad person," Cecilia said.

"He thought Childe was a bad person?"

"No, he thought *he* was, Joey. He saw himself as evil."

"So you knew these people a while before you ran away?" I made my way around to the driver's door of the Chevette. I was feeling strain from standing still. I wanted to wring Cecilia's neck, get her to tell me where they were *now*. But I knew pushing her might make her clam up, and I needed her talking.

"Friends," she said. "I thought they were friends. They aren't people."

Neither are we, Cecilia, I thought. "Go on about Joey."

"He started following Childe before I met him. I don't know what he was like before then. When Joey was in a good mood he would talk about what an evil bastard he was—saw himself as—about all the people he was angry at. When he was in a bad mood, he would sit and sulk. I think he amused Childe."

"Amused him?" I said as I slipped in and started the car. I didn't know how tight control between master and thrall was, but I felt that there was a good chance that this woman was directly under Childe's control. I was lucky she was volunteering information.

Whatever that control aspect was, my experience with my own influence, especially with Doctor Nicholson, seemed to be less absolute domination, and more of an erosion of the victim's will—or desire—to resist suggestions.

After being locked up with Joey, Cecilia probably didn't feel any excessive loyalty to Childe, or to Childe's thralls. If I was right about the way things worked, I could probably deal with her up until she met Childe again, and the domination reasserted itself.

"People amused Childe—" She shook her head. "I tried to leave him before. . . . Who are you?"

The sudden shift startled me. I was driving carefully, away from Lakeview, keeping an eye on the rearview mirror. "My name's Kane, Kane Tyler."

"Why is that name familiar?" She seemed to ask me and herself.

"I arrested your father once."

"You *are* a cop!"

"*Was,* a long time ago. I retired when a twelve-year-old blew a hole through my lung."

"Sorry," she whispered and touched my bicep. "Were you hurt badly?"

"I've been hurt worse since." I turned the wheel, more to escape her hand than to maneuver the car. Her touch made me uncomfortable. "You said you tried to leave Childe. Why didn't you?"

"He convinces you. That's what he does. He convinces you to do things, and once he does that, he owns you. Once you go with him, you can't go back; no one else would have you if they knew what he'd made you do."

"If someone forces you—"

"That's it. He doesn't force. Everyone's free to go, they just *can't.*" She bent over, palms pressing into her temples. "You can't imagine—" She stopped talking for a while, and just shook.

"I wanted to kill myself," she finally whispered. "You know why I didn't?"

"Why?"

"Because of what he has us do to the bodies."

Then, in a massive rambling lump, she let it all come pouring out.

Cecilia had been sucked into Childe's group because she was quite consciously searching for something diametrically opposed to her father's Catholicism. In a sense, for her, the neo-pagans that populated Cleveland Heights were just too good-natured for her.

In other words, she was exactly the kind of person Childe looked for. Childe pulled his followers to him by appealing to something evil.

Childe offered power to his followers, in return for their absolute slavery to him. Somehow the inherent contradiction of Childe's offer was overshadowed by his demonstration of blood-magick. His charisma was such, and his appeal so visceral, that no one who entered his inner circle ever left. He called himself Satan's agent on Earth, and the people he targeted were so alienated and nihilistic that such a proclamation was attractive, especially after Childe demonstrated the ability to transcend death.

Cecilia told me of a time when Childe offered a revolver and a box of ammunition to a doubter named Eric. Within a circle of twenty people, Eric loaded the revolver, and pumped off three rounds point-blank into Childe's chest. Childe's robes erupted with gore, and Cecilia remembered seeing, briefly, the walls of the wound going deep into Childe's chest. Childe smiled, took the gun, and fired a single round into Eric's head.

Eric had not taken Childe's sacrament; Eric died. After that demonstration, it was easy for Childe to order his followers to descend on Eric and feed—even those who had not yet become his thralls.

The pattern Cecilia related was common for all of Childe's followers. He would pull the victim in, gradually force the person to sever all ties to family and friends outside the group, show some demonstration of power, and slowly pull the person into steadily more degrading acts. Each event would increase Childe's power over the individual, until, by the time Childe decided to take the final step and grant his own blood to the victim, the person was already psychologically enslaved.

According to her, she had been locked in that mausoleum for two and a half weeks prior to the ceremony. She only had water. She was nearly driven mad by hunger and isolation—but Childe had done enough of a job on her to keep her from crying out.

When they opened the door for her, she had no choice but to walk out. But according to her, after the door opened, she had no memory until waking up, inside the tomb, with the zombie.

There were things in her story that didn't ring true. There's a difference in the way people tell their stories. And when I listen I can tell the difference between someone who's telling me something for the first time, and someone who's rehearsed. The pauses are more conscious. There's more awareness of the audience. I can see the words flow by as if by rote.

It doesn't matter how emotional or inarticulate a person is, I can see when they know the next word they're going to say. I suppose it was all those times hearing the difference between what people said during interrogation, and what they said on the stand after being rehearsed by their lawyer.

Listening to Cecilia made me wonder if she had been talking to a public defender.

But I had other worries. "So where can I find them?" I asked.

"You don't want to find them."

I slammed on the brakes and skidded the Chevette to the side of the road. Clouds had rolled over the moon, and a light snowfall was captured by the streetlights in front of me. Cecilia was curled up in her spattered, ragged, dress, staring at her lap.

"They have my daughter!" I shouted.

She winced and I softened my voice as much as I was able. "Cecilia, I *need* to find her."

"Too powerful. . . ." she whispered. I had to struggle to keep from grabbing and shaking her.

After the silence became too long, I said, "Lead me somewhere she might be, Cecilia."

She nodded. "I can't go in with you. You can't make me face him."

I placed a hand on her shoulder. "I wouldn't make you do that."

Slowly, very slowly, she said, "There's a house where he kept us—"

The house was in East Cleveland, on the economic downslope from the hills of Lakeview. I was expecting her to lead me to something a little less mundane. Instead, I pulled up across the street from a three-story brick duplex that had seen better days. The yard was fenced-in chain-link, the gutters were sagging, and I saw a few major dips in the roof. All the windows were dark, and in the sodium glow of the street lamps, I could see newspaper covering the insides of most of them.

"There?" I asked, looking at the dead windows.

Cecilia nodded without looking at the house. "Don't make me go in there," she whispered.

To me, the house looked empty. At least it was a hell of a lot emptier than its neighbors. There was loud rap music from at least two nearby houses. Lights blared from a party on our side of the street. Teenagers were crossing the street from house to house, ignoring the snow, ignoring us.

The clock on the dash read 1:30. The house across

the street loomed in silence like a tooth missing from a smile. I looked at Cecilia.

She looked terrified. I could feel the waves of emotion from her even without looking in her eyes. While that sixth sense felt the warm tide of fear, an older sense—a gut instinct that had hung with me ever since I was on the force—smelled a setup.

They had tied Cecilia out there for someone. Sebastian maybe. Maybe me.

I'd been able to bust the handcuff chain with no problem. If she had fed recently, wouldn't she be capable of a similar feat? Why had Gabriel left her there?

"What did you tell the man with the cane? What did you tell him that you haven't told me?"

"Nothing else," she whispered.

I wondered if that meant Gabriel was here. It was probably a mistake, but I couldn't gamble with my daughter's life. Still, I was second-guessing myself even as I said, "Don't leave the car."

I locked the Chevette behind me, leaving her curled up and hidden behind the snow-dusted windows. I stepped out into the slush in the middle of the road and looked around me.

It was so damn *normal*—obnoxious teenagers drinking, partying, and playing loud music. Change the black kids to white, and the rap music to neo-punk grunge, and this could be *my* neighborhood. The alienation I felt from that normalcy was crippling.

I walked to the one empty house, conscious of exactly how quiet it was. I was figuring geography in my head as I stepped through the snow-covered, carless driveway, so I wasn't surprised to see the rusty fence at the rear of the house, the woods beyond it, or the fresh-cut hole in the chain-link.

The ends of the cut wire were shiny, and fresh tracks marred the snow in a path between it and the rear door of the house. Too many tracks to tell if the most recent were coming or going.

It had taken me a while to figure, but it was clear to me now that this property bordered on Lakeview. Beyond that fence was part of the cemetery. Lakeview was a huge suburb of the dead, bordering Cleveland Heights and East Cleveland, as well as Cleveland proper.

Of course Childe would own a house that bordered on the cemetery's property. The question in my mind was, *was anyone home?*

The house gave no clue. It was silent and dark, most of the first-floor windows covered by wood or newspaper from the inside. If it weren't for the glittering wound in the rusty fence, and the trail at least as fresh as the last snowfall, it would appear totally abandoned.

I looked to the lighted yards on either side of this one, and saw no one watching me. I drew the Eagle and walked to the back door of Childe's house.

I tried the door. It was locked. I slowly leaned on it, forcing my shoulder between the lock side of the window and the doorjamb. I thrust with my legs, concentrating on using whatever paranormal strength I had.

The dead-bolt gave with surprising ease. Dry-rot showered me as the wood of the jamb gave. The lock broke as I'd wanted it to, with a bare snap. It didn't look or sound as if I had kicked the door in.

A metal object glimmered a moment, and I caught it with my left hand before it clattered to the ground. It was the half of the dead-bolt that I'd torn loose from the wall, screws and all. I pocketed it to avoid making any more noise.

I listened at the doorway for movement inside. I could sense some dim life—not heard, but felt as a dim wave of barely conscious emotion. The only thing I *heard* was the loud music next door.

I slipped in and shut the door behind me.

I found myself in the rear stairwell of a two-family home. Stairs before me led down into an ink-black basement. The stairs up led to the rear of the first floor apartment.

Where first?

I wanted to follow the impression of life I felt upstairs; it could be Gail. But I had a long instinct for not leaving my backside exposed. I descended into the basement, going slowly down the stairs to give my eyes a chance to adjust. Even my extreme night vision had problems seeing in the near-absolute darkness.

I held the Eagle before me, and before I made it halfway, I could smell the blood. At the foot of the stairs I had to pause for a long time before I could understand exactly what I saw.

At first all I saw was an abstract pattern of shapes piled against the cinder-block walls. I saw blotches of shadow, and deeper shadow, and oblong and round patches that rose out of the shadow. My gaze locked on a circular patch of off-white formed of symmetrical shadows.

I must have stared for at least half a minute before I realized I was looking at a skull, jawless and upside down, perched on top of a pile of other remains.

It was the same conceptual shift I remember from those optical illusions where suddenly a vase becomes a pair of faces. Suddenly I saw the random shadows as bones from maybe half a dozen human beings. Other piles resolved into scattered piles of sneakers and jeans.

I stopped breathing.

Blood dotted the walls like rust-stains. Odd bits of clothing, reduced to rags, were scattered everywhere. Ragged lumps of bone lay here and there. Most appeared to have been gnawed.

I began to see movement in the piles of remains, and

I nearly shot, before I saw a fleshy patch-furred thing trailing a naked tail.

Rats.

If I concentrated, I could hear their claws scratching on the concrete. They followed the edges of the basement, scratching and gnawing. But I saw them now, dead-eyed things, the smallest the size of my fist.

Central to the basement, extending the width of the room between the sinks and the rusted-out water-heater, was a table. I saw the stains, the marks, and the chains meant to restrain. I was overcome with memory.

The stains form a vaguely cruciform outline on the dining room table. Markings by the police give it a human shape. The table is scarred, knives perhaps, maybe even claws. I see wires that could have bound legs and arms. Some of the strings lead up to bloodstains on the ceiling.

The table was the same here, the same as the dining room where Kate had been killed. It served the same purpose, for many more people. A deep rage filled me, and fear for my daughter that bordered on agony.

28

As I ascended to the first floor, the air warmed, freeing something dead in the air. I bent close to the door on the landing and listened for movement. I heard the scratching of rats below me, the music blaring outside, little more. I stood for a few long moments, before I reached for the doorknob.

The knob spun loosely in its socket. I pulled gently. It slid out of the door. The door creaked open a fraction, and in the crack I saw a slice of the kitchen.

The scrabbling of rats continued, and the smell grew worse.

I pushed the door open with my foot, keeping the Eagle leveled at the dark kitchen. A rat the size of a brick exploded out of a pile of garbage by the door, shooting between my legs.

I froze, listening for reaction from the rest of the house. Nothing but the sound of music blaring outside and rats scratching inside the walls.

Yellowed newspaper sealed the kitchen's one window, filtering the only light. Piles of garbage, mostly clothing, covered cracked linoleum. The refrigerator, doorless, gaped at me, revealing an interior splattered with black stains. There was no stove.

I dropped the doorknob in the filth choking the sink, and inched deeper inside.

The place was empty, but I counted a half-dozen mattresses in the two bedrooms, where the windows were painted black. The walls in the living and dining rooms were covered with writing, or symbols, or something. Predictably, the marks were written in blood.

The bathroom was where most of the smell was coming from.

I dreaded approaching that place, but when I came near enough I realized that, whatever it was in there, it had been there since long before Gail had disappeared. It hung from a pair of handcuffs to the rear, over the bathtub. It was vaguely humanoid, and quite dead. About half of it had spilled into the bathtub.

The fact that it wasn't Gail was faint reassurance. The deeper into this place I walked, the more the fear gripped me. I backed out of there quickly, and retreated for the stairs.

I could feel that more was here besides me and the rats. What I felt came from upstairs. I mounted the steps, climbing to the second floor. I expected more of the same.

I was wrong, very wrong.

The first sign was that the door was locked. It wasn't a great lock, it broke when I put my shoulder to the door—but just the fact that the door was locked at all was a signal that the upstairs was different.

After the door broke, a security chain went with it, swinging and jingling as the door rebounded off of the wall.

I stood there, the Eagle covering a relatively clean kitchen with refrigerator, stove, and empty sink, and I listened. This time I heard more than scratching rats and Dr. Dre lyrics in the background. I heard a high-pitched whine. . . .

The sound stopped me in my tracks. It was something that might have come from a leaky radiator. It had the same weak breathless quality. But the tone of that sound struck me on an entirely different level, something that tore at the bowels, that made me want to curl up into a ball and shake.

The sound did not end. It droned on and on and on—

I thought of Gail and my stomach tied into a hard little knot. It was that thought that gave me the courage to move. The thought ran over and over in my head, *I woke something up.*

The doorway between the kitchen and the dining room was blocked by a heavy red drape. The sound came from beyond that. I steeled myself, and pushed it aside with my gun.

It was as if I had left this century and entered the previous one. I entered a twisted parody of Childe's apartment. The walls had been knocked out, down to the structural supports. Most of the second floor was now a giant velvet-draped space. Candles guttered everywhere, and threadbare Victorian furniture weighted stacks of balding oriental carpeting. Incense fogged the air, barely covering the smell of rot.

And over that, came that whine.

Ahead of me, across a room furnished from a nineteenth-century garbage heap, was a trunk, or a table, concealed underneath a tasseled red cover. Gold thread had come loose from the cover, leaving random stitches as almost-comprehensible hieroglyphs.

I took a step and I saw one of the tassels move.

That sound, an exhausted anguished cry, came from under that cover. And something underneath it was moving.

"Gail?" I whispered so low that I didn't hear my own voice.

Whatever the covered object was, it was set so its top was at waist height. It was at least seven feet long, maybe a yard wide. I approached it, hands shaking, feeling perspiration for the first time since the sewer.

I saw that the object was not perfectly flat. The edges were higher than the center, some sort of frame . . .

Within a foot the smell was almost intolerable. Not just from the incense-burning braziers that flanked this thing, but from the rot the incense was trying to cover.

The sound died. It didn't trail off so much as sever itself. Something pushed the red cover, brushing it slightly from underneath. It was a weak motion, and only the thought of Gail kept me from backing away.

I lightly tugged the cover away from the rectangular object. It only took a slight tug before the cover slid off under its own weight.

The object uncovered was as much a discard from the last century as the rest of the room. But it belonged in a insane asylum, or a torture chamber.

I reeled from the box, as the thing inside began keening again.

It was a flat cage of wood and iron, two feet by three feet by seven. The box sat, like an offering, on an antique table supported by a set of cracked jade dragons. The creature imprisoned within could not move more than a few inches in any direction.

It wasn't my daughter; the thing inside that cage had been trapped for much longer. . . .

Exposed, the thing within began thrashing and jerking, screaming louder. It was naked, and reduced to nearly a skeleton. Ragged holes were worn in its flesh, and the skin in its face had tightened to form a rictus grin. The eyes had sunken too deep in the skull for me to see more than shadowed holes. Its teeth were fangs, and its fingers formed six-inch claws—

I kept backing away from it.

It shook as if having a seizure, the claws on its hands slashing its sides. As I watched, the wounds tried to heal, seal themselves shut. However, the flesh would fester and boil instead, and leave another crater in its skin.

I had retreated all the way to the kitchen door when the caged thing arched its back and tore at a gaping wound that scarred most of its shriveled abdomen.

It screamed as it sank claws into its gut, and when its hand withdrew and slapped against the bars, it dropped something that fell through the bars and to the carpet. It was a rat, coat slick and black. It scurried off into the darkness to join its brethren.

I wanted to vomit.

The imprisoned thing sank into quiescence, not breathing, not moving, as silent as a corpse. Just looking at it made me feel filthy. Who would do this, to anyone? To *anything?*

I took a step forward, and it didn't move.

I walked back up to the cage. The creature was as physically devastated as a mummy. It was nearly impossible to determine sex—determining age was hopeless.

When I reached its side, the flesh the rat had fed upon had aged to match the other old sores that perforated its flesh. The motionlessness was so complete that it was hard to believe that I wasn't looking at an inert corpse.

"Raven?"

I jumped at the breathy whisper. It shocked me badly enough that I nearly put a bullet through the cage.

"*I see your name.*" It slowly turned its head, eyes burning red in its deep sockets. The voice was weak, paper thin, and it terrified me. I leveled the Eagle, aiming between those red eyes, but I didn't fire.

My hands shook.

"*Let us sup, you and I,*" it said. I felt gore-spotted talons clawing into my mind. I could feel its will pulling me down toward it.

Strength, I thought.

"No," I whispered, raising my gun and tearing my eyes away from the gaze of that thing.

"Sate my hunger and I will be yours," it whispered. I kept backing away, into the kitchen. I was relieved when I finally slipped away from that thing. There was something very special about that creature in the cage—

Before I had enough distance to think, I was interrupted by the sound of voices outside, behind the house. The thing in the cage must have heard them, too, because I heard something that might have been a laugh. The sound it made was little more than a whispery cough, but there was a malignant humor woven into it, a weight of malicious unreason.

It was hard to retreat into the stairwell. The corpse-thing pulled attention to itself, even when it had receded from view. It was hard to concentrate on anything else, knowing it was there.

The voices behind the house were close enough to be intelligible over the music blaring next door. It was the hard rhythm of gangster rap more than the voices that pulled me back into the present.

"—the fuck's the matter with Joey, man?" The voice was fast, high-pitched. It came from almost directly under my feet and I edged up next to the window across the landing from the kitchen door.

"Wake up, Joey. Say something!" Female voice, deeper, rougher than the first. When I was next to the window, I peeled some yellowing newsprint away from the window, so I could see down into the yard. The paper came away in a shower of dead flies.

I saw six figures, struggling along the path between the back door and the cemetery. They were half-dragging a bald man with staring eyes.

"What, Hel? Like Joey said anything before? We had to lock him up, remember?" This was another woman, back to me, who was leading the bald guy by the arm.

"Shut up!" Said the first female voice. There was a paleness to that woman, to all of them except the bald guy, more than makeup could account for. Their skin was near-translucent. Hel's skin was white enough to make her lips appear black by contrast.

Everyone's hair was black as well, again, except for the bald guy. The bald one was dressed in the same Goth-punk outfit as the rest of them, but rattier, mud-spattered.

It wasn't until they were close enough for me to see the hole blown in his shirt that I realized that I was looking at zombie-boy. That shocked the hell out of me, because there wasn't any of the leprous rot on him anymore. He wasn't even pale, like his escorts. Joey's skin was now smooth, pink, and as blemish-free as a baby's. I didn't see a speck of hair, or a sign of the bullet holes I had put into him.

However, his eyes were as blank as a dead television set. He stared straight ahead, being led by his fellows, showing no sign of anyone at home.

"We *are* vulnerable," I whispered. I had shot this guy in the head and all the mechanical damage, even to the brain tissue, had regenerated. The mind, it seemed, had not.

I swallowed, thinking about what would have happened to me had the late detective fired an inch or two higher into my face. I'd be dealing with more than a little amnesia.

However, the fact that the body had returned to a state healthier than when I had shot him, that I had trouble figuring.

I had two choices—run for it, or force a confrontation.

With Gail missing, I had one choice. The Eagle didn't counterbalance being outnumbered like this, but these were the beings responsible for the disappearance of my daughter, more so than Childe—whose fate I was only now beginning to comprehend.

I didn't want to meet with the cage-thing again, so I started down the stairs for the first-floor apartment. I listened to the two women argue over Joey as I ran down two flights of stairs. "Joey's nuts, Hel."

"Shut up. We'll get him better—we're promised that much."

"Yeah, for sitting on the missing newbie. Did you forg—"

"Shut up!"

I had reached the landing behind the kitchen door on the first floor when I heard a new male voice say. "Girls, we've got a problem." With the voice, I heard the rear door creak open. It was a voice I had heard before, from the rear of Sam's car, and Childe's answering machine tape.

I braced the Eagle in both hands as I approached the landing.

I heard one whisper from the woman who wasn't Hel. "Stace, stay with the geek." Then the voices silenced themselves.

The shadow from the door below slid by the wall next to me. I backed to the far corner from the door and tried to become part of the shadows. My Eagle was focused down the flight, toward the back door. Next door, amplification distorted a voice rapping about natural-born killers.

Three figures slipped into the stairwell. Even in the dark, the albino skin on the trio lifted their images out of the shadows. The clothing they wore faded into the blackness, making their heads and hands gray and disembodied.

The one in the lead, the male, looked directly toward me and said, "So what the fuck's this?" It was eerie to see this guy close up. He looked like someone playing at being undead, someone who could blend in with all the other teenagers who'd read Anne Rice once too many times. However, at this distance it was obvious that the pale skin wasn't makeup. I could see the shadow of his veins weaving under the surface. The vivid mouth could have been lipstick, but I suspected a play-actor would have chosen pure black or red, and not a shade exactly the color of clotted blood.

"Where is my daughter," I said to him.

The guy laughed. "You don't know what the fuck you're doing, do you?"

I kept my gun leveled at him. "Neither do you. I'm supposed to be dead, remember? *Where is she?*"

I looked past him at the two women. One, with hair long and black, was wearing a floor-length dress that looked extremely impractical for anything other than hiding bloodstains. The woman next to her was more punk than Goth. She had shaved the sides of her head, and wore about a pound of jewelry through various holes in her face. Like the lead guy, she wore a studded motorcycle jacket, self-consciously abused black denim, and a pair of Doc Martens.

Thirty years ago, Childe's disciples probably wore tie-dyed peasant shirts, granny-glasses and love beads.

The guy took a step forward, up the center of the stairwell. The two women slid to the walls and followed, a foot or so behind him. The punked-out girl was giving me a hungry, long-toothed smile.

"I'd stay where you are," I said.

The guy shook his head. "That gun can't do anything to us."

It was my turn to smile. These kids were more ignorant than I was. "Joey would tell you different if he could still talk."

Hel screamed and leaped toward me, and I would have put a bullet through her if the guy hadn't blocked her. Punk-woman was no longer smiling.

"I don't believe you," he said, his words slurring a bit behind a long grimace.

I felt a shriveling in my gut as I realized I was watching them change. Their skulls were shifting, favoring an inhumanly long jawline and carnivorous teeth. Their nails were lengthening, turning into black claws. The punk one was turning into a pierced version of the vampire from that silent German film, *Nosferatu*.

The moment I noticed, I could feel the skin in my face tightening in sympathy.

"A slug through the brain," I said. "The nerve tissue might grow back, but I doubt it knits into anything really complex."

He took another step, and Hel was pushing to get by him. Her eyes had gone blood-red with fury. She snarled like an animal, her skin had gone gray and twisted, and her skull was forming a muzzle.

"Stop!" I put what will I could into the word. I tried to force down the trio with my stare, as I had tried with Joey. I pushed, but with the three of them it was barely enough to force a pause in their advance. "I took third in marksmanship. I'll drop one of you, probably two, before you reach me."

They stopped advancing; even Hel stopped snarling for a moment.

"Where's my daughter?" I said.

"You know where she is, Kane." His voice had become high and hissing. Where Hel was changing into something animalistic, he was turning into something demonic. His forehead had distorted into a shape that suggested a crest and horns.

"Where's Gail?" I yelled at them. My own voice was slurring, my tongue was too thick in an oddly formed mouth.

There was something wrong. The demon laughed and I realized that it wasn't my will forcing them back. They were waiting for something.

It struck me all at once. There'd been six of them. Joey was guarded by someone out back. Werewolf, Demon and Nosferatu were in the stairwell with me—

Where was the last vampire?

I tensed, expecting it, and when the door to the kitchen exploded open, I fired the Eagle into the Demon's face before I began turning. I was tackled by a punk nightmare before I finished my movement. I had a visceral glimpse of chain and leather, then my back slammed into the wall, crushing plaster and splintering lathe. Claws pierced the wrist of my gun hand, pinning it to the frame of the window next to me.

More claws pierced my abdomen, just above the groin. I felt its hand slam against my spine in a white-hot explosion of pain.

My vision fogged red. I watched its face, which seemed small and distant through the pain, despite being an inch away from mine. He was somewhere between Nosferatu and the Demon, ugly, but still vaguely human. Even more jewelry hung off his face than the other punks. Rings and chains jingled, almost touching my face.

Its jaw levered open, revealing carnivore teeth in a waft of carrion breath. One gold tooth remained disturbingly human.

I forced myself to move through the shock. I reached up to push its face away with my left hand, and found myself with my hands on a chain that dangled between its right ear and the bony ridge that used to be a nose. I yanked to the left, toward the wall next to me.

The chain came free of the ear instantly, it seemed, and its jaw snapped shut short of my neck. Its nose was more durable, especially with the cartilage that seemed to have grown around the end of the chain.

Its head snapped to the side, following the chain, slamming into the wall, going through the plaster. Its hands fell away from my gut and my wrist.

I stumbled back, away from everything, up the stairs toward the second floor. I faced down the stairs, leveling the Eagle two-handed as the flesh knitted on stomach and my wrist.

I heard Hel before I saw her—a feral growl to my right, behind the wall separating the stairwells. I'd stumbled halfway to the landing above when the growling thing rounded the wall into view. Whatever it was, it was no longer even vaguely human. It was wolflike, a wolf with sickle claws and sharklike teeth. It loped toward me, clumsily, on all fours.

The Eagle barked in my hand, drowning the thing's growls. The kick from the gun slammed spikes of pain into my still-healing wrist. The wolf-thing was close enough to the muzzle-flash that I smelled its coarse fur smolder.

The shot took out a chunk of its shoulder above the left foreleg. It tumbled backwards into the punk I'd slammed into the plaster, who was just now unwedging itself. They both tumbled into a heap under the window on the landing below me.

I scrambled up on the landing behind me, my gut leaking despite my body's efforts to repair itself.

My ears still rang from the gunfire as Nosferatu rounded the corner. She was still recognizable, even with the long clawed fingers and the vast forehead, and that made the transformation seem even worse.

I realized I was snarling as badly as the wolf, and my remade hands were making it difficult to keep the gun level.

What the hell have I turned into?

Nosferatu looked up at me and held a hand back, gesturing her tangled comrades still. *"Everyone chill the fuck out!"*

Amazingly, her voice was unchanged, despite the radical dental work her front teeth had undergone. Everyone stopped moving. I was grateful for the pause, because I could feel parts of my stomach moving around by themselves.

"Now what?" I asked, keeping the gun leveled at her skull. I had to lean against the wall to keep my hands steady. It was a standoff, and they knew it. I was pretty sure they could take me, but only with a high cost. The trio gathered at the foot of the second stairwell; it was just wide enough for two of them to rush me.

No sign of the demon, or the one guarding Joey.

That one must have heard the shots, and I was worried about being blindsided again. I was next to another window on this landing, facing the driveway. I tried to keep an eye on it, as well as the half of the stairwell going up to the second floor. I was too exposed where I was, but I couldn't keep retreating upward without losing sight of the vampires below me.

"You better put the gun down, Kane," Nosferatu finally said. "You aren't getting out of here." I felt a dominating pressure behind the words, but it was almost perfunctory. It didn't even compare to the thing in the cage, much less the one glimpse of real power I had seen in Jaguar.

"My chosen name is Raven." I smiled, which felt odd with my altered jawline.

"You're outnumbered, in our domain. You belong to us—"

I shook my head. "It doesn't work like that. Your horned friend might have chewed on my neck, but I took nothing from him. I own my own blood." I shook my head. "Nothing here belongs to you. It all belongs to your master."

I felt a wave of contempt wash up the stairwell. I couldn't tell which of the three it was coming from, or if it was inner- or outer-directed.

"To our master, then—"

"No one's my master." I slurred my speech, but it was becoming easier to talk. I was getting used to the shape of my jaw, which was good, since no one seemed to be changing back. I hoped that it was related to stress, and I wasn't stuck as whatever I was now.

"That can change." Nosferatu had slipped easily into the spokesman role. I suspected she wasn't that unhappy that demon-boy had taken a bullet in the face.

The thought reminded me of Joey and his keeper. Where were they? For that matter, what about Cecilia? If she had any brains, she'd run for it, or had swiped the Chevette.

"We can take you, Kane."

"The Covenant would frown on my death—"

She chuckled. "Let Childe bear that responsibility, as he's borne so much else."

"Would it frown on the destruction of thralls that go to such effort to flout it?" I leveled the gun. "Anyone who stands between me and my daughter is going to die."

Hel growled, and the punk fondled the loose end of his nose-chain and looked bloodthirsty. Nosferatu smiled up at me with her surreal teeth. The ring piercing her lip glinted red. "That would be painful for both sides, more so than you think." The glint vanished as she spoke. "Surrender to my master's authority and I think we can avoid the pain. Both to you, and your Gail."

"What master is that? Childe, if he is that thing upstairs, appears no master at all."

The red glint had moved to the ring through her eyebrow as she laughed. "Childe? He's no longer my master—"

The glint had drawn my gaze to the window on the landing below. Like most of the windows, it was covered with newspaper. Enough had torn away in the scuffle for someone to see in, if they were in the right spot. As she spoke, I saw a tiny dot of red laser light track across some of the newsprint—

"Get down!" I yelled, a fraction too late.

The window exploded inward as a gunshot blew the contents of Nosferatu's elongated skull out the left side of her face. I never heard the shot.

29

I ran for it. I dashed up the stairs, holding the hole in my gut to keep from tearing open the just-healed wound. I heard growling behind me, and the sound of breaking glass. From somewhere I heard someone kicking in a door.

I passed by the door to the second-floor kitchen and heard a whispery laughing from beyond it. I kept going because I had no desire to confront the thing in the cage.

I shouldered through the door to the attic, dodging past the window on the landing, giving the sniper as little profile as possible. I was lucky. The window exploded, throwing glass, newspaper tatters, and dead flies across the landing, but only after I'd passed.

I smelled something bad upstairs, but the sounds of chaos below continued to drive me upward.

I ran up into a huge peaked space running the length of the house. Above were naked, uninsulated rafters, covering a floor of loose gray planking. The space was lit by bluish moonlight from the rear window, and the yellow sodium streetlight from the front window. Neither window had glass or newspaper, and the wind blew wisps of snow through the attic.

Staring at me, from places in the eaves, between the beams supporting the roof, were small white faces. There were a dozen children up here, dirty-faced, pale, and looking at me with a feral stare that was becoming too familiar.

None of them looked older than thirteen, and half were naked and nearly as bony as the thing in the cage. The smell up here was appalling, and there was no incense to cover it.

Seeing kids up there filled me with a mixture of horror and pity. The force of the emotion slammed against the panic driving me, striking me still where I stood.

The children did not move, but they watched, and from their combined stares I felt a pressure akin to what I felt when that caged thing spoke to me. I heard the thing's laughter from behind me, and it finally pushed me forward.

I advanced, slowly, toward the front of the house, becoming aware of how most of the beams up here bore the scars of claw marks. Gunshots and screams came from below, and I no longer heard rap music in the background.

The whispery laugh followed me to the window.

I kept an eye on the children; the sight of them was a weight in my gut. I edged to the window in the front of the house. I took a quick look out, too quick for anyone to get a shot off at me.

What I saw, however, was enough. I saw four cars pulled up down there, and one was a familiar-looking Oldsmobile. I also saw my Chevette, empty, with the passenger door hanging open. Sebastian was as good as his word. He was taking his revenge on the people who had taken his daughter. On Childe. He was going to save his daughter's soul.

I felt the growing weight of my own guilt. Not only had I drawn my own daughter into this mess, I had led Sebastian to his daughter—and he was going to kill her, unless she had had the sense to run for it.

I had to get out of here and find Gail. She wasn't here with Childe's thralls. Where was she, then?

"You know where she is," he said.

What had he meant by that?

"You are not of the other?" I spun around at the voice, and found myself leveling my Eagle at a naked six-year-old girl. At least, she looked like a six-year-old girl, except for her eyes.

"The other?" I stammered, unsure where to point my gun.

"The one who keeps our master from us," said a scrawny ten-year-old.

I shook my head, unsure of what they were talking about. I was shaking from the enormity of everything. They were *children.*

"We are bound here twice," said another child's voice.

"Once to master."

"Once to other."

There were more screams from the first floor. Diving out the window was looking more and more attractive. These children frightened me worse than the chaos below me, almost as much as the caged thing. And there was the porch roof one floor below me. I'd made worse jumps. I rubbed the wound on my gut. The skin felt raw, but intact.

The kids were all talking at me, their words running together as if they were one person speaking.

"Are you here to free master?"

"Or kill him?"

"Who do you bring?"

"Who do you serve?"

"Will you free us from master?"

"Or other?"

"One must die now."

Their words pressed me against the wall, even though none of them took a step toward me. The assault was verbal, but there was a psychic pressure behind the words to the point where I wasn't even sure I was *hearing* their voices, in the normal sense of the word.

"Stop it!" I yelled, with all the force I could muster.

The babble ceased, and I heard movement below me. Someone was walking on the second floor. Dimly I heard a voice. "Shit, what the fuck is that?"

"Gimme that cross," said another voice. The whispery laughter below had ceased. In its place I heard that same paper-thin voice say, *"Come."*

That one word filled me with dread, despite the fact that it wasn't addressed to me.

"Come," the whisper repeated, an undeniable force behind the voice.

The children, all of them, turned away from me, toward the stairs at the rear of the attic. "Master," said the one nearest me. There was reverence in that voice.

Below me I heard a panicked voice saying, "Murphy, what the fuck are you—get the fuck away from— *SHIT!*"

There was an agonized liquid scream, and three rapid gunshots.

The children began slowly walking toward the stairwell. "He will come."

"Free us from the other."

The kids had begun another monotone babbling. I missed most of it because someone downstairs was putting shots through the floor. Two boards too close to me exploded outward, exposing splintered bullet holes shafted with candlelight from below.

The laugh was back. It no longer sounded like the laugh from a corpse. It was loud, vulgar, unashamed. The man with the gun was screaming something incoherent. It took a moment, between the gunshots, to realize that it was the twenty-third psalm.

"Yea, though I walk through the valley of the shadow of death!—" *Blam!* "—fear no evil: for Thou *art* with—" *Blam!* "—rod and Thy staff they comfort me—"

His voice was choked off, and there were no further

gunshots. The laughter ceased, and was replaced by a wet sucking sound.

I shuddered, and one of the children standing around the head of the stairs turned to face me. "He will wish to see you, Raven. He will come to free us from the other."

That monotone sentence still hung in the air when I heard the sound of fabric tearing, glass breaking, and wood cracking apart. I looked out the window, below me, in time to see a body tumble onto the porch's roof. The parts of the corpse I saw were completely dessicated, shriveled to the bone. Its neck hung open, and it left red tracks in the snow as it rolled off the roof to the right, into the driveway.

It had been thrown through the window below mine, and tatters of red velvet drapery and newspaper were still floating to the ground in the front yard. A gold cross glinted in the snow.

If I wanted to move, I had to do it now. I jumped though the glassless window, to the roof of the porch below. I bent my knees as I hit, keeping the gun away from me. The impact shuddered my body, but no bones broke, and my abdomen didn't split open—though it felt as if it wanted to.

I rolled twice, to the left, slowing. I was just about to jump to my feet when I ran out of roof. There was a sickening lurch as I went into free fall above the driveway of the next house. I fell five feet onto a car below me.

The car's roof caved in with the impact. Safety-glass exploded underneath me. I froze for a second or two, as the pain of the collision washed through my body and evaporated. The car's owners, occupants of the neighboring house, were nowhere to be seen. They had vanished with their music.

I forced myself up, out of the concave roof, and the

hood below my feet dimpled with a bullet's impact.
The sniper was still out there.

I rolled off of the roof, scrambling to my feet, and
ran through the snow in front of the house. The sniper
had to be behind the house, somewhere in the cemetery, and Childe's house offered the best cover I had—

As I ran, I almost collided with more of Sebastian's
thugs, running out the front of the house. I raised my
gun, but they barely paid attention to me as they beat a
panicked retreat. There were four of them, and two
were busy carrying a wounded comrade.

They piled into an illegally parked Dodge, which
began accelerating away before the doors were shut.

I ran for the Chevette, thinking, *Did I black out for a
moment? All the damn cars are gone.*

From the looks of it, every one of the cars had pulled
way at top speed. Snow had been sprayed across the
side of the Chevette.

"What the fuck did you do to her!" I yelled at the
now empty street. The Chevette was empty; the passenger door hung open with a shattered window. I was
filled with a futile rage at Sebastian and Childe, and I
didn't know if I was screaming for Cecilia, Gail, or the
six-year-old girl in the attic.

When did those bastards catch up with me?

I looked up, the car between me and Childe's house.
Standing in the attic window was a naked man. He had
a Van Dyke beard and shoulder-length hair that blew in
the biting wind. He was soaked in blood from the neck
down. The face he wore belonged to the pictures I had
seen of Manuel Deité.

He saw me looking, and smiled. . . .

Small forms were darting about in the shadows
around the house, larger than rats.

I dove into the Chevette, fear gripping my chest. I
fumbled the ignition and accelerated away without
looking at the house again.

* * *

I raced the Chevette through night-empty streets. I had blown it. I was furious with myself, mad enough that I was halfway to Shaker before my body reasserted its normal appearance. I had led Sebastian's people straight to Childe's house.

Hadn't I?

I had a gut suspicion that the whole scene was staged, from act one up to Sebastian's untimely arrival. I thought of Cecilia's story, her convenient imprisonment on the site of the sacrifice I had witnessed.

Where the fuck had Gabriel been? He had been *looking* for Childe, he had seen Cecilia before I had, and Cecilia had led me straight to the maniac. That whole house seemed designed to piss off Gabriel, the whole unsubtle setup. Childe had been starved in a box so he couldn't interfere with what was going on, letting his thralls go on a rampage, causing all sorts of havoc.

I now knew where Childe had disappeared to, and where Cecilia had disappeared to—and it didn't fit.

I could visualize the box trapping Childe. A strong vampire could break out of that thing, but if he'd undergone a massive injury, and was locked in there— I could picture his body feeding on its own resources in the absence of blood, the body wasting away to become the skeletal thing I had seen. From the actions of his thralls, Childe had been in that box since before I'd ever heard Cecilia's name.

Nothing fit, unless Cecilia was lying. If someone had set Childe up, shut him up in the box up there, that same person had staked out that ritual site for me to witness; that same person had shut Cecilia up in the mausoleum with Joey; that same person had control of Childe's thralls and had staged the house for Cecilia to lead someone to.

All the talk of two masters was beginning to sink in. I was dealing with another vampire. The person who

had transformed Cecilia, who had infected her, *wasn't*
Childe. She wasn't the kind of person who Childe
would take. Her father was a powerful man who would
believe the bloody clues left for him, and would react
accordingly.

That was what my wife and I were, bloody clues left
to ensure that Sebastian would act. The vampire who
had taken Cecilia, who had staged the sacrifice, he was
my enemy. He was the one in the cowled robe, not
Childe. He was the one who had taken my daughter.

I knew two vampires who had some grudge against
Childe. Who would want some summary justice delivered for his breaches of the Covenant. Gabriel was the
first and the most obvious, but his world revolved
around the Covenant. Would he stage all this to give
himself an excuse to dispose of Childe? It seemed
unlikely now. More than that, if he had set up this cha-
rade, why was Childe still alive?

Someone else had set up Childe for Gabriel's benefit.
And at the last minute, after talking to Cecilia, Gabriel
had not risen to the bait. Cecilia had told him what she
had told me, but I could see Gabriel talking to her as he
had me. I could see him asking who her master was. I
could see her lying. I could see him taste her blood, as
he had mine—and maybe he could taste who her master
really was. The old ones seemed to see, to sense, more
than I could.

If it wasn't Gabriel, that left me one other suspect.
The person I'd seen with the thralls, the person who
was free to follow Gail to Sam's apartment, the person
who'd been feeding me information on Childe all
along. . . .

Bowie.

Bowie had shown up too conveniently at the Arabica
right after my run-in with the thralls, he had broke me
out of Sebastian's in a way that was sure to inflame
him, he had disappeared right after I had sent my

daughter to so-called safety. The bastard had been using me all along, using me to lead everyone to suspect Childe, everyone from Sebastian and Gabriel to the cops.

The demon thrall had said that I *knew* where my daughter was. I thought of the first time I'd seen Bowie and Leia together. I slammed the brakes and skidded the car around to head toward Shaker Heights.

30

I pulled the Chevette to a halt angled across the tree-lawn of the Ryan house. I threw open the car door and rushed the front of the house. I shouldered my way into the house as Doctor Ryan ran down the hall toward me. He wore a blood-spattered lab coat.

"What's going on here—"

"Where is she?"

Ryan stopped short, about ten feet down the corridor from me. He eyed the splintered doorjamb behind me. "Who?"

"Don't bullshit me Doc," I said. "I want my daughter, and I want the man responsible for all this."

"Look, perhaps you should calm down."

"Fuck calm!" I drew the Eagle and leveled it at the doctor. "I want my daughter or I'm emptying your skull into the wallpaper."

"Mr. Tyler. . . ." The doctor backed to the wall. I advanced until the barrel of the Eagle was pressed against the white stubble on his cheek.

"Hey, man, you really ought to calm down," came a familiar voice from behind me.

I whipped around, keeping the barrel of my gun pressed into Ryan's neck. Bowie emerged from the den behind us. He stopped and leaned against the doorframe at the foot of the stairs. He looked unconcerned about Ryan.

"Give me my daughter," I said through clenched teeth. "Give her back, or I swear I'll kill him."

Bowie shook his head and tsked at me. "It doesn't work like that."

I chambered around and said, "Fuck that, you bastard. You've used me to set up Childe, and it ends now—"

Bowie kept shaking his head. "No, it doesn't. That's why we have her. With all the pieces out there, Sebastian, the cops . . . Childe will self-destruct if he hasn't been killed already."

"It's over. Childe's freed himself, and Gabriel's on to you."

Bowie laughed. "Sure he is. But do you see him here? He won't stick his neck out for Childe. He wants the status for Childe's head."

"But—"

"If Gabriel's the cavalry, where is he?"

I kept the gun pressed into Ryan's neck, and he muttered, "Please."

Bowie shook his head. "Put the gun down."

"Why, damn you?" I shouted. "Why take her?"

"What's she ever done to me, she's never hurt anyone, she wasn't a threat. . . ." Bowie straightened up and took a step toward me. "That's what you mean ain't it? Christ, ain't it obvious? Sebastian held her over you, and pretty damn soon you'd twig to what was happening, and we couldn't have you talking to Sebastian or the cops when you figured it out."

"Who's 'we?' " I breathed. Anger was twisting a hole in my gut.

"Me and my master," Bowie said. "And you have her word that no harm will come to your precious Gail if you just subjugate yourself to her."

Her?

"Put down the gun," came a voice from up the stairs, between me and Bowie.

I turned so I could keep an eye on the stairs as well as Bowie. Leia stood at the head of the stairs, glaring down at me. She was as pale as ever, and deep in her eyes I felt a tug that could only come from one source.

"Put down the gun," she repeated. I felt her will, like a mental undertow on my arm. I resisted it, despite the weight my arm felt. My hand shook, and fear from the doctor washed away any emotion I might have felt from her.

"You?" I felt the anger again, the stress. I felt bones dislocating, muscle tearing and reknitting, skin splitting and flowing back together.

So obvious, so damn obvious. I suddenly knew what was wrong with the pictures on the wall of Ryan's office. There hadn't been a single picture of Ryan's wife. There'd been him in England, him and his granddaughter Leia, but none of a wife. What had *really* sparked his interest in vampires?

What if Leia wasn't his granddaughter?

"Yes, me. I've waited half a century for Childe's humiliation. You aren't going to stop it."

"My daughter or he's dead!" came a half-animal yell. I glimpsed a shadow of myself on the wall, and saw a hunching back, lengthened arms, and a distorted skull evolving a muzzle. I could feel myself willing the changes now. Everything was tinted with blood-red anger. I snarled.

"No," she shook her head. "And you harm him, and you'll watch me tear out your daughter's heart."

I was fighting an internal urge to drop the gun and rip out the doctor's throat. My body was burning itself with the effort of the change, and it sensed the heat within the doctor's flesh. It wanted that flesh.

Leia kept staring at me, and it was becoming difficult for me to concentrate. The gun shook in a clawed, leathery hand. The world seemed to be twisting away from me, as if the scent of the doctor's blood, even through the skin, were making me high.

"Childe is evil; he has to be punished. Punished, then killed." Leia took a step down the riser.

I tried to say, "Gail." But all I produced was a breathy growl. My clothes split and shredded.

"You weaken yourself with your anger," she said, and I found my neck turning so I could stare into her eyes. She was halfway down the stairs now, her cloying perfume in advance of her. Now, however, my sense of smell had become infinitely more acute, and I could smell the corruption that perfume cloaked.

She kept descending until near the end, where her eyes were even with mine.

"Look at what Childe did to me," she said. She grabbed the collar of her turtleneck and yanked it down. The fabric tore as she uncovered her left shoulder, neck, and breast—

A gaping, festering, wound sank into her flesh. I saw the outline of a collarbone, glistening red.

I felt something stab into my side, opposite the doctor. I turned to see Bowie plunging the contents of a hypodermic into my side. I yanked myself away, breaking the needle, but I was too late. The hypo was empty. I readied to lunge at Bowie, the doctor all but forgotten—

"Look at me," she said.

I could not avoid looking.

"That blood's just to soften your will." I was locked in place, unable to draw my attention away from her. Heat rippled out from where the needle had pierced my skin, and my body sucked in the heat, along with something else.

"Fetch his daughter," she said to Bowie. He ran up the stairs. She turned back to face me. "You will be harder than a thrall. You have to accept my blood willingly."

She took another step down the stairs. "You ask me why? Childe took my blood and left me with this—" her hand went to the wound that ate into her shoulder and chest "—he seduced me, used me, and then left me to die from a long, suppurating infection. I lived for a month."

I remembered Ryan's words: *"In most humans this entity can't survive the first twenty-four hours in a living host. Though, if another infection weakens the immune system, the entity can survive much longer."*

The warmth in my side had spread to every part of my body. I shook with a feverish heat, sweating, dizzy, my body beginning to tear itself back into a human form. I tried to recapture the emotions I had been feeling, but they slipped through my mental fingers like so much air.

My back collapsed against the wall, and the gun tumbled from my fingers. Everything seemed very far away, even the pain of my bones reshaping themselves.

"Death wasn't the end," a far away voice was saying, "I was left cursed with this unhealable wound. Every night for fifty years I've woken up to this pain. Every night for fifty years I've been tied by this political contrivance they call a Covenant. Every night for fifty years I've been waiting for Childe to slip, to give an opening for those who hate him. Even his own race wish him gone, and will happily destroy him for a misstep. You know what Childe is, you know he had to be stopped. Punished. Crushed."

I shook; my body was fighting off an alien infection.

The master-slave relationship, and the control it created, flowed from the blood, blood linked to a specific mind. The blood in my veins, the vampiric infection throughout my body, gave me control to the point where I could heal gunshots and restructure my entire body. Allowing another vampire's blood into my body, allowing another infection, could give that "other" similar control, both body and mind.

That was how she had taken control of Childe's people.

That was happening to me now. With that flash of realization, I tried to push back the encroaching apathy and disorientation that blazed across the surface of my fever.

"Cross," I muttered through a mouth that was still animalistic.

Somewhere, far away, I saw her nod. "My maiden name. My brother, the chief inspector, was responsible for those police files your detective friend ordered from England. Detective Weinbaum is almost as useful against Childe as Sebastian is. Now either they will kill him, or Childe will kill them, bringing all the force of the Convenant down upon his own head."

I barely heard her as I tried to concentrate, tried to gather together the tatters of my will against the fever. My body stopped changing back.

"With my brother's death, I knew Childe would never stumble on his own. I had to take his thralls."

I felt her breath against my sweaty cheek. My half-human body was vibrating with fever, drenched in sweat. Inside myself, I fought to retain my own identity, my own perception of reality, against the force this woman was exerting.

The pressure of the fever, the blood, and her will, was becoming impossible to fight. Her mind was as strong as my own, maybe stronger, and she was aided by the traitor infection that Bowie had injected.

I saw Bowie descending the stairs, bringing Gail with him. Gail stared blankly, going where Bowie led her.

"You have a choice," Leia's face was within an inch of my own. I felt her words brush my ear, burning it. "Take my blood. Become one with my blood as your daughter has. Or your daughter dies. The Covenant protects no thralls."

Gail. She showed no reaction upon seeing me, as if she were in a trance.

Leia had taken her. She had forced my own daughter to become one of them. A sound, somewhere between a cry and a howl, emerged from my throat. A spark of rage ignited, my own fire, and I concentrated on it.

Her arm extended in front of me, the vein opening for me as Jaguar's had. There was a flood of fire, a pressure willing me to taste, to drink. I wanted the blood, and I knew that it was the desire that was the key. The second I stopped resisting the desire, the burning hunger that she was pulling out of me, I would be lost.

She had taken Gail.

I felt the knot of anger harden.

I was not a thrall. I was not a human any more. I was a vampire whose chosen name was Raven. I was this woman's peer. She had had half a century to focus her will, but my own wounds were fresh.

I felt myself bend over her arm, felt the bones begin again to rewrite the structure of my jaw. I could smell her blood, and it was the sweetest thing I had ever smelled. Below me it leaked from her arm, a warm ruby glow, radiating with life.

Under it all I could still smell the taint of corruption.

She had taken Gail.

The world stopped spinning around me, and my sense regained a sharper focus.

"Take of me, Mr. Tyler. Your daughter has an eternity before her, don't let it end."

She had taken Gail.

Focusing on Gail allowed me to retain myself. Doctor Ryan had found a weapon for her, but the weapon wasn't absolute. The tainted blood increased her power over me, but it did not make me her slave. I was the master of my blood, not a thrall who carried another's blood in his veins already.

I held her arm with both hands. My nails were talons in leathery skin, my jaw a savage muzzle, my nose wrinkling at the sweet smell of blood. I knew, instinctively, that to give up control, even for a moment, would make me her slave.

"Drink, Kane—"

Raven, it is Raven now.

"—you should not be fighting me—"

My name is Raven and I am master of my own blood.

A voice came from out of the darkness within me. I heard myself whisper.

"From childhood's hour I have not been / As others were—"

I raised my eyes to meet hers. Leia stopped talking. I slammed the tatters of my will against her own.

"I have not seen," I whispered, "As others saw—"

I dropped her arm. I could feel her try to turn away, but I held her gaze with my own.

"I could not bring / My passions from a common spring—" I could feel the fever burning itself out within me. "From the same source I have not taken / My sorrow—" The blood inside me burned like a magnesium flare, brief, intense, leaving nothing but ash in its wake.

"I could not awaken / My heart to joy at the same tone—/ And all I lov'd—I lov'd alone . . ."

I was still me. My mind felt tempered, all the impurities burned away. I felt all the anger, the fury, the endless rage and fear burning through my skull. All of it focused on Leia in front of me.

Leia began to scream.

Bowie began moving toward Gail, who still stared into space.

"No!" I growled. My hand slashed in front of me, at Leia. Every last trace of emotion within me powered

that swing. My hand was not a hand anymore, it was a weapon.

My talons sank into Leia's neck, tearing across her throat. Her scream gurgled to a halt. She slammed into the wall next to me.

Bowie had grabbed Gail, and she seemed to wake up from her trance. Gail yelled, and I leaped at him. His hands were on her throat as he looked up at me.

I saw fear in his face.

He raised his arms too late to defend himself, and I sank my teeth into his throat. I tasted blood, but I didn't drink. I tore at him, shredding flesh, tearing at him tooth and claw, driving him away from my child. Gail scrambled, panicked, up the stairway.

Bowie pounded at me, and I felt his bones shift under my assault. His spine separated under my teeth before he could transform into anything threatening. I threw Bowie's corpse into the den to shatter through the French doors. His head stayed in the doorway.

I heard a renewed scream behind me. I turned around in time for Leia to grab me with a pair of clawed hands. Where I had turned into something wolflike, she had turned demonic. She threw me high against the wall. My back cratered the plaster, and a picture shattered underneath me. I slid to the ground, Ryan diving out of my way.

Leia dove upon me and slashed with obscenely elongated hands. Her nails were a foot long and tapered like swords. I raised an arm to defend myself and I felt the claws sever the muscles down to the bone.

I grabbed her wounded neck with my other hand, holding her at bay. It didn't work as well as I intended. My gut exploded in pain as her other hand slashed into my abdomen, burying itself in my stomach.

I roared, and Leia hissed at me in a way that was too reminiscent of the way Childe had sounded in his box.

She pushed away my other arm, its muscles severed

and immobile, and began slashing at my face and neck.
I saw my own blood spray across the hallway, splashed
by her blows. As I weakened, I felt my body rebel
against the alien shape.

Each slash knocked more of the beast out of me, and
more leaked out of the fiery hole in my gut. My hand
on her throat did more to pin me than it did her. As I
began regaining a human form, she started laughing
at me.

Then the world exploded as someone fired my
Desert Eagle. Leia's face exploded across me. She
stopped laughing. However, her hand kept slashing at
me, as if by reflex.

The gun fired again, numbing my ears. Leia's head
caved in with the impact. Her arm still moved.

Again it fired.

Leia's arm dangled by her side.

I was frozen in that tableau for nearly a minute, as
my body shifted, sucking all its resources to return me
to my human form. Above me, Leia's head was
nothing more than a chunk of rotten meat above her
lower jaw, good as decapitated. As I watched, her
oozing blood faded from livid red to a sick, dead,
black.

I let go of her neck, and her body tumbled to the
ground.

Gail stood there, in the center of the hall, holding my
Desert Eagle in both hands.

31

Gail held the gun, trembling, tears streaming down her face. "Dad?" she whispered.

I slowly pushed my back up the wall. I looked down the hall to where Ryan stood, shaking, staring at Leia's corpse with wide eyes. He didn't move.

I looked back at my daughter and said, "It's all right, it's over."

"Over?" she repeated.

I walked up and took the gun from her hands.

She buried her face in my shredded shirt and cried. "I'm sorry, Dad. I didn't want to lie, but they made me."

"You're free now," I said. I looked down on Leia's body. All her blood was now the black of death. Ryan had knelt down next to the corpse and was whispering. "Come on, honey," he mumbled at her, "wake up, wake up—"

I looked at Gail.

"You are master of your own blood now," I said to her. "Let's leave this place."

I walked her out the front door, out into the snow, toward the Chevette on the lawn. I was limping, feeling as if most of my flesh had been torn from the bone. For my injuries I must have looked almost as bad as Joey had.

Gail was shaking her head, and I thought of all she had to go through. For what?

"So pointless . . ." I whispered to the night.

"Things usually are," replied a cultured voice with an English accent.

I turned to face the Ryan house, and leaning up against an ivy-covered wall was a well-groomed gentleman who appeared to be in his fifties. He had a slight touch of gray at the temples of his shoulder-length hair, and his chin sported a Van Dyke.

"Childe?" I said.

The man made a slight bow. "My reputation precedes me."

I glanced back up at the house. Gail turned to me and whispered, "Oh, God."

Childe shook his head. "He has little to do with it. No, we're discussing Jaguar, actually." He smiled grimly and followed my glance up at the house. I saw erratic shadows cross the windows, semi-human in form. Nearly a dozen of them. No sound came from the house.

"Jaguar?" I said.

"The English of an otherwise unpronounceable Mayan name. I would think you'd remember meeting him."

Jaguar, my raceless visitor. I nodded as the lights went out in the house. "He told me Doctor Ryan was buried in the flesh."

"Some of us more so than others." Childe held out his hand. "Perhaps you two should come with me."

"What is he doing in there?" I asked.

"Fixing things."

I stared at Childe and after a moment said, "That was you, in that box."

He started walking away from the house said, "I have made better impressions."

"I should have killed you."

He paused for a moment and looked back over his shoulder. "Yes, by your lights, perhaps you should have. But come."

He waved us after him.

"I could have," I whispered.

He kept nodding. It was difficult to picture this man as the thing within the box. But I'd had that glimpse of him in the window, and he was unquestionably the same being. The same person whose picture was faxed from England.

How many of Sebastian's men had it taken to bring him back?

"For God's sake, why?" Gail said.

He turned around, and I noticed that the suit he wore had to cost close to a grand. The scarf and gloves he wore spoke of the same expensive taste. "Why ask for nepenthe of some strange black bird crossing my threshold? Is there balm in Gilead?"

Childe addressed me, giving me an odd grin. "I know something of you now, and you shan't offer such balm."

"What do you mean?"

"Don't make the mistake Leia did. She was one of us, but she wasn't *of* us. Applying a human morality to us is akin to applying that bird's morality to a human."

He turned around and resumed walking. "What souls we have, what minds, are chained within this flesh. All resides close to the surface. We become what we are. Our thoughts mold ourselves, our flesh, our reality. Our choices bind us—"

I nodded, not understanding all I wished to. Though I began to see how vampiric psychology could affect the flesh; from Joey's zombie-rot to Leia's wound, self-image molded the body.

"What she did," Childe continued, "forcing herself on the bodies of my thralls, with her blood, that was a worse act than killing me would have been." He shook his head and wiped snow out of his hair.

"All of them chose to be *yours*?"

The corner of Childe's mouth twitched upward. "I

do not force the worm within my breast upon anyone. They each had time to decide."

We turned a corner and approached a black car. "What happened with her?" Gail asked.

"At the end of the war, I offered something to a woman. She gave freely, but when it came time for her to *take,* she refused to deal any more with me. I am always clear about what a relationship with me costs."

We stopped at the car, a Rolls Royce, one of the earlier models, before they started looking like Lincolns. Childe shrugged. "Her husband was a doctor, but she hid the marks too long. They became septic. She died. She lived. Her mind kept the scar alive, and she blamed me." He shook his head. "She existed for half a century, and all must have seen that wound in her heart. None sponsored her, took her into the community, or gave her a name." He gave me a meaningful look. "You're very lucky. Rogues come to bad ends."

I felt a small flare of anger at the society I had thrust myself into. "She was such a loose cannon, why didn't Jaguar, Gabriel, or *somebody,* stop her before it came to this."

"Her husband was useful, I suppose. He had a good, if incomplete, model of our existence. If she was removed, so was the motive for his work. Also, I am not loved. They may have waited to see what my fate would be."

"They let this happen?"

"To an extent. But, thanks to you, this conflict began attracting too much attention to ignore." Childe looked up the street, back toward the Ryan house.

"Jaguar will fix this, as I had to clean my own house." I looked up and I began to see a flickering glow through the trees.

"I owe you something," he said, interrupting the memory.

"What?"

He opened the door to the Rolls. "They were mine, those who did this to you. By our law, I *am* responsible for what happened to you. I may indulge you in something compensatory—"

Gail hugged herself closer to me, and I said, "You can't bring Kate back."

Childe shook his head. "Do you desire something more within my power than forgiving your violence against my own? That I have already done."

What could I want from this creature?

I looked up at the sky, remembering how the moon looked as it hung low over Lakeview. If there was only one thing I could ask from Childe, I knew then what it was.

"Cecilia," I said.

"What?"

"If she still lives, free her from her father. Free her and sponsor her."

Childe appeared interested. "This will not change what she is . . ."

"She does not deserve Sebastian killing her. Your protection should be worth something."

Childe looked at me a long while, then said, "This I'll do, to cancel our debt." He slipped behind the wheel and said, "Shall I give you two a lift somewhere?"

I shook my head and said, "No. We have our own car."

I took my daughter and began walking back.

"Indeed," Childe said. I heard the door shut behind me, "But perhaps, my dear Raven, you'll indulge me a moment more?"

I stopped walking, and without turning around, I asked, "What more is there to say?"

I heard the Rolls' quiet engine start, and I heard the tires grind snow as it advanced to pull even with us. The wheel was on the wrong side, so Childe was sitting just on the other side of the door from us. "A story," he said through the open window, "an old one."

"What—"

"Shh. This predates that American drunkard you're so fond of by two millennia, and it is just as much part of your soul now."

I turned to face him, and Childe looked off, out the windshield. It began sinking in, as he spoke, what Ryan said, about Childe being so old.

"This occurred in the east, in the mountains there. Perhaps India, perhaps China. I prefer to think of it as Tibet. The thirst came upon a young man in a monastery. There was no one to tell this man what had happened to him, and when it overpowered him, finally, he killed his teacher and drank of his blood. The young monk was horrified by his deed. He ran off into the night, hiding in a cave far away from any other person. He sat in that cave, and vowed to sit there until he died."

He paused and stroked his beard. He still didn't look at me.

"This monk had a strong will, perhaps as strong as any other man's had ever been. Stronger when tempered by his horror at his teacher's fate. He did not move from his spot in the cave. Days came and went, the sunlight never reaching his flesh. He did not feed, nor did he move. Within a month, the monks found him there, after half his flesh had withered. They demanded answers from the young monk, for the death of his teacher."

Childe finally turned to look at me. When his eyes met mine, I could picture the scene. The cadaverous monk in a lotus position, and the robed elders, holding candles and shouting questions. I was unsure if the imagined scene was from my mind, or Childe's.

"The young man did not answer, and the only part of his body he moved was his eyes. The questioning went on for days, during which he did not move, or eat, or speak. He could smell the blood of the monks around him, but he held his hunger inside. The others saw this, and decided that the young man had achieved enlightenment."

Childe grinned as if this were his favorite part of the story. "They left him there, with his hunger. The young monk stayed unmoving for a year, then another. Word spread across the countryside about his enlightenment. Soon pilgrims visited the mountain, to ask their own questions, to which the young monk would offer no answer.

"The thirst gnawed away at him for a century, withering him away until he was barely a skeleton held complete by the force of his denial. As every day passed, his will strengthened along with the thirst. And the pilgrims still came, dozens, hundreds—all asking questions with no answers.

"The monks built a shrine around the cave, and the pilgrims began to worship at the young man's bones. They held him sacred now, though none knew that he still lived, and still kept his vow.

"A city grew up at the base of the mountain, below the monk's shrine. Eventually, the cave itself was walled up, for fear of anyone disturbing the young monk's remains.

"Slowly, though, the young monk was forgotten. The pilgrims ceased coming. Eventually, it was forgotten why the city was where it was. And, nine centuries after the young monk had walked into the cave, he moved.

"In the space of one night, every single person who lived within the walls of that great city died. A thousand, ten thousand. A quarter awoke the next night, with their own thirst, and found the shrine destroyed, and the young monk nowhere to be seen."

Childe tuned back to face the windshield. "You can't deny yourself, much as you want to."

"That justifies all the killing?"

"It means what it means," Childe said. "There are hundreds of versions of that story. Will over thirst, thirst over will. Fate, destiny—" Childe shook his head. "There's just more there than I've said, and there's more here than you've seen."

He pulled the Rolls away from the curb, leaving us alone in the snow-dusted night.

"What did he mean?" Gail asked.

"I'm not sure," I said. "But we'll work it out, somehow."

We walked back to the Chevette. When we reached it, I could hear sirens in the distance, and the Ryan house was already engulfed by fire. I could picture another fire burning in East Cleveland, destroying Childe's house, burning away everything that might not be mundane.

I thought of Leia, and Bowie, and Ryan. I hugged Gail's shoulders and counted ourselves lucky. Leia had been right. Revenge is not a happy pursuit.

Elizabeth Forrest

☐ **PHOENIX FIRE** UE2515—$4.99
As the legendary Phoenix awoke, so too did an ancient Chinese
demon—and Los Angeles was destined to become the final
battleground in their millenia-old war.

☐ **DARK TIDE** UE2560—$4.99
The survivor of an accident at an amusement pier is forced to
return to the town where it happened. And slowly, long buried
memories start to resurface, and all his nightmares begin to come
true . . .

☐ **DEATH WATCH** UE2648—$5.99
McKenzie Smith has been targeted by a mastermind of evil who
can make virtual reality into the ultimate tool of destructive power.
Stalked in both the real and virtual worlds, can McKenzie defeat
an assassin who can strike out anywhere, at any time?

☐ **KILLJOY** UE2695—$5.99
Given experimental VR treatments, Brand must fight a constant
battle against the persona of a serial killer now implanted in his
brain. But Brand would soon learn that there were even worse
things in the world—like the unstoppable force of evil and destruction called KillJoy.

S. Andrew Swann

HOSTILE TAKEOVER

☐ **PROFITEER**   UE2647—$4.99

With no anti-trust laws and no governing body, the planet Bakunin is the perfect home base for both corporations and crimi-
nals. But now the Confederacy wants a piece of the action—
and they're planning a hostile takeover!

☐ **PARTISAN**   UE2670—$4.99

Even as he sets the stage for a devastating covert operation,
Dominic Magnus and his allies discover that the Confederacy
has far bigger plans for Bakunin, and no compunctions about
destroying anyone who gets in the way.

☐ **REVOLUTIONARY**   UE2699—$5.50

Key factions of the Confederacy of Worlds have slated a takeover of the planet Bakunin . . . An easy target—except that its
natives don't understand the meaning of the word surrender!

OTHER NOVELS
☐ **FORESTS OF THE NIGHT**   UE2565—$3.99
☐ **EMPERORS OF THE TWILIGHT**   UE2589—$4.50
☐ **SPECTERS OF THE DAWN**   UE2613—$4.50

Welcome to DAW's Gallery of Ghoulish Delights!

☐ **DRACULA: PRINCE OF DARKNESS**
    Martin H. Greenberg, editor
A blood-draining collection of all-original Dracula stories. From Dracula's traditional stalking grounds to the heart of modern-day cities, the Prince of Darkness casts his spell over his prey in a private blood drive from which there is no escape!   UE2531—$4.99

☐ **THE TIME OF THE VAMPIRES**   May 1996
    P.N. Elrod & Martin H. Greenberg, editors
From a vampire blessed by Christ to the truth about the notorious Oscar Wilde to a tale of vampirism` and the Bow Street Runners, here are 18 original tales of vampires from Tanya Huff, P.N. Elrod, Lois Tilton, and others.
                                                                UE2693—$5.50

☐ **WEREWOLVES**
    Martin H. Greenberg, editor
Here is a brand-new anthology of original stories about the third member of the classic horror cinema triumvirate—the werewolf, a shapeshifter who prowls the darkness, the beast within humankind unleashed to prey upon its own.
                                                                UE2654—$5.50

☐ **WHITE HOUSE HORRORS**
    Martin H. Greenberg, editor
The White House has seen many extraordinary events unforld within its well-guarded walls. Sixteen top writers such as Brian Hodge, Grant Masterton, Bill Crider, Billie Sue Mosiman, and Edward Lee relate of some of the more unforgettable.   UE2659—$5.99

☐ **MISKATONIC UNIVERSITY**
    Martin H. Greenberg & Robert Weinberg, editors
Miskatonic U is a unique institution, made famous by the master of the horrific, H.P. Lovecraft. Thirteen original stories will introduce you to the dark side of education, and prove once and for all that a little arcane knowledge can be a very dangerous thing, especially in the little Yankee college town of Arkham.
                                                                UE2722—$5.99

DAW

Attention:

DAW COLLECTORS

Many readers of DAW Books have written requesting information on early titles and book numbers to assist in the collection of DAW editions since the first of our titles appeared in April 1972.

We have prepared a several-pages-long list of all DAW titles, giving their sequence numbers, original and current order numbers, and ISBN numbers. Also included, of course, are the authors and book titles, as well as reissue information.

If you think that this list will be of help, you may have a copy by writing to the address below and enclosing two dollars in stamps or currency to cover the handling and postage costs.

DAW Books, Inc.
Dept. C
375 Hudson Street
New York, NY 10014-3658